MURDER ON THE TRAIN

A gripping crime mystery full of twists

FAITH MARTIN

Detective Hillary Greene Book 21

Joffe Books, London
www.joffebooks.com

First published in Great Britain in 2024

Cover art by Nick Castle

ISBN: 978-1-83526-545-1

CHAPTER ONE

At just gone ten thirty on a bright and sunny June morning, Hillary Greene snapped shut the lid of her suitcase with a sigh of satisfaction and put it on the floor by her single bed.

As she glanced out of the porthole of her narrowboat's window, a heron landed on the opposite bank of the Oxford canal, where she was permanently moored in the village of Thrupp. The bird peered hopefully into the base of a small stand of reed mace that it had spotted growing there, no doubt hoping to snaffle an unwary stickleback or two for its breakfast, or even a dace or bream.

'Good luck, mate,' she murmured to it, pleased to see the bird after whom her boat, the *Mollern*, had been named. But the fish on this stretch of the water were very much accustomed to anglers and their cunning ways, and she doubted that even one of the feathered variety would have much joy.

She hauled her case out and onto the bottom of the steps that led up to the stern of her boat, then doubled back to do a quick inventory. All windows closed and locked — check. All gas appliances turned off and safety valves employed — check. Water valves likewise firmly closed — check.

It felt odd to be leaving her home, knowing that she wasn't going to be returning to it for another two weeks. But then, she hadn't been on a holiday in years.

After a last, swift look around, she picked up her case and hefted it up the short set of metal steps and onto the tiny platform that was the rear of the boat. Having made sure that the padlock which secured the iron door (the only entrance and exit onto her boat) was snapped firmly in place, she hitched her handbag over one shoulder, picked up the suitcase, and stepped off onto the towpath.

Cow parsley frothed in a creamy line alongside the nearest farmer's field, and butterbur and burdock competed to encroach on the narrow pathway. In the hedge, a whitethroat abruptly stopped singing as she passed, but she didn't take it personally, and as she approached the Boat, one of the village's two pubs, she felt her spirits positively lift. And why not? She was off on a holiday — well, of sorts, anyway — and for two weeks her life would not involve murder victims or murder suspects, work colleagues, people lying to her face, or (worst of all) paperwork. Mind you, being somewhat cynical by nature, she was still expecting people to lie to her face, but you couldn't have everything, could you?

Crossing the car park of the pub — where she had ongoing permission from the landlord to leave her trusty and rusty car, Puff the Tragic Wagon, overnight — she delved into her bag for her set of keys, musing that now would *not* be a good time to discover that she'd left them inside the *Mollern*. Especially given the fact that the key to the boat's padlock was on them.

But no, they were in the side pocket where she always kept them, and within a few moments she had stowed away her case in the boot, opened the driver's door and was sitting facing the steering wheel and making herself comfortable.

'Right then, Puff,' she told the ancient Volkswagen Golf, patting his dashboard affectionately. 'We're off to Wales.' She turned the key in the ignition and was instantly rewarded by the sound of his engine (which could not always be guaranteed to be the case). 'There may be hills,' she added in a whisper, hoping that he didn't quite catch it. No point alarming the old boy before he was presented with a *fait accompli*.

She reached into the glove box and withdrew an AA road atlas, on which she'd previously mapped out the route. She refused to use a satnav, having heard too many horror stories from other drivers about where they could take you, and contemplated instead her list of written instructions. Pleased to note that she'd be on relatively familiar ground for the first hour of the journey at least, she reversed out of the car park and headed down the narrow lane that would take her, within moments, to the main Oxford-Banbury road.

As she waited there for a pause in the long line of traffic so that she could safely pull out, her mind drifted back over the events of what had led her to this morning.

Six months ago, on a cold January day that had never seemed to get properly light, she had gone into hospital to have a non-cancerous tumour removed from her lung. Never having been a smoker, she remembered feeling rather hard done by and resentful of the need for the whole process, which, on reflection, now rather amused her.

Naturally, she had been forced to take sick leave from her job as a civilian consultant to the Crime Review Team at Thames Valley Police HQ in Kidlington, which was situated less than a mile away from her current location. (As a recently retired DI with thirty-odd years of experience under her belt, she now took a second look at old murder cases, with the help of another 'retired' police officer, Claire Woolley, and former soldier Gareth Proctor, who'd been forced out of the army after being disabled by an exploding bomb and was now finding his feet in a new career.)

A self-confessed workaholic, she'd always known that taking time off work would present her with a major challenge, and so it quickly proved. Which meant that when, not two days into her convalescence, a letter bearing a publisher's logo had arrived containing some surprising news, she'd been delighted.

Many years ago, and like several police officers before her, Hillary (who'd taken a degree in Literature from a non-affiliated Oxford college) had got it into her head to write a crime novel. Titled *The Farringdon Conundrum*, it was based *very* loosely on one of her first murder cases, which she'd highly fictionalised and sent off to a publisher with a strong crime fiction list, and she had never heard a word about it since.

But now, it seemed, someone with the splendid name of Tegan Quartermaine had rediscovered it. There were obviously 'issues' that needed to be 'addressed' first, but all in all, the first draft showed 'some' promise.

Thoroughly amused, intrigued, and desperate for any kind of distraction, Hillary then read the attachment to the letter, which was little more than a mile-long list of 'suggested' changes that would need to be made. Would the author be interested in doing some more work on it?

And Hillary Greene, sitting in her very quiet boat and ready to start chewing on the furniture, was more than ready to snap the hand off anyone who could have offered her an alternative to three weeks simply vegetating.

She'd written back the same day saying that she'd be happy to start work on the book immediately. And so, after much swearing, some (OK, more than *some*) wine drinking, and the exchange of a variety of 'lively' emails between herself and the annoyingly demanding Tegan, *The Farringdon Conundrum* was finally finished to their mutual satisfaction.

Contracts had then been drawn up and signed, the upshot of which being that now, five months later, her first ever book had just been let loose on an unsuspecting public.

She was determined not to obsess about it, however. So, since her usual annual holiday leave was looming, Hillary took the decision that rather than just stay at home on the boat as she usually did, this year she'd distract herself by taking a proper break away.

No fan of holidays abroad (travel was such a pain) or beach holidays (too boring), she was thinking instead of going somewhere much closer to home. Somewhere that she'd always wanted to go but had never got around to visiting — Hay-on-Wye. The town in Wales that had more bookshops than almost anywhere else. For a bibliophile like herself, what could be better than spending all day browsing through bookshops? If nothing else, it would certainly give her the opportunity to stock up her library (well, her two bookshelves that were crammed under her starboard porthole anyway).

And if she took some copies of her book with her, she might even be able to drum up some interest in it, an idea that had been heartily (some might say forcefully) backed by her editor. Yes, all right, she admitted to herself crossly — she wanted the book to sell, damn it! And as a bonus, being just three hours or so away from Oxford meant that she could also come back home quickly and easily if she was needed back at work on short notice for any reason.

Spotting a gap in the traffic at last, Hillary pulled out of Thrupp and she and Puff set off jauntily westward. Turning on the radio, she found a station that played only sixties tunes, and humming along to the Hollies, who were sharing their umbrella at a bus stop, finally caught the holiday mood.

She was off to parts unknown, the sun was shining, and she had just given herself permission to spend far too much money on books.

What could possibly go wrong?

* * *

It was just about half past one when she found herself approaching Hay-on-Wye. In the distance she could see mountain ranges that looked high enough above sea level to make her ears pop should she have to go over them. She sincerely hoped that wouldn't be necessary, as the only thing Puff was likely to pop — if he had to do the same — was his clogs.

For some time now, she'd noticed the word 'ARAF' painted on the roads and — being a top-notch detective — had deduced that it was a Welsh word, meaning that she'd now crossed over the border. Furthermore, since it usually appeared just before villages or sharp bends, it probably meant 'slow'. (See, she was learning a foreign language already!) So, on seeing it again, she glanced at her speedometer and realised that Puff didn't really need instructions to keep his speed down.

She made her way past the Swan Hotel and up Church Street, periodically checking the map of the town that she'd printed off the day before, then took a turn down Lion Street. Her bijou hotel, the Riverside Inn, seemed to be located not far from the Old Black Lion hotel, and after a few false turns, she finally found it at the end of a narrow lane lined with picturesque cottages.

Festooned with attractive black wrought ironwork and a rampant wisteria, it overlooked a long, fairly broad but shallow river that Hillary strongly suspected must be the River Wye. Unless, of course, the committee set up to name the town had had an unexpected sense of humour. The building looked very much like a former rectory and had definitely been built in Georgian times, and thus possessed all of that era's sense of quiet decorum and perfect proportion.

She parked under a bright yellow-flowering laburnum and climbed out from behind the wheel with a little wince. Although the journey had only taken about two and a half hours she was glad to finally stretch her legs, nevertheless. She'd left most of the dark suits that she favoured for work behind, so was dressed in a light mint green and white summer dress that showed off her bell of chestnut hair to perfection. She was even wearing flat white sandals, which had proved to be surprisingly easy to drive in.

The weather was perfect — and, as she knew after checking the long-term forecast, was due to be warm and sunny for almost the whole of the next two weeks. Which was a relief, since the end of the previous week had seen a cold and wet spell that she had feared might ruin things for her.

Retrieving her case from the boot, she looked around with a sense of well-being. A small gravelled and circular driveway swept past the front entrance — a black-painted door set above three shallow circular steps. The small front garden consisted primarily of low boxed hedges with different-coloured roses in their centres. The sash windows of the square house lined up in perfect symmetry — one either side of the door, and three above.

She knew from the website that the hotel only catered for six to eight guests at a time, which suited her just fine. The price for her stay had been eye-watering, but she was beginning to suspect it would turn out to have been worth it. Here, off the beaten track and by the river, all was peace and calm, and birdsong was the predominant sound.

Walking up to the door she turned the handle, found it open, and pushed her way inside. This must have triggered a warning somewhere, because before she'd got halfway across the attractive black-and-white tiled hall, a door opened off to her left and a woman appeared, a wide smile of welcome on her face.

'Hello? Mrs Greene is it?'

Hillary, with an inner grimace, admitted to being Mrs Greene. She had yet to become accustomed to being addressed as anything other than 'Inspector' or 'boss' or 'guv' and she still squirmed inwardly whenever she was reminded of her late and very unlamented husband; a bent copper she'd been in the process of divorcing before a car accident had saved her the time, trouble and lawyer's fees.

The latter she had been particularly pleased about.

As a cop, she had very little time for members of the legal profession whose sole reason for being was to get off the very people that she'd been working so hard and diligently to get into court in the first place. And whenever she was forced to endure them in an interview room they often brought to mind something that she'd once read by Addison Mizner — namely, that 'ignorance of the law excuses no man from practising it'.

But on a lovely summer's day like this, about to book into a swanky hotel in a pretty town that she'd never visited before, she didn't want to think about any unpleasant things. So, she smiled and said, 'Mrs Pringwell?'

'Yes, but please call me Judith.'

Hillary knew, again from the website, that the woman running the hotel had owned the building for many years, and was something of a one-woman band, for she was also the cook. Aged around fifty, she was five feet ten and solidly built, with short layered fair hair and pale grey eyes. Clad in slate-grey slacks and a silky-looking blouse in a paler, pearly grey, she looked smart but practical.

At a small desk tucked in the recess under a modest oak staircase, Hillary went through the procedure of booking in, producing her card details, and being given a proper brass key, with the usual large piece of wooden block attached to it, to discourage her from losing it.

After Judith Pringwell rang the quaintly old-fashioned bell sitting atop the desk, a young lad appeared from down a short corridor and picked up her bag. He was almost certainly a student earning some extra cash, and as she followed him up the stairs she wondered if she was expected to tip him. It had been so long since she'd had a 'proper' holiday that she wasn't sure of the protocol anymore.

On a small landing, he pushed open a door and stood aside for her to enter, offering a shy smile as she did so, and she found herself in a spacious, well-appointed bedroom. The large sash window was already open, letting in the warm summer air, and she gravitated to it automatically, pleased to discover that her view was of a medium-sized flower-and-shrub-bedecked back garden. Beyond that lay a small flower meadow, and then the river itself. In the near distance, the mountains seemed to stretch away to infinity, blue-grey and massive, underneath a cloudless azure sky.

'Beautiful view,' Hillary murmured.

'Yes, madam, I hope you enjoy your stay,' the lad said, sounding rather like an uncertain recruit in an am-dram production. No doubt he enjoyed calling someone 'madam' about as much as she enjoyed being called it, for his cheeks were slightly flushed as he gratefully fled the room.

Hillary, with a wry smile, began to unpack her clothes into a large old-fashioned wardrobe with an exquisite burr walnut veneer. It had probably been in the house for more than two hundred years, and Hillary, for one, was glad that it still survived. The bed was a generous double and on testing it cautiously, she discovered that it was neither too hard nor soft. The dressing table had all the curves of French antique furniture at its best. On it resided a glass vase with fresh carnations in it.

The colour scheme was predominantly green, cream and apricot, with curtains that reached all the way to the floor. Whilst lovers of modern minimalism would be weeping into the feather pillows by now, Hillary felt that this room suited her down to the ground.

What's more, after living on board the *Mollern* for so long, she felt almost lost in the vastness of the space.

Suddenly, something occurred to her, and she almost ran to the connecting door and opened it. A quick look around the bathroom had her almost purring. A proper bath! Also a shower, but this she ignored. How long was it since she'd had the luxury of an actual bath? Although she loved her boat, and couldn't now imagine living anywhere else, it had only a tiny cubicle for a shower, and she did sometimes miss the option of soaking in a tub.

A quick inspection of the pristine white tiled shelf offered up the usual complimentary shampoo and shower gel — and there, in a small bottle, 'luxury' bubble bath. She gave a long, contended 'aahhhh'.

That was her next half hour sorted. Setting in the plug and running the hot water, she poured the gardenia-scented bubble bath into the base of the steaming water and almost gave a whoop of joy. She was going to stay in those bubbles until she resembled a prune!

As she began to strip, she started to hum. And to think, within just five minutes' walk from here, she had bookshop upon bookshop to peruse — a bibliophile's nirvana.

And for once, she felt almost kindly towards her editor!

* * *

Although Hillary had paid for the bed-and-breakfast option, after a long, leisurely stroll along the river, she decided to dine in the hotel, rather than go to the bother of trying to find somewhere in the town itself.

Consequently, at just gone seven o'clock, she located the charming dining room in what must once have been the spacious front parlour. Round walnut tables set for two were littered across the parquet flooring, with plenty of room for the wait staff to manoeuvre around them. Here the colour scheme was predominantly burgundy and white with accents of powder blue, and a pair of French windows set in the far wall led out into the back garden. These had been wedged open to let in the warm evening breeze, and a small tortoise-shell butterfly was fluttering in confusion against the glass of a closed sash window next to them.

Hillary made her way to it, opened the window and then gently guided the insect to freedom. As she did so, she became aware of two sets of eyes watching her curiously.

One belonged to a tall thin man with hair so white that it almost looked dyed, and bright blue eyes set in a suntanned face. Hillary instantly suspected that, though he only looked to be in his early fifties, he was probably one of those men who would turn out to be much older than he seemed. Seated opposite him was a woman who looked to be in her late twenties and who had facial features so similar that they had to be related. She was willow thin to the point of being gaunt, and in her case her hair wasn't white but that shade of very pale blonde that was so near white as to make little difference. Her skin too was pleasantly tanned, but not to such a degree as her companion, and whilst the older man's blue eyes had warmth and curiosity in them, hers looked bored and impatient.

'I hate to see butterflies trapped inside rooms too,' the man said with a smile as their eyes met, and half-rising from his chair, he introduced himself with an air of open friendliness. 'I'm Jasper Van Paulen — as you can tell by the accent, we're from the United States. This is my daughter Jasmine. You staying with us long?'

Hillary admitted to being there for the next two weeks, and Jasper advised her of various 'must-sees' in the area — with the picture-postcard view from Symonds Yat being high on the wish list.

They exchanged more pleasantries for a few minutes, before Hillary excused herself and made her choice of table. Set halfway along one wall, it gave her a good overview of the whole room. She had just taken her seat and was reaching for the menu when two men walked in, side by side.

Although neither one was very tall — one couldn't have been more than five foot three, whilst the other only topped him by a few inches — unlike the Van Paulens, they couldn't have looked less alike. The smaller one was maybe twenty-four or five, Hillary gauged, but his dark hairline was already receding. He had a well-fleshed look that made him appear 'cuddly' but might soon become a real weight problem. He wore small, almost frameless glasses, faded jeans and a 'tweedy' jacket that should only have been seen on someone of Jasper's age. He wore a 'bookish' air about him that would make him blend in — almost to the point of invisibility — within the market town's plethora of literary shops.

His companion was older — somewhere in his mid-thirties — with lots of luxuriant brown hair that curled riotously across his head. He was small-boned and so thin that he gave the appearance of being as light as thistledown, but as they walked past her, his Irish accent was loud, startlingly robust, and good-humoured. As they made their way to a corner table, she got the impression that the younger of them was used to not being able to get a word in edgeways.

Amused, Hillary turned her attention to the bill of fare, and was happy to note that, whilst the choice of dishes was not huge, everything on it looked good.

She was still contemplating whether to have a starter, when a waft of expensive perfume made her look up. A woman in her late thirties drifted by. She was doing her best to look in her late twenties and mostly succeeded, largely due to her elegance and elan. She appeared to glide rather than walk, an effect that was helped by the fact that she wore one of those floating, ethereal-looking full-length summer gowns in lemon, white, cream and silver. At five feet ten, she was around the same height as Hillary. Her hair, in contrast to her gown, was jet-black and cut in one of those chic, geometric styles that left two sharp points pointing to her jawline like arrows. Her eyes were dark chocolate and they swept over Jasmine without pausing or looking impressed.

In fact, Hillary thought that her red-painted lips might just have twitched, as if at some inner amusement.

She looked like 'someone' but Hillary — who was definitely *not* into celebrity culture — had no idea who she was. Somewhat to Hillary's surprise, it was no handsome male companion who arrived to join her at the table a few minutes later, but instead a woman in her seventies. She was lean and fit-looking, with short white hair and deep-set dark eyes. She looked elegant and affluent in well-tailored white slacks and a short-sleeved pastel-pink blouse, and the pearls she wore at her throat were undoubtedly the genuine article.

The two women greeted each other with mild but genuine warmth, and Hillary instinctively felt that the friendship between the two had only begun when they'd met here, at the hotel.

* * *

It wasn't until after dinner, when she'd made her way to the small, select bar adjoining the dining room, that Hillary began to learn the names of her fellow guests, and something about their lives. The Irishman, she learned, was named Patrick Unwin. A former 'alas, my darlin', very unsuccessful professional jockey' he now spent his life in Scotland, working for a large oil-rig supply company. 'Lucky for me, I don't have to go out to oil rigs in the North Sea often, mind. But I can tell you exactly what they're made of and what they need to keep 'em going.'

She learned that he had been the first of the current crop of guests to arrive, having made the journey down during the cold wet weather that had preceded the current heatwave. 'Motorways were practically waterways,' he'd told her with a grin, trying to raise her hair with tales of near misses with articulated lorries aquaplaning all around him.

His dining companion, being far less outgoing and vocal, was harder to get to know, but from picking up on various conversations going on around her, she nevertheless learned that his name was Barry Kirk. He came from somewhere in the Midlands, Hillary guessed, going by his accent when he did speak (which was seldom), and how he earned his daily bread was apparently a mystery. And one that he was in no hurry to solve. He had arrived two days after Patrick, and finding themselves allocated the same dining table, had struck up a friendship of convenience.

The 'celebrity' turned out to be a celebrity only in Canada, in the world of lifestyle magazines, blogs and podcasts. A 'social influencer', she apparently had a large online following of wealthy women of a certain age and was a much-sought after 'professional guest' on the west coast of Canada's social dinner party scene.

A rather catty Jasmine Van Paulen informed Hillary that, though she called herself a journalist, the woman really made her living off alimony payments (having gained and ditched at least three wealthy ex-husbands already) and answered to the name of Belinda 'Bel' John-Jacques. At least, that was her professional name. 'In my opinion, she's about as upper class as an alley cat,' Jasmine had muttered, slurring her words slightly after her fourth Martini. 'And if she's Canadian royalty then I'm the Queen of Sheba. You ask me, she probably started out as Betty Nobody from Nowheresville Nova Scotia.'

The transatlantic contingent had been the last of them to check in, and luckily for them, the warm weather had already taken charge.

The eldest of the guests was Imogen Muir, and the classy name somehow suited her. Hillary was not surprised to learn that she was a wealthy widow, the only offspring of staunch middle-class parents who'd defied them to marry a self-made man who'd made his fortune in scrap metal. No doubt her parents had never talked about him in polite society! She had the habit of expecting the best, and always getting it, and Hillary noticed that Judith Pringwell in particular treated her with an air of wary deference.

She also noted from the chilly looks that Jasmine would periodically send Imogen's way that the young American seemed to dislike her for some reason, and that even her father Jasper Van Paulen — who reminded Hillary of a friendly dog desperate to like and be liked by everyone — was not his usual effervescent self around her either.

Perhaps Mrs Muir, with her polite but reserved demeanour and general air of disinterest in her fellow guests, had had previous reason to rebuff them? She had arrived at the inn barely hours after the loquacious Irishman, but it was perhaps not surprising that closer acquaintanceship with him hadn't exactly led to mutual cordiality. Instead, she seemed to regard him with a cool and wary eye. But then, Hillary mused, she didn't look the type to enjoy being teased or appreciate Patrick's so-called Irish charm.

But whilst Hillary was content to allow the information about her fellow guests to wash over her as it pleased, she was careful never to talk about herself. There was nothing like letting on that you worked for the police for being a buzzkill. Instead, when really pushed — mostly by the relentlessly friendly Jasper Van Paulen — she admitted to having written a novel which was due out next month, hence her presence in town to promote it. But although everyone seemed genuinely and flatteringly impressed by the news, demanding to know the entire plot and when and where it could be bought, she felt uncomfortable around their enthusiasm.

Not usually prone to nerves, she couldn't shake off the absurd feeling that she would somehow jinx the chances of the book being even a modest success if she bragged about it in any way.

Perhaps sensing her embarrassment, the talk quickly turned to other topics, settling on a discussion of the merits

— or otherwise — of the various excursions everyone had been on so far. Jasmine had been reluctant to praise anything in 'this quiet backwater of a place', whilst Patrick had stressed that he was there mainly in order to catch up with various relatives in Wales, so hadn't done anything much touristy yet. Jasper was boyishly keen on all things British, in stark contrast to his offspring, and waxed lyrical about mountain walks he'd taken.

The sun had just begun to set when Patrick Unwin brought up the subject of Beggar's Leap. And if Hillary had had a crystal ball that was even partway accurate, she'd have got up and walked out of the room then and there.

CHAPTER TWO

'Since I haven't been doing much sightseeing so far, I thought I'd treat myself to something I've always wanted to do, and that's go on a steam train,' Patrick said. 'There's a line not far away that sounds like a great day out.'

Not surprisingly, his words instantly caught the attention of Jasper, who was keen to try all things British. 'Say, that sounds grand. I've heard about your British steam trains but have never seen one.'

Producing a standard leaflet from his trouser pocket, Patrick passed it on to the tall American who read the blurb with infectious eagerness.

'It says the line opened in 1905 and has operated for nearly 120 years. Built originally to carry lead ore, it's been a tourist railway since the 1950s. It passes through the southern edge of the Cambrian Mountains, which is an area of outstanding natural beauty. You hear that, honey?' he broke off to say to his daughter, who merely rolled her eyes and gave an exaggerated yawn.

'Sounds interesting,' Barry Kirk roused himself to actually speak. 'How long is the journey?'

The American turned over the leaflet, then shrugged. 'Doesn't say. There's a map though. Sounds as if you have to head to the coast a ways, past some place called Devil's Bridge. Now how spooky is that, before you even start? You pick it up there. It then climbs to over six hundred and eighty foot above sea level to some waterfalls called Beggar's Leap. Says here the place got its name because back in the old days, it was a popular suicide spot for disappointed lovers or people made destitute.'

'Charming, Dad,' Jasmine drawled. 'Sounds like a real cheery place.'

'I think it sounds romantic,' Belinda sighed. 'A trip up the mountainside, waterfalls with a tragic past. Fantastic scenery. What more could you ask for? I think I might go as well, if you don't mind, Patrick?'

'And why would I mind? The company of a beautiful woman was never a hardship to an Irishman. And if you want real romance, darlin', it's the sound of a steam-train whistle that you'll be needing. Even if you've never heard one before, it's mournful and haunting and twangs the heartstrings like you wouldn't believe.'

'It *is* an iconic sound,' Barry Kirk murmured.

'Well, count us in,' Jasper said. 'I'm sold. Says here it travels so high you're above the treetops. Hope you don't mind heights, Pat?'

'Not me,' the Irishman said with a grin.

'I can't say as I care for them,' Imogen mused.

'Say, does anyone else want to come? You don't have to pre-book, you just buy your ticket at the station. I'll have room in my old jalopy for three passengers, if anyone doesn't fancy driving themselves up and over the mountains,' Patrick volunteered.

Hillary, thinking she quite liked the sound of the excursion herself — and since someone was offering to spare Puff the arduous trek — why not take advantage of the offer? She held up a hand. 'I wouldn't mind taking you up on that offer, Patrick. And I'm happy to give you something towards the petrol.'

'Yes, it sounds like it'll be an experience,' Barry Kirk said.

'Oh what a pity,' Jasmine drawled. 'That only leaves one seat left, Dad. I guess we'll just have to bow out.'

'Not on your life,' Jasper said, grinning at his daughter. 'I quite fancy a drive over the mountains myself. I didn't hire a four-by-four so that we could just pootle about down tame country lanes.'

'I'll come too,' the Canadian said. 'It'll make a great article for a magazine editor I know who's always on the lookout for something novel by way of a travel piece. Pat, do you mind squeezing me in as a fourth?'

'Nonsense, Bel,' said Jasper, 'you can ride with us. That way we'll have three people per car — a much more comfortable and roomy arrangement.'

Bel smiled graciously as Jasmine looked daggers at her oblivious parent.

Surprisingly, Imogen Muir took the opportunity at that moment to admit that she was also intrigued by the possibilities of the excursion, and Patrick, ever the gentleman, graciously insisted that she should be given pride of place in the front passenger seat beside him.

Imogen gave him a rather enigmatic look, and the Irishman grinned back at her broadly.

Imogen turned to Belinda. 'Bel, dear, would you mind if I stuck close to you? I don't suffer from vertigo or anything like that, but I *am* a little wary of heights. It would be a shame to miss out though, so if you wouldn't mind . . . ?'

Belinda reached out and grasped her hand. 'I'd be glad of some company myself. And don't worry, I'll stick to you like glue. If your head starts swimming, just let me know — I'll make sure you don't get too near any cliff edges!'

And on that note, Hillary finished off the last few sips from her glass of red wine and bid everyone goodnight.

* * *

The next morning Hillary, who usually only had a cup of coffee and perhaps a slice of toast for breakfast if she had time, ate enough food to last her the rest of the day. (What was it about holidays and the breakfast buffet? And who ever ate a full English Breakfast anyway, unless you were in a hotel?)

They had arranged to leave the Riverside Inn by nine o'clock at the latest. According to the brochure, the steam trains ran at two-hourly intervals on the odd hours, so they were aiming to make the eleven o'clock train journey. And since Patrick had estimated that the commute should take them no more than an hour and quarter at the most, this would give them plenty of time to find the station, purchase tickets and find a good seat, and all without having to hurry.

Since Patrick, on his visits to various relatives, had picked up the lay of the land more than most of them, Jasper was amenable to following behind the Irishman's surprisingly expensive top-of-the-range saloon car in the shiny black four-by-four he'd hired.

Hillary, consigned along with Barry Kirk to the back seat of Patrick's sumptuous car, settled herself comfortably and only hoped that she wasn't going to regret the impulse to commit herself to the day in her fellow guests' company. Not normally one to be a part of a crowd, she reminded herself yet again that she was on holiday and her habitual rules of wariness and mild pessimism needed to be put to one side for the duration.

'Not a cloud in sight,' Barry Kirk mused. 'So long as it's the same where we're headed, we should have a good view of everything.'

And with that happy thought and a jaunty pip of the horn, they were off.

The trip over the mountains did indeed make Hillary's ears pop. And, just as people had been telling her whenever they learned she was off to Wales, she did see a lot of sheep. The roads were a joy though, with barely a pothole in evidence. But then, since they met hardly any cars in either direction, she wasn't surprised they were in such good shape.

Patrick turned out to be a competent driver, and she noticed that his curly-topped head often lifted as he checked in his mirror to make sure that the Van Paulens, driving behind, hadn't come adrift. Imogen remained characteristically silent at first, but she was clearly enjoying the scenery, and after a while she unbent enough to tell them that she had actually been born in Wales, but her parents had moved to Cheltenham when she was a child.

'I don't really remember much about my homeland, so I thought it was about time I came back for a visit,' she admitted. 'My husband, Derek, in the early years of our marriage, actually visited these parts quite regularly during his scouting trips for scrappage, funnily enough,' she added.

Hillary, sensing that a rather lonely person lurked behind her somewhat 'hands off' demeanour, gently drew her out some more, and they subsequently learned that she had only one son, who'd emigrated to New Zealand whilst in his early thirties, and that she often flew out to visit him and her grandchildren.

Patrick then entertained them with some outrageous anecdotes of his horseracing days, relating undoubtedly slanderous tales about the shenanigans of various jockeys, trainers and racehorse owners, then went on to ruefully give them a list of 'bones I have broken' from the number of times he'd found himself sailing over a fence all on his lonesome, whilst his mount had snickered at him from the other side of the obstacle that it had steadfastly refused to jump.

'A wall-eyed, knock-kneed sow of an animal, so it was, and I swear it bit me more times than the bloody mosquitoes did,' he was moaning at the conclusion of one such tale, even as Hillary spotted the entrance to the steam railway station and pointed it out to him.

Once safely parked, the two teams of travellers met up inside the station to purchase their return tickets, with the men instantly going out to the track to inspect the small black steam locomotive that was waiting to take them up the mountainside. The vintage carriages stretched out behind it were from the 1920s and 30s and looked tiny by today's standards.

Peering inside one, Hillary noted that they had only six seats per carriage — two sets of three seats lined up in single file alongside the windows, with a small aisle between them for access to the seats at the back and front of the carriage. With high wooden backrests, they each had high wooden panels at the side too, which had padded leather armrests atop them for comfort. The upholstery wasn't original, but the fabric chosen for the refurbishment was an authentic-looking design in red and blue. The door to each carriage was one of those whereby you had to pull down the top glass partition to reach inside to open the mechanism.

'Hardly the *Orient Express*, is it?'

It was, typically, Jasmine who made the sardonic remark with her usual churlish lack of charm, and Hillary wondered why, if the American girl was so bored with her parent's choice of holiday destination, she had bothered to come at all.

'Oh, I don't know, honey, I think it looks quaint,' her father protested. 'Say, have you seen the engine? I want to take a picture of you in front of it.' Then he added wistfully, 'Your mother would have loved this.'

Jasmine, thus chided, shrugged and dutifully went off to be photographed.

'Do you think, if her mother hadn't died when she was so young, she might have better manners?' Imogen spoke quietly — not to Hillary, but to Belinda, who had wandered up to join them.

'I doubt it,' the Canadian responded dryly, and the two women exchanged knowing looks. 'Are we getting in this one here then?' she added, glancing inside the carriage thoughtfully. It was a warm day, and although the place wasn't exactly packed with tourists, the carriages were beginning to fill up with passengers. 'I reckon we should claim it fast, or we won't get seats together.'

Although the transatlantic accent was pronounced, Hillary's ear thought it picked up a slightly off tone somewhere in its make-up. Perhaps, like Imogen, she'd been born elsewhere and migrated when still young?

'Well, they all seem to be much the same, so we might as well,' Imogen concurred. 'I was told it might be chilly up in the mountains if the clouds come down,' she remarked idly, 'but I think we're going to be lucky.'

Hillary glanced around her at the blue sky and the few fluffy white clouds meandering across the horizon. She could understand why the older woman had taken the precaution to dress in black woollen trousers and a dark navy cashmere jumper though. She remembered that her own grandmother had felt the cold more keenly as she'd aged.

Imogen warily eyed the rather high, narrow wooden step leading up into the carriage. She reached out to get a hold on the open door and nervously put one foot out to test the height.

Before Hillary could do so, Barry Kirk quickly stepped in and put a reassuring hand under her elbow and stood close behind her. 'Up you go, Mrs Muir, I won't let you fall.' There was something about the firm but respectful way he handled the woman that made Hillary suspect that he'd had a lot of practice with older ladies. But then, he had the look and air about him of a man who might never have left home, and still lived with his mother.

Hillary did a quick bit of mental arithmetic as the Van Paulens returned and Patrick shot off to take a quick photo of the locomotive for himself. With the American father-and-daughter team, plus Barry, Patrick, Belinda and Imogen that made six — and the carriage would be full.

So, on the basis of last-in-first-out, Hillary told everyone that she'd find a seat in another carriage, and set off to do just that, waving aside their polite offers to move to another carriage themselves. In truth, she had no objection to taking the journey free of their company. It wasn't that they were a bad lot, but she sensed various undercurrents in the group that she had no interest in exploring.

She walked a little further up the line of carriages towards the engine, and finally found one that was child-free.

Smiling at two pairs of older couples and one middle-aged man (dressed in a safari suit, of all things), she took the last free seat and settled back, looking out of the window at the uninspiring car park.

She suspected she was about to find out whether or not she had a real head for heights and had just opened her bag to retrieve a mint to suck on when the train, right on time, gave a little shudder and began to move.

From somewhere ahead of her, the unmistakable and thrilling sound of a steam whistle rent the air.

And they were off!

* * *

The first part of the journey was on relatively flat land, where horses and sheep grazed. After a few minutes a river appeared on the scene, meandering along beside the tracks for some miles. It was hard to estimate their speed, but Hillary doubted it got much above twenty-five miles an hour. But then, speed was not the point. The clanging of the wheels and the swaying of the carriages was strangely soothing, and even though she was no romantic, the nostalgia inherent in this old-fashioned form of transport was by no means lost on her.

Soon, however, the bucolic scene started to change as the train began to noticeably climb. Now the river became nothing more than silver ribbon, receding further and further below, and the trunks of trees became the middle branches, and then the treetops. The farmhouses and cottages below began to take on the aspect of children's toys, sheep became mere white dots, and all the time, the edge of the track began to inch closer towards a sheer drop.

Her fellow passengers, by this time, had all long since got out their mobile phones and were busy recording the passing scenery, some standing up to cross to the other side when the view was significantly better, politely asking if this was all right with the passenger whose lap they were leaning across. And in typically British fashion, this invasion of private space was naturally always all right. Even the man in the safari suit raised no objections and seemed to get into the spirit of things, even standing up once or twice to allow an especially eager spectator better access to 'his' window.

'Oooohs' and 'ahhhs' quickly became the order of the day, as at one point a red kite flew close to them, travelling parallel for some moments, raising the phone/camera usage to fever pitch.

Hillary was the only one not filming. She had long since concluded that trying to capture an image often meant that you missed experiencing the moment in reality. Besides, when did a filmed image ever really measure up to the real thing? No, she was content merely to watch and absorb and allow her memory to do its job should she ever wish to recall these moments again.

She also kept one wary eye not only on the ever-widening view below, but also on the way the nearness of the precipice inched ever closer to the railway tracks. What had been a foot of ground a few minutes ago, then half a foot, now seemed to be mere inches. They must now, she estimated, be almost at the highest point of the journey and the end destination, given that the line seemed to have been hewn into the rock itself. Indeed, for those sitting on the nearside, they could have reached out the open window and patted the mountainside rock itself, had they so desired.

She resolutely refused to ponder what would happen should there be a rockfall or landslide. What was the point? You never knew what was around the corner no matter where you were. So what if she was in a small carriage, halfway up a mountain, with a sheer drop on one side and a rockface on the other? With nothing but a small, valiant, ancient steam engine to get her out of it? She had been in far more danger than this just going about her normal routine back at Thames Valley.

Hillary gave an inward chortle. What was it Kingsley Amis had once said? 'As a means of shortening your lifespan, I heartily recommend London' or something like that? Well, at least she could take comfort in the fact that she wasn't there!

The track, every now and then, began to twist and turn at a sharp angle, and by looking obliquely through the window, she could see the steam train engine ahead as it became briefly visible going around the sharp bend first. As it did so, it invariably blew the whistle, presumably to warn anything on the other side that it was coming. Although what that could be Hillary had no idea. A lost mountain goat? A gormless backpacker, more lost than the goat?

Naturally, everyone in the carriage was determined to capture this particular spectacle, and whenever it happened there was almost a stampede to whichever side of the carriage happened to be the best-favoured. At one such point, the man in the safari suit went so far as to tread on her toe. He was most apologetic and sounded German. Hillary told him it was quite all right. Of course it was. She was British and to make a fuss would have been unthinkable.

After several minutes of laboured effort on the steam engine's part, Hillary began to hope that the train would soon pull into the final station, and was moderately relieved when, a few minutes later, it did just that. Although she wasn't sweating, and she had (more often than not) enjoyed the experience, she vowed that on the downward journey she would choose a seat on the side that was predominantly nearest the rock!

She let her fellow passengers get off first, before climbing carefully down the somewhat tricky narrow step and jumping the fairly deep drop onto the platform. A man in uniform was patrolling, helping various passengers who looked nervous of doing the same. By the time Hillary had walked back down the long line of carriages, she wasn't that surprised to find nearly everyone in 'her' pack grouped together on the platform, exchanging horror stories of vertigo or delight in capturing the bird of prey in flight.

It took Hillary a moment to realise that there were only five of them there. Standing on tiptoe, she peered inside the carriage and saw that Imogen Muir was still in her seat. Perhaps she was waiting for the railway volunteer worker to get down this far to help her onto the platform? She was looking out of the window across the flat expanse of the station, one shoulder leaning negligently against the high back of the chair, and one arm pressed between her body and the armrest's wooden panel.

She looked somehow . . . *wrong*.

And as Hillary continued to look at her, she felt a moment of presentiment steal over her. It was a cool, quiet, unpleasant sensation, and she wanted, for just a moment, to ignore it. But, of course, she couldn't. Not saying anything to the others, she put one foot on the wooden step and went inside.

'Mrs Muir?' she said quietly, hoping — but not expecting — to see the woman's white-haired head move in her direction. But there was no response. 'Imogen?' she said, already stepping forward.

The other woman had selected the last left-hand seat in the far back of the carriage, so Hillary had to walk down the short aisle past the other two sets of seats to get to her. She didn't touch the older woman, but instead half-crouched down to get a better look at her. Her deep-set eyes were open but nothing in them moved. Hillary, carefully reaching out a finger to check the pulse at her neck, felt nothing move there either.

As she'd suspected, Imogen Muir was dead.

She stood up, frowning. Perhaps she had a heart condition? And on the journey, had she discovered that fear of heights was worse than she'd at first thought? If she had, pride alone would have prevented her from admitting it to her fellow passengers. Or it might have been any other number of things. A sudden stroke or aneurysm perhaps. One thing was certain — whatever had caused her death, she had left this life without alerting her fellow passengers, who were even now still excitedly chattering about the journey up here on the platform just yards away.

Hillary sighed. They would have to be told, and she wasn't looking forward to it. It would rob them of all the pleasure of the past hour or so. And a doctor would need to be called. She'd have to alert the railway staff and . . .

Through the glass window, the sun suddenly emerged from behind a rare cloud, and revealed a shiny patch in the middle of Imogen's dark blue jumper. Hillary went very cold and very still as she saw it. Slowly, without touching it, she put her face closer and stared at the stain. Given the dark shade of the wool, she couldn't tell what the colour of the liquid was that had soaked into the cashmere, but she could make a damned good guess.

Unlike the scene in so many a television series or film where the fictional detective puts out a finger to dab it into some unknown or mysterious substance, then withdraws it and stares knowingly at it for a moment — maybe even sniffs it — and then gives a knowledgeable, wise pronouncement, Hillary kept her fingers firmly to herself. The SIO called out to the scene — not to mention any of the SOC officers — would have her guts for garters if she contaminated their crime scene in such a way.

Hillary straightened and automatically glanced around her but could see no sign of a weapon of any sort. She was looking almost certainly for a knife or else any long, sharp blade of some kind. She was by no means a medical expert, but she was sure as she could be, given the circumstances, that Imogen Muir had been stabbed neatly and cleanly through the heart. And the fact that there was so little blood on the scene told her that her heart must have stopped beating almost instantaneously.

She checked the area immediately around the victim's feet and then the area on the seating surrounding her and nodded. No tell-tale drips or pooling anywhere.

Hillary glanced at the open window and sighed, knowing that one of the SIO's first instructions would be to have the railway tracks from here to the original station searched for a weapon.

And rather them than her.

She backed out slowly, trying to leave as little trace of herself as possible behind, but realised that any forensic team was already going to be well up against it when it came to getting anything useful in here. For a start, just how many people must have used this carriage during the tourist season?

She negotiated the step back down, then looked up and down the platform, wondering who her best point of contact would be. She had to get the train sealed off as soon as possible, and it definitely needed to be prevented from making the return journey with its fresh set of waiting passengers, who were beginning to assemble even now for the return trip.

As she stood firm guard at the entrance to the carriage, she noticed that Barry Kirk was watching her with a speculative look in his eye. He was the only one who was. Patrick was busy showing his footage of the red kite to Jasper, who was watching his own version of it and joshing the Irishman that his was better. Belinda was looking around her down at the far end of the platform, but Jasmine had already wandered off somewhere.

At that moment, Hillary saw the chap in the uniform walking slowly her way. He was checking that the carriages were empty, and shutting any doors that had been left open. She didn't know whether this was his paid job, or whether he did this as part of the group of volunteers and enthusiasts who were responsible for keeping so many of Britain's heritage steam train lines operational.

He looked to be in his early fifties and had a pleasant, open face. Even as he approached the carriage, he was smiling a greeting at her, clearly enjoying the warm summer day, and the delight of her fellow passengers. He probably had nothing more on his mind than getting some lunch and maybe calling up his wife or kids for a chat or settling down with a paper to do the crossword or something else as pleasant and innocuous.

And she felt absurdly guilty that she was just about to ruin his whole day.

CHAPTER THREE

As he reached her, Hillary held out her hand and beckoned him closer. 'Hello. Look, I'm sorry, but I'm afraid we have something of a situation here,' she began calmly.

The pleasant smile faltered a little as she moved a step closer, lowering her voice to inform him that there was a dead woman in the carriage, and that he needed to call an ambulance, the police and his boss, in that order. Naturally enough, this made him instinctively crane his neck to look inside the carriage, where he noted the still figure in the seat.

'I should check on her, madam. I'm trained in first aid,' he said. He started toward the door to the carriage, but Hillary gently blocked him. The fewer people who left their traces in that carriage, the better.

'I am too, and I can tell you that she's dead,' Hillary repeated flatly. 'I really must insist that you call the police. And I'm afraid nobody can get on this train until they've arrived, which means that you'll need to make some sort of announcement to that effect — and maybe start to organise an alternative route back to the station? Do you have contingency plans in case of a technical failure? Maybe hire a bus or something? I take it there is road access up here?'

The unhappy railway employee agreed that there was, but still visibly hesitated. No doubt he was wondering if she was a crank, or if she and the woman inside were playing some sort of practical joke on him. But one look at Hillary's steady gaze seemed to decide him otherwise, for he nodded, reached for a mobile phone, and wandered off a pace or two and began to use it.

By now, her fellow guests had become alerted to the fact that something out of the ordinary was going on, and Jasper and Patrick both sidled up to her. Barry Kirk, she noticed, did the exact opposite and turned and wandered off in the direction of the café. The building was a charming, wooden-chalet type affair that probably charged the earth for a cappuccino and a slice of cake.

'Something up then, m'darling?' Patrick asked cheerfully, but there was an alarmed flicker marring the look in his blue eyes.

As he spoke, Belinda came up behind him and frowned. 'Is Imogen coming?'

Hillary saw no point in beating about the bush. 'I'm afraid she's . . . er . . . passed away.'

Jasper went pale, then stiffened, went red, then wilted. He opened his mouth, but when nothing came out, he closed it again. Patrick's eyes merely flickered even more. 'The old ticker, was it then? What a shame — she seemed a game old bird,' the Irishman said, but his eyes were on Jasper. Hillary might have been wrong, but she was sure there was speculation in his gaze as he did so.

'You didn't notice anything? On the journey up?' Hillary asked them, unable to help herself. She knew, of course, that she really had no place interviewing suspects and witnesses, and if she didn't knock it on the head, she'd get a proper rollicking (and quite a deserved one, too) from the SIO when he or she rolled up. The one thing that was vital in any investigation was to interview everyone concerned as quickly as possible, and ideally, before they'd had a chance to try out their responses beforehand on everybody else. After a second or third time of telling it, a witness's recollections could take on a kind of storybook aspect that became more and more embellished at each telling, to the point of becoming almost useless as testimony.

But she was so full of curiosity that the question had shot out of her automatically and before she could stop it.

'No,' Patrick said instantly. 'She seemed OK to me. Jasper? Did she seem ill to you?'

Jasper merely shook his head. He seemed to have settled on being pale and silent, but his hands, Hillary noticed, were trembling visibly.

'Look, why don't you go and have a sit down and a cup of hot sweet tea, Jasper, you've had a shock,' Hillary advised. 'Perhaps Belinda . . . ?'

The Canadian woman gave a little start, then nodded. 'Oh yes, I could do with something too. My knees feel like they've turned to jelly. You'll keep me company, Jasper?'

Hillary watched them head off, then turned to Patrick. 'I'll stay here and . . . er . . . supervise things. We'll probably all meet up again somewhere later, yes?'

Whilst she didn't like it one little bit that the five other people in that carriage were now free to roam around alone, she also knew that she had no authority whatsoever to detain them. Besides, where were they going to go? They were at the top of a mountain, and their transport was going to be out of commission for some time. So unless one of them had arranged to have a hire car waiting for them up here, it wasn't as if they could go anywhere. Besides, she knew their identities and where they were staying. If one of them did decide to make a run for it, the local police would have their name and description before they could get very far. Not that she really believed that was likely to happen. She was pretty sure that whoever had just killed Imogen Muir in that railway carriage had to be one cool customer, and it was unlikely that their nerve would break that easily now. 'Right, I think I'll go and join the others,' he muttered.

Left momentarily alone, Hillary pondered their reactions. They'd all expressed shock — except for the silent, watchful

Barry Kirk. Had his departure merely been the reaction of a timid man who didn't want to be involved in unpleasantness — or the result of a far more sinister need to put distance between himself and the silent figure in the carriage?

Hillary's musings came to a sudden halt as the railway official finished talking on his phone and made his way back to her.

'All right — the police and ambulance are on the way,' he said unhappily. 'And someone from the station is coming to, er, check things out.'

Hillary nodded. The train operators could send who they liked, she thought mutinously, but nobody except the attending SIO was going to be allowed into the train carriage. 'That's fine,' she said levelly. 'We'll just wait here until someone comes, shall we?'

The man in the uniform glanced around at the growing number of passengers waiting for permission to board the train and sighed. 'I'd better start telling them that they're going to have to be here a little longer than they thought,' he muttered. 'They're not going to like it though,' he predicted.

He was right. They didn't.

* * *

The first police officers to arrive on the scene were a pair of uniformed constables, probably sent to do an initial look-see from the nearest police station. Whilst one of them talked to the railway officer, the other one walked up to speak to Hillary.

She gave him all the details he needed to know to do an initial assessment, but he would insist on boarding the train to see for himself that the woman was dead, and not in need of medical assistance. She sighed heavily. 'All right. But try to keep your contact to a minimum,' she warned him. 'This isn't likely to be a case of death by natural causes, and the less you contaminate the scene, the better your superiors will like it.'

The young man gave her a surprised look, but went inside, and Hillary was relieved to see that he did exactly as she had said. When he came out, he looked serious and thoughtful, and got on his mobile to call for reinforcements. Every now and then he shot her covert glances, which amused her.

Unless she missed her guess, he had already placed her in the 'prime suspect' category.

Hillary ignored him and glanced at her watch. Barely twenty minutes had passed since the train had pulled into the station. It already felt more like an hour. This, she thought grimly, was going to be a hell of a long day.

* * *

Not quite fifteen minutes later, a black man somewhere in his late twenties or very early thirties arrived. He was in plain clothes, and looked like he might play some sort of sport very well, and Hillary instantly had him pegged as a sergeant. Smartly dressed in a dark blue suit, he approached the train and gave Hillary (who was still standing guard in front of the carriage door) a surprised glance — then sought out the uniformed constable who was standing a little to one side of her.

The constable had never let Hillary out of his sight, and this too had amused her. Did he really think she was going to try to leg it? The thought was enough to keep her entertained for minutes at a time. A few years ago, she might just have been able to put on a fair enough sprint to give him a bit of a challenge, but nowadays she doubted she could even make it out of the car park before he'd rugby-tackled her to the ground.

She didn't much blame him for his caution though — she knew well enough that from his point of view, her cool demeanour and determination to insert herself into the action was suspect. It was not exactly unheard of for a killer to hang around at the crime scene, either in an attempt to explain away their DNA or fingerprints, or simply so that they could get some sort of sick, vicarious thrill out of it. His colleague, though, was busy helping the stationmaster (or whatever his title was) to keep curious passengers at bay.

'Constable,' the newcomer said, nodding at the PC, who stiffened to attention slightly, and nodded back.

'Sarge.'

'What have we got?'

'The train pulled in at its usual time. The guard was informed by this lady,' he nodded his chin towards Hillary, 'that a passenger in this carriage was deceased. She asked him to call us. When I arrived, I ascertained that the passenger — a woman in her seventies I would say, was indeed deceased. This lady,' he again jerked his head in Hillary's direction 'was insistent that the cause was suspicious and refused to leave the scene.'

So he hadn't noticed the dark stain on Imogen's chest, Hillary mused. But then, that wasn't surprising. She had almost missed it herself, and she'd had years of experience of murder cases behind her.

'Right,' the sergeant said, giving Hillary a more thorough look. As she stood there, her best poker face firmly in place, she pictured just what it was that he was seeing. A woman in her mid-fifties, whom she hoped he would describe as 'well-preserved', wearing a pair of lightweight apricot-coloured slacks and a burnt-orange and white blouse. She had a white, long-handled canvas bag slung over one shoulder and was wearing white sandals.

As their eyes met, their gazes both unwavering, she could almost tell, to the moment, when the sergeant became seriously interested in her. His brown eyes narrowed slightly, and he nodded briefly at the constable before approaching her. As he walked, he switched on some sort of recording app on his mobile. He also took out a notebook and pencil.

'Can you tell me your name please?' were his first, crisp words.

'Hillary Greene.'

'Address?'

'I live on a narrowboat called the *Mollern* at a permanent mooring on the Oxford canal in the village of Thrupp, Oxfordshire.'

'Did you travel up on this train?'

'I did.'

'In this carriage?' he pointed behind her with his pencil.

'No. There were only six seats per carriage, and there were seven in our party. I offered to find a seat in another carriage.'

'So you know the deceased?'

'Slightly. I met her yesterday, when I arrived at the Riverside Inn at Hay-on-Wye. She was already resident, as were all the other members of our party today. Her name is Imogen Muir. I believe she's a widow, with one son, resident in New Zealand.'

She was careful to give only the facts as she knew them to be, and to keep her own thoughts and opinions to herself. After years of being called out to crime scenes as the senior investigating officer herself she knew how much easier it made your life when you were gifted with coherent and succinct witnesses! It felt distinctly odd being on the other end of this process though.

'You say there were five others who made the journey in the carriage with her?'

'Yes. They were a Mr Jasper Van Paulen and his daughter Jasmine. Both Americans. Mr Patrick Unwin, an Irishman, but I believe he currently resides and works somewhere in Scotland, Mr Barry Kirk — English, and a Ms Belinda John-Jacques, a Canadian, who may be a journalist of some sort,' she added significantly. Nor did the warning pass him by, for (as she well knew) the last thing he needed was to have a nosy media professional muscling in, and the sooner he was warned of the danger, the better. Bitter experience had told her how quickly a case could go south once the press got the bit between their teeth.

Yet again he looked at her closely. 'Is she now?'

'She might also be something of a small celebrity in her own sphere — social media and such like. I have an idea she might be freelancing for more upmarket magazines and periodicals rather than for any particular newspaper.' But for all either of them knew, she might already be relaying the news via a public platform.

According to Patrick, neither he nor Jasper had noticed anything odd, so it was feasible none of the others had either. Unless they were all involved in a conspiracy of silence. Which was all very *Murder on the Orient Express* and all that, but in her experience, very unlikely. Why would any one of them, let alone all of them, keep silent if they'd seen anyone deal the fatal blow?

'And how did you come to discover that the lady was dead?' The sergeant's question dragged her mind away from her speculations, and she forced herself to concentrate on doing all she could to make his job easier.

Carefully, Hillary took him through her discovery of the body, leaving nothing out, but keeping it short and simple for both his recording device and his notetaking. She suspected he realised that she was doing this, for once or twice she found him watching her with a growing sense of puzzlement.

'And nobody else who travelled in there with her noticed *anything?*' he asked, sounding very sceptical indeed.

Hillary merely shrugged. 'Patrick Unwin claimed not to have noticed anything, and Mr Van Paulen agreed that he hadn't either. If Belinda has any information, she didn't volunteer it. But by the time I'd arrived here, Jasmine Van Paulen had already gone off exploring. And Barry Kirk left before I could talk to him.'

For her own part, Hillary wasn't as surprised by the seemingly collective blindness of the witnesses as the newcomer. It was possible Imogen hadn't been killed until the journey was all but over, limiting the time frame when someone might have noticed Imogen's ominous silence and stillness. And from her own experiences on the way up, she had already formed her own ideas as to how the thing might have been done with a minimum of risk of detection on the killer's part. If Jasper and the others had acted in the same way as the people in her own carriage had, any one of them could have killed Imogen without it being noticed.

Imogen had also selected one of the two back seats, and the one nearest the window that had had predominantly the best views. Any one of the passengers, recording the journey, could have asked permission to lean over her to get a prime shot of the action. And if the killer chose their moment well — when the bird of prey had flown so close to them, say, or when the engine had briefly come into view going around a corner — then everyone else's attention would have been firmly fixed elsewhere.

It wouldn't be that hard to slip a very sharp implement into the old lady, using their own body to hide what they were doing, then simply flick the knife or whatever weapon was used out of the still-open window. Since most people preferred to record things without glass in front of them, it was almost impossible to believe that all the windows weren't similarly open at the time of the murder.

Of course, the killer had to take the risk of the old lady crying out. Which begged the question — was that stab to the heart a lucky break, or had the killer some medical knowledge? Either way, given the clackety-clack the train made when it went over the points, plus the excited chatter of the others all around them, it was unlikely that the old lady would have been heard unless she'd actually had the chance to scream blue murder. And somehow, Hillary didn't think that that was how the medical examiner would sketch it out in their report. It had looked to her as if death had come too quickly for that. The old lady's clothes hadn't been in a state of any disarray at all, so the likelihood of any kind of physical tussle seemed very small.

No, she thought, at most the victim might have given a quiet gasp or a surprised grunt, but nothing more.

When she glanced back at the sergeant, waiting for his next question, she found him watching her with a look of intense concentration, and it was obvious to her that he might almost have been listening to the mental cogs turning in her brain. Luckily for her, she had her poker face still firmly in place.

The sergeant nodded. 'All right, let's take a look.' He turned and climbed into the carriage. Through the glass, both Hillary and the constable watched him bend closely over the dead woman's body. Like Hillary, he made no move to touch the stain on her clothing when he eventually spotted it. He backed out of the carriage carefully, then leapt lithely down onto the platform.

Hillary wished she'd been able to do the same, but nowadays thought her knees wouldn't have thanked her for it if she'd tried it.

The sergeant nodded at her. 'Can you give me a physical description of all those people you just mentioned. Height, weight, hair colour, eyes, any distinguishing features?'

Hillary did so and he noted it all down meticulously. When she was finished, he nodded at her abruptly. 'Thank you, Mrs Greene. You can leave now.'

If the constable looked surprised at her sudden dismissal, Hillary merely nodded at the sergeant and walked away. Having ascertained that he had murder on his hands, she knew he had things he needed to be doing — and that meant prioritising.

And right now, he had other things to attend to than keeping a wary eye on her.

Naturally, she wanted to stay so badly that she could almost taste it. It had been some years now since she'd been present at an immediate homicide, and she could feel the old familiar song singing in her veins. But she was not a DI anymore and would only be in the way. She was a witness, nothing more.

And she was on holiday. Right?

And this was none of her business. Right?

* * *

The moment she walked away, the sergeant — whose name was David Soames — did two things. Firstly, he reported back to his HQ that this was a very suspicious death indeed and that they would need an SIO and a full forensics team up at the station as soon as possible.

The second thing he did was use his phone and google the name of Hillary Greene and Thrupp. It didn't take him long to find her. And the more he read, the wider his eyes grew.

* * *

Sergeant David Soames knew DI Ian Jones only by sight. The inspector had recently transferred from a station near Swansea, and they hadn't had the chance yet to work together. But the things Soames had heard about the man had been positive so far, although some of the more traditionalists didn't think much of his university degree and his rather rapid rise through the ranks.

This didn't bother Ian Jones much, as he was inclined to put it down to the usual case of sour grapes. His degree was in Sociology, but his real passion was hill running. At six feet one, he was scrawny and fit as the proverbial butcher's dog and had lived in the Welsh countryside most of his life. Recently divorced — and still a little shell-shocked by it — when he'd been given this case by his guv'nor he'd been more than ready for the challenge and distraction it offered him.

He had two previous homicide investigations under his belt — a domestic, and a youth killed by a rival gang member over territory. Both cases had been straightforward, with the suspect in the first case obvious from the start. But this had the feeling of something very different about it, and he'd have been lying to himself if he didn't admit to feeling a certain amount of trepidation.

Any murder was rare in his experience, and when he'd been informed that this victim was a tourist, an old lady found dead in a steam-train carriage no less, his first thought had been that someone was pulling his leg. That, of course, had quickly proved to be not the case, and on the drive past Devil's Bridge and up into the Cambrian mountains, he knew the pressure would be on to get results.

His previous cases had both been during his secondment to Cardiff. But this one, out here in the beautiful countryside, felt almost surreal. The beauty of the passing scenery and the gloriously sunny weather — combined with his tourist-trap destination — did little to help dispel this slightly disorientating feeling of unreality.

It wasn't until he walked down the station platform and was approached by the serious-faced DS Soames that it suddenly became all too real. Within moments he was standing over the dead woman and wishing that she didn't remind him quite so much of his own grandmother, who was thankfully still very much alive and a demon bingo player in Abergavenny.

With some difficulty he could just make out the now congealing stain in the middle of the dead woman's navy jumper. When he complimented the sergeant on his skills of observation, the inspector was to get the first of many surprises that day when his colleague informed him that it was not himself, nor the first responder, who had spotted the evidence of a possible stab wound, but another passenger on the train.

'Her name is Hillary Greene, sir. And I'd better warn you right from the off — she's not your average witness.'

* * *

Hillary was sitting in the shade under a large chestnut tree. The sun had decided to shine as if it really meant it, and she was drinking a generic brand of apple juice from the café's refrigerator when she saw the sergeant, accompanied by a tall lanky man with a mop of brown hair, heading her way. She saw herself being pointed out and wasn't at all surprised when the two men made their way to the wooden bench on the other side of her picnic table and sat down.

'Mrs Greene, this is Detective Inspector Ian Jones. I'm Detective Sergeant Soames.' Both men held out their ID. Hillary studied them carefully and nodded.

'First off, I understand you used to be on the job,' DI Jones began without preamble. If he thought his knowledge would surprise her, he was to be disappointed.

Hillary, who wasn't about to give herself any pats on the back for figuring out that the sergeant would be quick off the mark in establishing her identity, merely nodded.

'Yes. With Thames Valley,' she agreed. 'I retired at your rank and now work as a civilian consultant in the CRT department.'

DI Jones nodded. 'Yes, so I understand.' He had just been reading a file all about her — including her medal for bravery after being shot on the job. 'I have to say, your record for closing cases is . . . impressive.'

Impressive, he thought wryly, was hardly the word. After learning all about their chief witness, Ian had done what any sensible copper would do on learning that he had a decorated, high-ranking former police officer on the loose at his crime scene.

He'd called upon the cop network to find out the talk about her.

Ian didn't know anyone working at Thames Valley, but every copper always knew someone who would know someone who would know someone, and so he'd put out a call to an old Fraud squad pal he'd met in training college whom he knew had been deployed in Oxfordshire. And this mate had duly promised to get back to him with word on the former DI Hillary Greene as soon as he could manage it. So — be it good, bad or indifferent, before long he was going to know all he needed to know about the woman seated in front of him.

And until he knew just what and who he was dealing with, he decided to proceed with caution.

He nodded at Soames, who restarted his recording app and got out his notebook.

'I'm sure you, of all people, know how important the first hours are on any investigation, so I'm hoping you can help me hit the ground running, DI . . . er . . . Mrs . . . er Ms? Greene?'

Hillary looked at the young detective, who already looked as if he wanted to kick himself after getting flustered at the very start of his interview and smiled wryly.

'Call me Hillary — it'll be easier. And I'll do all I can to help.'

Something in her voice had the inspector's tense shoulders relaxing a little.

'Thank you. First of all, can you explain why you're here in Wales, and how you came to be on the train today?'

Hillary reluctantly admitted to writing a crime fiction novel, and very briefly explained her intent to help the book get into the local shops. She passed quickly on to her arrival at the Riverside Inn and her impressions of his five suspects. 'Unfortunately, having literally only known them a matter of hours . . .' She ended on a shrug.

'That's more than I could have hoped for,' he assured her. 'Now, can you remember what these people were wearing when they boarded the train?'

Hillary half-closed her eyes and began to recite. She knew herself how vague or inaccurate witness statements could be and was rather pleased and proud of herself to be able to provide him with detailed descriptions of everyone's clothing that day. It was not that she'd knowingly taken inventory, but she'd had decades to hone the habit of observation and now it paid off.

As Soames and his DI exchanged pleased glances, she knew why she'd been asked the question, of course. The clothing of all those people in the carriage would be gone over minutely by forensics, and he wanted to know if anyone had changed clothes since getting off the train.

She suspected that he'd already sent off reinforcements to round up his suspects and take them back to his home station, but she didn't think that would present any difficulties. The descriptions of them that she'd previously given to the sergeant would help, and anyway, the sole attraction here were the Beggar's Leap waterfalls. And anyone not there taking photographs would either be in the café, the gift shop, or one of the other little shops selling souvenirs, postcards, fudge and other sweet treats that seemed to proliferate at this sort of place.

And if any one of them was wearing different shoes or tops to those being noted down right now, things wouldn't be looking good for them.

'I'll require a formal statement as soon as possible. When I have a car available, I'll have them take you down to the station and then back to . . . Hay-on-Wye, wasn't it?'

'Yes. Thanks, that would be helpful. I don't think there's a regular train station there, and I have no idea what bus routes would be available.'

The inspector nodded, thanked her and left.

Hillary watched him stride away, full of purpose and energised, and was wryly aware that she'd probably never felt more envious of another person in her life before.

But this was not her case. Not her business. Right?

CHAPTER FOUR

By the time Hillary returned to the Riverside Inn it was nearly five o'clock, and Judith all but pounced on her. She'd barely set foot through the door and into the hall before the proprietor was by her side.

'Oh, Mrs Greene, you're back! I've been so worried. A policeman came to the door and showed me papers saying that I was authorised to pack a change of clothes for each of my guests, except for you, and then he took them away with him. What on earth's going on? The policeman wouldn't tell me anything.'

Hillary gave her what she hoped was a reassuring smile. She knew that procedure dictated that you told civilians nothing at all about a case if you didn't have to, and doubted anyway that the uniformed constable assigned to such a duty would have been able to explain, even if he'd wanted to. 'Don't worry, it's all in order. You know, I really could do with a very large glass of wine, Mrs Pringwell, if the bar is open? I have some rather bad news for you. I'm afraid Mrs Muir has been killed.'

Hillary saw her go pale and sway a little. 'Mrs Muir? She's *dead*?'

'Yes, I'm sorry.'

Leading her gently towards the bar, she persuaded Judith to have a drink herself, and for the next ten minutes or so Hillary gave her a gentle and carefully edited update on what had happened. By the time she was finished, the hotel owner looked both sombre and worried — as well she might. But although Hillary had no doubt that the canny businesswoman was already considering just how much damage this would all have on her hotel's future bookings, she also got the feeling that there was something other than that bothering her.

'Did you know Mrs Muir before she came here?' she asked quietly. They had taken their drinks to a table overlooking the garden, and Judith was sipping from a bulbous glass of brandy whilst absently watching a pied wagtail hawk for flies along the lawn's edge.

'Hmmmm?' The other woman dragged her eyes from the erratic antics of the little black-and-white bird and looked at Hillary with a vague smile. But there was nothing vague about the look behind her eyes, Hillary noticed. 'Oh, I never met Mrs Muir before she booked in here last Wednesday,' she said. It might have been the effects of the brandy, but Hillary had the feeling that her choice of words had been very carefully selected. 'But she seemed to me to be a nice, pleasant sort. The last kind of woman that you'd expect who would . . . well . . .'

'End up murdered? Yes, I agree,' Hillary said dryly. 'But I'm afraid we'll have to face facts. And since she was alive and well when she went into the carriage, and dead when it arrived at its destination, I'm afraid we'll also have to face up to the fact that one of her fellow guests here was responsible for it.'

Although Judith paled even more at this, and took another hasty sip of restorative brandy, Hillary didn't get the sense that her blunt words had caused any real shock or surprise in the hotelier. But she was an intelligent woman and had probably figured that much out for herself already. A quick thinker then, and capable of keeping a cool head in a crisis.

'Tell me, did she ever seem to you as if she was afraid of someone here?' Hillary asked, as casually as you can ask such a question. 'I know I only arrived yesterday, but it seemed to me, although everyone acted friendly enough, that there was a slight undercurrent somewhere amongst the others?'

Judith gave her a considering glance, and Hillary knew that she was carefully weighing up the pros and cons about just how much discretion she should use. She needed to nip any inclination to reticence in the bud if she was to get anywhere. 'I'm not asking to be nosy, or anything like that, but I'm afraid things are bound to get more and more complicated for us all as the investigation goes on, so we need to be prepared. I expect the police will be here soon to search Mrs Muir's room, for instance. I daresay the police officer who came asked you to lock the room and give him the key?'

'Yes, yes he did. How did you know . . . ?'

Hillary didn't want to show her true colours just yet so she simply gave a wry smile and a shrug. 'Well, I've just written a crime novel, as you may know, and I had to do a lot of research. Besides, it's just common sense, isn't it? They're bound to want to know everything there is to know about Mrs Muir and all the others, aren't they? And their first port of call to find that out, I'm very much afraid, is going to be right here at the Riverside — which means you and me. I've already been taken to the station to give a formal statement, and I imagine you'll be asked to do so tomorrow as well. It might make things easier if you think about what you need to say in advance.'

She paused to let that sink in. Judith frowned a little, then sighed. 'I suppose so. And you're right, in a way, there did seem to be something a little strained about this batch of guests. Usually, you know, most of my guests get on well, perhaps because they only meet at breakfast and dinner! They don't have the time to fall out with each other.'

'But these guests have?'

'I'm not sure. At times I thought there must have been an argument or disagreement or something going on between them, but I might have been imagining things. I think a lot of it can be put down to simple personality clashes; certainly between Jasmine and Belinda, and Jasmine and—'

She stopped herself abruptly.

'Mrs Muir?' Hillary prodded calmly. 'Yes, I thought I detected a certain coolness between them too.'

'You'd noticed that already?' Judith sighed heavily. 'I hate it when that sort of thing happens — it can ruin everyone's holiday. Jasmine's problem, in my opinion, is that she's always been spoilt. She lost her mother young, I gather, and as an only child, I think her father overcompensated for it by not disciplining her properly, and by giving her too many *things*. A combination that's just asking for trouble, to my mind. You know — treating her like his princess who can do no wrong? From what I can gather, Mr Van Paulen is a very wealthy man, and she's always had the best — clothes, jewels, holidays, expensive schools. But that sort of privilege can sometimes create its own problems, can't it?'

'Yes. A sense of entitlement for one,' Hillary agreed. 'Being the centre of someone's world can make you think the *whole* world should revolve around you. And it comes as a shock when you learn that it doesn't.'

'Exactly. Jasmine's beautiful too, which doesn't help matters. Mr Unwin actually flirts with her and poor Mr Kirk goes red whenever she talks to him.'

Hillary grinned.

'But then there's Ms John-Jacques . . .' Judith rolled her eyes slightly.

'And suddenly Jasmine found she had some real competition?' Hillary interpreted the eye-roll with ease.

'I'll say! A beautiful woman — in a very different way from herself — and although an older woman, one with a more sophisticated back story than her own and a natural elegance about her. It put Jasmine's nose right out of joint, as you can imagine. She started off with sly digs about her, and then became downright catty towards her.'

'And how did Belinda react to that?' Hillary asked curiously. Although they weren't yet talking about the murder victim, nevertheless, the interrelationships of all those who'd been in the carriage today interested her inordinately.

'Oh, I think she was more amused than anything, to be fair to her,' Judith said with a slight shrug. 'She never responded in kind — mainly, I think, because she had enough sense to see it would only make her look ridiculous. Oh, sometimes she could lose her patience with the girl a bit, and then she'd come back with a witty put-down that made Jasmine furious. Eventually they seemed to settle for a mutual, mostly silent antipathy — you know, like two jungle cats meeting accidentally in a clearing and warily sidling around each other with just the odd warning snarl or two.'

Again, Hillary couldn't help but grin. 'Sounds exhausting for them and trying for everybody else. I noticed that Belinda and Imogen Muir shared a dining table, and seemed quite friendly though?'

'Oh yes, I'd say so. Mrs Muir had arrived two days, I think it was, before Belinda, and I've noticed that it's often the case that two single ladies will pair up with each other — especially when they share a table. Our dining room's too small for everyone to have their own, you'll have noticed. Your table was fully occupied before you arrived, father and daughter made for one duo, and the two boys made up another, so it was rather inevitable.' Judith gave a shrug.

'But they seemed to genuinely get on as far as I could tell, rather than just find it convenient to pair off?' Hillary baited the hook carefully.

'Oh yes, I think so. In my opinion . . . Mrs Muir was naturally a lot older than Belinda, but they seemed to share the same sort of outlook on life, if that makes sense? Both were elegant women, both liked good but not flashy clothes, both were well heeled and liked the same sort of things. Considering they lived on different continents and were decades apart in age, they actually seemed to have a lot in common. They played cards like demons for instance — I'm not sure what the game was though. Canasta maybe? Something more complicated? Either way, they got very intense about it — but never argued. Just competitive, but in an enjoyable sort of way. They didn't play for money or anything like that, but whoever lost would buy a bottle of champagne for dinner the next day, that sort of thing.'

'And what was Jasmine's problem with Imogen?' Hillary asked curiously. 'I can see why she'd have issues with someone like Belinda, but with an old woman? I'd have thought she'd barely be a blip on Jasmine's radar.'

Judith shifted uneasily on her seat. 'Oh, I have no idea about that,' she said, and for the first time, Hillary was certain that she was lying — or at least, temporising. She might not know exactly what the deal was between the murder victim and the American girl, but Hillary was pretty sure that Judith could have given a damned good guess if she'd wanted to.

But Hillary was wise enough not to push it. Whatever the problem had been, she was sure she would winkle it out in the days to come. All she had to do was observe. She was fairly confident that she could pump each of her fellow guests in turn and, before long, could assemble a fairly accurate picture of the life and times at the Riverside Inn in the days leading up to her own arrival here. Enough to be of use to DI Jones, anyway.

Unless one of them was confessing to the crime right now, and the case was over before it started. But somehow, she didn't think it was going to be that easy.

And it wasn't. Judith received a phone call to say that none of her guests would be there for dinner that night, or would spend the night in their own beds, and the worried hotelier passed the information on to Hillary.

Of course, it didn't surprise Hillary that all of them were detained overnight. She knew Jones could keep them for quite some time, given the circumstances, but she doubted it would do him much good. If, as she suspected, they all insisted they'd seen and heard nothing, then he was really up against it.

He might *know* one of them (or perhaps two in collusion?) had killed the old lady, but proving it, Hillary feared, was going to give him a monumental headache. She doubted, given his age, he could have had much experience with murder inquiries, but he'd nevertheless struck her as being both intelligent enough and patient enough to realise that letting them loose and then observing their behaviour would do him more good than keeping them detained in the interview room.

Well, she would do her best to help him out all that she could, however he wanted to play things. Whilst being careful not to step on his toes, of course. She was hopeful that he would become amenable to the idea that he could call on her past experience and expertise any time he wanted it. He certainly hadn't struck her as egotistical, or so macho that he couldn't bear to listen to the advice of a former senior — albeit female — officer. In which case, she might be able to stay clued in on how the investigation was progressing and offer a few helpful suggestions along the way.

That evening, rather than put Judith to the time and trouble of cooking just for one, Hillary took herself down the road to a pub specialising in Italian cuisine. Tomorrow, she *had* planned to start her goodwill tour of the town's many bookshops, but that could always wait.

Later that night, as she settled down in her comfortable bed in the eerily quiet bijou inn, she wondered what luck forensics were having with the suspects' clothing. If they could find significant bloodstains on any one of them Jones might be home free. But Hillary didn't think she was being over-pessimistic in believing that it would probably turn out not to be the case. There had been so little blood at the scene to begin with, it was far more likely they'd only find microscopic traces on all five of them, which would prove absolutely nothing, since all five had been in the carriage for some time and might have picked up traces of it just by moving around.

No two ways about it, the killing of Imogen Muir was an odd one, Hillary mused. On the one hand, it must have been premeditated and planned carefully. The killer would have needed to bring the weapon with them for a start. Which indicated someone capable of cold, calculated murder. And yet, there was also an undeniable element of risk involved. To stab someone at close quarters with five potential witnesses required nerve and a certain amount of bravura.

Had the killer travelled that train before? If a previous reconnaissance *had* been made, then the killer would doubtless have observed what Hillary had seen on her own journey up the mountain; the likely behaviour of fellow passengers, plus the optimum moment to strike on one of those photogenic turns in the track.

She'd have to drop a hint to Jones to see if the rail company kept any kind of records of ticket sales. Not that she was particularly sanguine that it would lead to much. The killer might have been too wary to have done a dry run. And as she'd seen for herself, even if he or she had risked it, there was no pre-booking involved, so there'd be no computer trail. You simply turned up and bought a ticket at the station. It was just *possible* that the ticket sellers — on being shown photographs of the five suspects — might recall having seen one of them before today. But realistically, how likely was it? They must sell hundreds if not thousands of tickets over the summer season.

But the big question that really baffled her was — *why*? Why kill someone in such circumstances that you were bound to be amongst those suspected of committing the crime? That just made no sense to Hillary at all. They were not living in an Agatha Christie novel, after all. There was no imperative to create a classic whodunnit-style locked-room mystery.

So why hadn't the killer planned to wait until the train had arrived at its destination, followed Imogen Muir to the main attraction — the high waterfalls — and then just taken the opportunity to kill her there, by the simple expedient of pushing her over? True, Imogen's plea to Belinda to stay close to her *might* have brought about a radical change of the killer's tactics.

But Hillary just couldn't believe that. Surely the killer could rely on the fact there would be times when Belinda and Imogen would be apart? After all, the old lady would only have needed a hand to hold whilst exploring the falls themselves, but not for the rest of the time.

For a start, surely waterfalls on tops of mountains were surrounded by quiet, conveniently private woods and pathways, providing plenty of opportunity for a killing strike before Imogen got anywhere near a cliff edge and sought out Belinda to hold her hand? Then there were all the other amenities to consider.

At some point, Imogen would have had to visit the ladies. Then there was the café — and probably a gift shop? The sharp knife or implement used to kill Imogen in that railway carriage could just have effectively been used anywhere at Beggar's Leap — and with far less danger of discovery. And — far more importantly — would have left the field wide open. If Imogen's body had been found anywhere at the tourist site, then poor DI Jones would have hundreds of possible suspects on his hands.

And yet that hadn't happened. So, as things now stood, either Belinda, Barry, Patrick or one of the Van Paulens *must* be the killer. The idea of some outsider, waiting on the precipice of that narrow track, ready to throw a knife through the open window of a passing steam train beggared belief (no pun intended). Apart from the fact that you'd need the skills of a circus-quality knife thrower to even be sure of killing your intended victim, you'd have every person on that train getting a good look at you as it passed. There was simply no way to make yourself inconspicuous trudging along *that* railway line.

Was it just conceivable the killer had climbed one of the trees, concealed themselves behind a branch and then . . . At that point, Hillary gave herself a good talking to. She was thinking sheer tosh!

So . . . back to her original conundrum. If you were going to kill someone, why do it in such a way that you were just asking to come under close scrutiny by the police right from the start? There had to be a point to it. Unless, of course, the killer of Imogen was a genuine basket case, and if that was so, all bets were off!

At some point in the early hours, Hillary resigned herself to the fact that she'd have to return to Beggar's Leap again and thoroughly check out the lay of the land for herself to get a better idea of things.

Continuing to toss and turn, it took some time to calm down her racing mind enough to the point that it would allow her to fall asleep. Even then, she awoke at around 6 a.m.

* * *

After taking a quick shower, Hillary let herself out and wandered down to the meadow and through the buttercups to the river, enjoying the early morning mist and warm sunshine. She was determined to make the most of this calming interlude, suspecting that it might be the only respite she had that day.

And she was right. When she returned to the inn, she noticed that a police patrol car was now parked out front, and when she walked into the hallway, Judith was standing at the reception desk, looking up at the stairs with worried eyes.

Seeing Hillary, she hurried over to her. 'They came ten minutes ago with a search warrant to search one of the guest's rooms,' Judith began in a rush. 'Four of them this time. I had no choice but to allow it.'

Hillary stiffened to attention. 'Only one warrant? They haven't come to search all the rooms?'

'Thankfully not.'

Hillary thought rapidly. There must have been developments. DI Jones must have got a scent of something to be so targeted. She pushed down a growing sense of frustration at being on the outside of things and having to peer in, reminding herself that she was just going to have to get used to the feeling.

But that didn't mean she was totally without resources. 'Whose room are they interested in?' she asked casually. Even so, the hotel owner gave her a knowing look.

But Judith Pringwell obviously felt more in need of an ally than the sense of satisfaction that came with being discreet, because after only the briefest of hesitations she met Hillary's eye with a worried expression.

'Jasmine Van Paulen's,' she said quietly.

Hillary merely nodded. That was interesting. Very interesting.

'You'll be wanting breakfast soon, I'm sure,' Judith abruptly became businesslike again. 'Shall we say in half an hour? I don't know if I should cater for . . . any of the others? I haven't had any phone call to say when I can expect the rest of my guests.'

'That would be lovely, thank you. As for the others . . .' Hillary could only shrug unhelpfully.

She'd just come down to breakfast, however, when a commotion in the hall told her that Judith's wayward guests had, after all, been allowed to return and would probably want feeding.

It was as she'd suspected. DI Jones had had to let them all go, pending further enquiries. He'd have kept the passports of all those from overseas, naturally, and must have warned the UK residents to remain available for questioning.

She wondered if the officers searching Jasmine's room had managed to finish the task before the occupant of the room had returned. If not, she couldn't see the American girl being best pleased.

Hillary sipped her coffee patiently, and awaited developments. Someone had been murdered and that was utterly deplorable, but she would have been dishonest with herself if she didn't acknowledge the fact that she hadn't felt this alert and eager for years. Did that make her a 'bad' person? On the other hand, it could be argued that she was morally obligated to use her skills and expertise for a good cause. She wasn't sure. And right then, she was not in the mood to philosophise.

She had a killer to catch.

No. *DI Jones* had a killer to catch, a little voice in the back of her head reminded her. And then she gave a brief grin and wondered — just who was she trying to kid?

* * *

An hour later, Hillary was sitting under the shade of a large-leaved ornamental tree in the back garden. The white-painted wrought-iron garden furniture looked quaint, but she'd been surprised to find the chairs were also rather comfortable.

Further upriver, tourists were sitting out at tables belonging to a riverside café and were taking advantage of the bankside view, whilst downstream a small flotilla of kayaks and canoes were busily disappearing off down the Wye. But thankfully, the chatter from neither gathering reached her. A moorhen chick was anxiously making contact calls to a parent that had just disappeared into a reedbed, and overhead a buzzard soared ever-upwards on a thermal, its mewing call getting fainter and fainter as it headed towards the blue-coloured mountains in the distance. In a bed of marigolds, bees droned contentedly.

If circumstances had been different, then she really would have felt as relaxed as she must have appeared to the man who approached her and then drew out the matching chair opposite her table. As it was, Hillary had noted DI Ian Jones's presence from the moment he'd first stepped out of the dining room's French windows and into the garden.

She'd already made a mental note to go back inside in another half an hour. Knowing how investigations worked, she had estimated that the SIO or his second-in-command would give the released suspects only a brief breathing space before invading their home turf, so to speak, and she had wanted to be on hand to observe their reactions when they found themselves once again under official scrutiny.

But she was just a little surprised, however, to discover that she was one of the first ones that the SIO had sought out.

As the only one not to have travelled in the same carriage as the victim, she should, surely, be very low on DI Jones's list.

Pretending to notice him for the first time, she moved her bag obligingly to one side to give him room to put down his mug of coffee on the table's flat ironwork top. He left the smart leather satchel that he'd been carrying leaning against one of the legs of his chair. 'I see Mrs Pringwell is being hospitable,' she said with a smile, glancing at his beverage, for the discreet white mug bore the Riverside Inn's image on one side.

'Yes, freshly ground too,' he murmured, taking an appreciative sip. 'And thanks for the statement yesterday by the way. It was just right — full of detail, but nothing extraneous. Did it feel odd to have to be making it?' he asked curiously.

Hillary grinned. 'It did, rather,' she admitted. 'It's the first time I've been in an interview room on the receiving end.'

Before he could respond, she heard the ringtone of her mobile phone calling from inside her bag and grimaced an apology as she reached for it. It wasn't a 'personalised' tone, just the generic, irritating warble that had come with the phone as standard, and she frowned a little as she retrieved it.

She wasn't one of those people who lived on their phone, and carried it only for work. True, several friends had the number, but she'd told no one she was going away, and they never called her during working hours, not wanting to interrupt her at what might be a critical moment.

So when she saw the very familiar number it was displaying, she scowled even harder. What the hell were Thames Valley doing calling her here? Working cold cases, it couldn't possibly be anything urgent; besides, the super was the one who'd told her to totally 'switch off' on this break and get in some proper R&R.

She hit the green phone symbol expecting to hear either one of her team or her superintendent, Rollo Sale, but the voice that came over the line belonged to neither.

Without realising that she was doing it, Hillary straightened instinctively in her chair; her shoulders went back, and a shutter came down over her face, leaving it totally expressionless. To the younger Welshman watching her, it was a fascinating display.

'Yes, sir,' Hillary rapped out smartly.

Ian Jones reached for his mug and took another sip. He knew who must be on the other end of that conversation, and why, and he was feeling rather tense about it. He was hoping that Hillary Greene was going to take the news being given to her well, but he was prepared for her anger if she didn't.

He saw her sherry-coloured eyes cut to him briefly before returning to her contemplation of the river, which he was sure she wasn't really seeing.

'Yes, Commander, I understand that,' she said flatly.

At the name of the very high rank, DI Jones also found himself — rather absurdly — stiffening to attention. He had assumed that the matter would have been dealt with by someone far less high up on the food chain. Now he began to seriously worry. Had he somehow really put his foot in it? It had seemed like such a good idea at the time, and his own superintendent had been happy enough to agree with him. He watched Hillary anxiously now as she continued to give her flat-eyed stare out at the surrounding vista.

'Yes, Commander, I understand completely,' she said. Her tone of voice was one that puzzled him slightly, because he couldn't seem to place it in any specific category. Not quite amused. Not quite subservient. Not quite irritated. Not quite . . . well not quite anything that he could put his finger on.

Again, her eyes cut to him. And this time her lips twisted into a smile. Or maybe a grimace? Or a grimacing smile? He took another swallow of his coffee and tried his best to look nonchalant.

'Yes, sir, I'll do my best,' Hillary said. She listened briefly, then gave a little nod to herself. 'Yes, I'll be sure to do that, Commander. Goodbye.'

She pressed the red phone icon with a swift jab of her finger and very carefully laid the phone down on the table. DI Jones became aware that he was sweating a little, a fine prickling of his skin that made him want to wriggle uncomfortably in his chair.

Hillary slowly removed her eyes from the river and looked at DI Jones. 'That was Commander Marcus Donleavy,' she said flatly. 'It seems your guv'nor phoned my guv'nor this morning, with a rather unorthodox request. So unorthodox my super had to pass it up the chain.'

And in Thames Valley HQ, everyone knew that meant Commander Donleavy. DI Jones couldn't know it, of course, but it had been Donleavy who had fought to stop Hillary retiring from the police service in the first place, and Donleavy who had been instrumental in getting her back, offering her the plum job of taking a second look at murder cases in CRT.

They had a long and not-quite-understood history together, neither by the rank and file, her superiors, nor even, she often suspected, Marcus Donleavy and herself.

Some suspected she was his hatchet man, but that was not quite accurate. Some suspected she was his spy, and that definitely wasn't accurate. But there was no denying that Donleavy rated her far above what a humble DI should have been due, and there had been times in the past when they had worked closely together on some very sensitive issues that never did filter down to her regular colleagues.

And even now that she only enjoyed civilian status, everyone knew that the commander would always take a telephone call from Hillary Greene as a priority. It was even rumoured that his secretary had interrupted one of his calls from the ACC when Hillary had insisted on it, but some assumed that story was apocryphal. Some didn't.

'It seems,' Hillary continued, her voice alarmingly mild, 'that your superintendent thinks that I can be useful to you, and that my status as a civilian consultant to Thames Valley should — temporarily — stretch to include that of the Welsh borders.'

Ian decided there was little point in beating around the bush. He pushed his half-finished coffee to one side and looked her in the eye. 'Look, I've been asking around about you, and I liked what I've heard. More than that — I liked what I saw and heard for myself yesterday. And after checking out your solve rate when it came to homicide cases . . .' He shrugged. 'Let's face it, I'd be an idiot if I didn't take advantage of what you've got to offer. Wouldn't I?'

'Not inclined to look a gift horse in the mouth, hmmm?' she asked dryly.

Ian smiled. 'No, ma'am. But on the other hand, if you really resent having your holiday interrupted like this, you don't have to put in too much time. By that, I mean your hours will be your own. I'll just be grateful for any help or advice you can give.'

Hillary looked at him and considered this latest turn of events. He sounded genuine enough. And she wasn't surprised that he'd put out feelers on the old cop network to get the inside information on her. If the positions were reversed, she'd have done the same. And if he was not inclined to look a gift horse in the mouth, well then, neither was she. Hell, just half an hour ago she'd been thinking up subtle ways in which she could inveigle herself into this man's investigation. And now here he was, inviting her in — and not only that, she had the blessings of both his boss and hers as well.

She could tell by his body language that he wasn't sure yet which way she was going to jump, so she needed to put him out of his misery and relaxed back into her chair. 'Well I suppose I could lend a hand,' she said, with an air of nonchalance.

DI Jones sagged a bit in the middle, then grinned. 'Welcome on board, Mrs Greene. Ma'am.'

'Call me Hillary,' she reminded him at once. Then added 'sir' after a slight pause.

Ian instantly shook his head. 'Oh no — I'm not having that! If you're Hillary, then I'm Ian.'

Hillary nodded. It was early days, but she was willing to accept him at face value. However, if the rather odd professional dynamic that was being suggested was to work, she knew that communication was going to be key. 'OK. But let's just set the parameters right away, so there's no confusion. You're the SIO and in charge, but I take it you want me to have an overview?' When he nodded, she carried on. 'And give you advice if and when I think you might need it? Discreetly, of course,' she added, when she saw him hesitate.

His hesitation was natural, of course. He had to maintain the respect and discipline of his team, she understood that. 'So, you've been given enough officers for a murder inquiry?' she asked.

'I'd like more, but with budgets . . .' He shrugged.

Hillary didn't need any telling about budgets. She merely sighed. 'All right then. What have we got so far?'

CHAPTER FIVE

Before they began, DI Jones rose and took off his jacket — a dark blue cotton one that matched the rest of his suit — and hung it over the back of his chair. He also loosened his tie before resuming his seat. Hillary admired his pragmatism; it was far better to be comfortable, and besides, she reminded herself with a wry inner smile, she was hardly anyone he needed to impress.

'Right — the wound,' he began. 'As you suspected, it was a single stab wound to the heart with something long, thin and very sharp.'

'A stiletto?'

'Possibly — but the pathologist thought it more likely to be something surgical or maybe a very thin skewer. It could even have been something especially tooled for the job. Which would suggest an expertise none of our suspects, on the face of it, would seem to have.'

Hillary nodded thoughtfully. 'An improvised weapon might suggest an ex-con,' she said, sipping her coffee. 'You know how good they are at making weapons out of almost anything, and ones that can be quickly disposed of. I take it you've got boots on the ground walking the sides of the tracks looking for it?'

Ian sighed. 'Yes. But I'm not holding my breath. Our killer would have picked his or her spot well, and if they tossed it out the window at the right point, it could have sailed straight down the mountainside for who knows how many feet. Hundreds, knowing my luck. And then it could have bounced and skittered about and ended up who knows where. I'd need an army to cover all the ground, and even then, it could take them weeks.'

Hillary was already nodding. If the Welsh police funding was anything like that in her own neck of the woods, the inspector would be lucky if his bosses would let the search go on until the weekend. 'All right. Worst-case scenario, the weapon's never found.' She shrugged. 'You've run a background check on all five of our suspects. Any of them have form?'

'None of the UK contingent. I'm still waiting back to hear from Canada and the States. We've done all the usual internet searches, social media, that kind of thing, and so far it's not looking good that one of them might turn up trumps. Belinda John-Jacques is who she says she is. The lady's been married and divorced three times already, and each ex-husband was successively wealthier than the last, but she *is* something of a celebrity over there in her own right. Writes for high-class magazines about how to live the life of an A-lister on a C-lister budget, that kind of thing. How to have your cake and eat it too. Fake it to make it. Get the picture?'

Hillary nodded. 'Yes — I can see she'd have a following for that kind of thing amongst a certain age group with aspirations. She's got a sort of effortless French-style chic about her that's the ultimate in self-advertising.'

'If you say so,' Jones said. 'When I interviewed her, she reminded me of a wet cat.'

Hillary nearly spluttered over her coffee at this mental image.

'The point is, if the lady *has* ever served time over there, I can't imagine that her fans or enemies wouldn't have unearthed it by now and splashed it all over the place.'

Hillary nodded — it was a good point. 'And the Van Paulens? They as wealthy as they seem?'

'Yes — as far as that goes. The father recently sold his various prosperous businesses and took early retirement. And I know what you're thinking — where there's a successful businessman there's scope for slippery financial dealings. But so far, nothing downright illegal has come to light about him. Not even a short spell for tax-dodging. Now, his daughter is a different proposition.'

'Ah yes, I heard you'd got a warrant to search her room,' Hillary said.

The Welshman gave her a knowing look. 'Did you now?' he said. 'I daresay you provided Mrs Pringwell with a sympathetic shoulder to cry on?'

'Might have done,' Hillary agreed nonchalantly.

Her companion flicked her a wry smile and nodded. 'Our Jasmine has had issues with drugs and alcohol. What you might expect from a spoilt rich kid, I suppose. According to her hometown police chief she's got a number of warnings under her belt, but no time actually served. This was when she was between the ages of sixteen and eighteen, when possession of some pot or other non-prescription low-level drugs isn't usually prosecuted to the max. But she was warned, when she hit twenty, that that sort of leniency wouldn't still apply. She had a driving ban for a year when she was caught just over the legal limit, but has kept her nose clean since. Or maybe not.'

Hillary cocked her head a little.

'The reason I got the warrant — when we brought them in, our evidence officer recognised her name. Apparently, the station received an anonymous letter about her only two days after her arrival here.'

'A letter? What, written on actual paper with an actual pen?' Hillary asked, sounding mock-shocked.

'I know. It wasn't even printed off a computer or anything. But the words were all block capitals. A handwriting expert might still have been able to make something of it, if we'd been inclined to give it that much effort — which we weren't, at the time.'

'What was the gist?'

'The writer claimed to have seen what looked like a suspicious transaction taking place between Jasmine Van Paulen and an unknown male, in which the unknown male handed over something small enough to fit into the palm of his hand, in exchange for what appeared to be a substantial amount of cash from Van Paulen. A detailed description of the man was given in the letter, and the general consensus amongst our officers working in that area is that it fits a small-time dealer called Peter Hardiman.'

His lips twisted in a wry smile as he said this, and Hillary cocked an inquisitive eyebrow. Catching it, Jones shook his head. 'Hardiman is one of Marvin Bodicote's minions, and Bodicote is something of a rancid joke amongst our drug squad colleagues.'

'Huh?'

'He's a bit of a nutter, by all accounts. Goes around as if he's living in a different world most of the time — a world where he's some sort of supervillain forging an empire for himself. Watches too much television, I suspect. Anyway, in spite of being an oddball, a lot of his contemporaries genuinely fear him. And so do our lot too, for the same reason. He's got a volatile temper and nobody quite knows what he's likely to do from one moment to the next.'

'He sounds like a right charmer,' Hillary drawled.

'Yeah. Unfortunately for us, Bodicote's also clever and dedicated to his career, which means he's rising up the ranks fast. All in all, he's definitely *not* the sort that rich Americans holidaying abroad should be consorting with.'

Hillary sighed. 'So it would appear she hasn't learnt her lesson after all. Well, well, who'd have thought it. Mind you, it was quick work on her part in finding a connection so soon after her arrival — even one as dodgy as this Bodicote character.'

'I agree. Usually, users need a like-minded pal to provide them with an introduction, or otherwise learn by trial and error where you need to go to get what you fancy. Which just goes to show our girl is determined, intelligent and motivated.'

Hillary wasn't about to argue with his logic. 'Was this tip-off not followed up on at all?'

'Oh yes, it was followed up,' Jones said instantly and somewhat defensively. 'She was stopped and searched at random the next day by a constable — but naturally she was clean.'

'Naturally,' Hillary concurred. You had to be very lucky to get a result from a random stop-and-search of that nature. 'I take it she was given the usual warning, meant to keep her away from undesirables?'

Jones spread his hands. 'You know as well as I do that's often the best we can do. But if people are determined to use . . .' He finished with a graphic shrug. 'At least we marked her card and let her know she was on our radar. Given that she's in a foreign country, and not back in her comfort zone where her father can wield some influence, we thought that it might just be enough to discourage her from indulging until she returns to the States.'

'And did it?'

'Didn't appear to. She gave the constable some lip and threatened to sue him for harassment and all the rest.'

Hillary sighed. So far, it all sounded par for the course. 'So the warrant you issued to search her room was to see if you could find drugs? That's all very well, but I don't see the connection to our murder case. Or was she being obstructive during questioning, and you were hoping to find something to use as leverage against her?'

The smile Jones gave her then reminded Hillary of a drawing she'd seen of the Cheshire Cat in a tatty old book that she'd once browsed through in a now vanished book shop. 'We were hoping for a bit more than that,' the Welshman said smugly. 'The sighting of the drug deal was right here in Hay-on-Wye, and the letter was posted in a local post box.'

Hillary's eyes sharpened as she caught on to the significance of this at once. 'And since Jasmine's new to the area, it's unlikely that a mere resident of the town or a visiting member of the public would know her from Adam, let alone be able to name her. Which means . . .' She trailed off thoughtfully.

'Yes. It must have come from here, right?' Jones gave a jerk of his head, indicating the building behind him. 'Who else but her fellow guests at the inn would recognise her? And if we poor dunderheaded policemen could figure it out . . .'

'She could too,' Hillary nodded.

'And you yourself told us in your statement that Jasmine seemed to have issues with both Belinda and Imogen Muir. So what are the odds that she suspected one of them of dobbing her in it? And if it was Imogen . . .'

'And sending a letter, as opposed to a digital message, sounds like something that someone of an older generation might prefer to do. Do you know if the victim had a smartphone?' It was always possible that Imogen had been a silver surfer.

'She didn't — at least, not on her, and we haven't found one in her room. Unless the killer lifted it out of her bag at some point and tossed it out of the window as well as the murder weapon,' he said. But before Hillary could even shoot him a sceptical gaze, he was already shaking his head. 'And that seems very unlikely to me. Rummage through her bag and pinch her phone? Forget it. The killer would have to be mad to risk it.'

Hillary nodded. 'I can only tell you that I never personally saw her use a mobile, but then, I only knew her for one evening and the following morning. Have you informed the next of kin — her son in Australia or New Zealand?'

'Yes — he's arranging to fly over. When he does, I'll ask him if his mum had at least a basic mobile to use for emergencies. I can tell you she didn't use internet banking or do any online shopping. Our tech people have already ascertained as much, so it doesn't look as if she was hip enough to enjoy modern gadgets much.'

Hillary wondered when the last time was that she'd ever heard someone described as 'hip' and inwardly smiled. 'I can probably find out for sure by casually talking to my fellow guests. Belinda would know if she ever texted or used a mobile. By the way, speaking of the others — let's not go out of our way to tell anyone what I do for a living, hmmm?' She knew it was inevitable that they'd suss her out eventually, but the longer she could pass for 'one of them,' the better she'd like it.

'I agree,' he said promptly.

'Especially since they all know me as an author only out here to help promote my first book. And if I sort of let them run away with the impression that I've retired on a low-level civil service pension . . . well.' She gave a shrug.

'A book? Really?' Jones looked impressed.

For some reason, Hillary felt herself flushing and feeling a little flustered. 'Oh, just a bit of crime fiction. Nothing to write home about. If you'll pardon the pun. So, forensics?' She brought him back to business quickly.

Jones put aside the folder containing the post-mortem report that he'd been reading from, and retrieved a bulkier one. 'Well, as you can imagine, fingerprints galore, including all five of our suspects and our victim. Of the hundreds of others, we've eliminated most of the train and station staff, and that's as far as we've got.'

Hillary shook her head. No doubt the others belonged to tourists who had long since scattered to the four corners of the globe. In other words — useless.

'Next,' she said succinctly.

'Blood stains — and lack thereof. The pathologist reckons the old lady died almost instantaneously on being stabbed. Which means, as I need hardly point out to someone with your experience, no arterial spurting. There must have been some blood flow at contact, but after that, very little seepage at all.'

Hillary nodded glumly. Hadn't she seen for herself how little blood there'd been at the scene? 'How about the clothes they were all wearing?'

'Microscopic traces on all of them. But that doesn't surprise me. Do you know what they all admitted to doing?'

'Bending over the old lady to take recordings through her section of window?' Hillary asked, enjoying his look of surprise. 'No, I'm not psychic,' she assured him, then went on to explain the behaviour of the people in her own carriage.

Jones looked even more downcast. Even his mass of curly brown hair looked deflated. 'I was hoping that their stories about doing that were a bit far-fetched, but if *you* can confirm it's not as unlikely as it sounded . . .'

'Sorry. At one point a red kite flew parallel to the train for a while, and I practically had someone in a safari suit sitting in my lap to get the best shot.'

'A *safari suit*?'

'Don't ask. So, forensics isn't going to help us out. And there was no preponderance of blood around the sleeve area of any one of our suspects?'

Jones was already shaking his head.

'Anything else standing out to you?' she asked.

'Not to my eyes. But here,' he nudged the report across the table to her. 'You can read it at your leisure later. It's a copy.'

'I'll go over it tonight in my room, away from prying eyes. Oh — and can you let me have a copy of the inventory of Imogen's belongings?'

Ian agreed to email it to her, but he'd already looked at it and didn't think she would find it particularly useful. It contained only what one would expect of an older woman who was on her holidays. Predominantly lightweight, pale-coloured summer clothing, medicine for a thyroid condition, some pieces of nice jewellery, the usual credit cards, toiletries, evening shoes, sandals, and a pair of reading glasses. And that was about it.

'Well, I expect you want to see what they're all up to in there,' she looked across at the entrance to the dining room. 'Although they're probably all taking a catnap. I take it none of them got much sleep last night?'

Jones smiled wryly. 'What do you think?'

But Hillary was wrong in her assumption that all of her fellow guests would be trying to catch forty winks, for as she and Jones walked through the French windows and into the deserted dining room, raised voices could be heard coming through the far door leading out into the small hall.

Raising a collective eyebrow, they made their way silently to the hall and tracked the sound of heated conversation to the lounge next door.

'Daddy, don't be such a . . .'

'Watch your language, my girl! Swearing at me only makes me dig my heels in even harder, remember?'

The voices clearly belonged to father and daughter, and Hillary and Ian stopped short of the open doorway, careful not to be seen or heard, and commenced to listen in without a qualm.

'Well, sometimes you make me so mad I want to spit. Especially when you say something so damned stupid!' Jasmine shot back, the contempt in her voice almost shocking. It was not so much that a daughter would talk to her father in that way — some of the things Hillary had heard family members say to each other would have made even a psychiatrist blanch — but the fact that the twenty-something woman sounded almost exactly like a spoilt brat of thirteen or fourteen.

For the first time, Hillary began to wonder if Jasmine had grown up at all. And if not, was there a medical reason for it — either physical or mental? Or was she simply one of those women who became so addicted to being 'Daddy's Little Princess' that she was subconsciously struggling to remain a child? If so, her drug and alcohol problem made sense. What could ensure that Daddy would always look after her more effectively than providing him with such ample proof that she needed looking after?

'You know damned well that I never say stupid things, my girl. And that I always mean what I say. Your allowance is cut off for the duration of our vacation.'

'But, Dad, I've told you and told you and told you 'til I'm blue in the face. I . . . did . . . not . . . buy . . . any . . . damned . . . drugs,' she exaggerated the pause between each word and punctuated each word loudly and sharply. 'Did that cop find anything on me when he stopped me and checked out my purse and pockets? No, he did not. And have any of this lot found anything in my room this morning? No, they have not. So why are you punishing me?'

Both Hillary and Ian clearly heard Jasper's heavy sigh. 'Jas, honey, can't you just . . . Never mind. You want to go on thinking I'm blind and stupid, go right ahead. But right now, I need you to listen to me and listen real good. This is not a two-bit drink-driving ticket we're talking about here, or being found in possession of a few paltry pills of E or whatever the hell it is that you kids are messing with nowadays. Right here, right now, we're both mixed up in a murder case. Do you understand that, Jas? A *murder* case!'

There was a sudden sense of movement from the other room and then Jasmine yelled. 'Ow, that hurts! Daddy, get your hands off me. I don't need shaking like I'm some rag-doll. I—'

'Oh but you do, Jasmine — you need some sense shaken into you! Don't you get it? Imogen Muir is *dead*. And you, my girl, are their number one suspect.'

For a second there was total silence. Hillary raised a questioning eyebrow at Ian. *Was she?* Ian gave her a brief shrug in response, then put his hand in the air, palm flat downwards and rocked it from side to side. *Maybe yes, maybe no.*

Inside the lounge, they heard Jasmine give a little gasp. 'Dad, you don't really think so, do you?'

'I wouldn't say it if I didn't mean it,' Jasper responded heavily.

Hillary and Ian exchanged another significant look. Both of them found it very interesting that the girl's father should immediately suspect his daughter. If, Hillary mused cynically, he actually *did* believe so. It could just be that, like nearly all parents, he was instinctively protective of his child, and was anticipating the worst and preparing for it. He was a wealthy man, and no doubt a powerful one locally in his own community, and as such would be used to taking charge and getting his own way. But over here in the UK, he had to be nervously aware that he had none of his usual advantages. Perhaps he was just taking the pessimistic view in order not to get caught out?

Or he knew something they didn't.

Had he actually seen something that made him suspect Jasmine had killed Imogen Muir?

Of course, there was another alternative altogether. He had done it himself. And if that were the case, Hillary speculated, he would want to make very sure that Jasmine never suspected as much. He couldn't help but be aware that someone as volatile and juvenile as his daughter would give the game away almost immediately if she ever did.

'It isn't fair,' Jasmine wailed, right on cue, like a kid who'd had her sweeties snatched away by the playground bully. 'Why are they picking on me?'

Once more, they heard Jasper give a heavy sigh. 'Because of the letter,' he said flatly.

Hillary saw Ian Jones almost quiver to attention at that, like a gundog spotting a pheasant falling out of the sky.

'Oh that! Nobody takes that seriously,' Jasmine dismissed scornfully, but there was definitely an element of uncertainty making its way into her voice now.

'Of course they're taking it seriously,' her father challenged immediately. 'The moment you heard about it you assumed that Imogen had written it. And don't pretend you didn't. You hardly made a secret of it, did you? You accused the woman to her face, in fact!'

'But the old cow denied it,' Jasmine shot back.

'And did you believe her?'

Now there was an eloquent silence.

'And do you think,' Jasper swept on, 'once this investigation starts in earnest, and the cops start putting the pressure on Bel, and Pat and Barry and Mrs Pringwell, that they won't eventually cough up all they know about it? Because you weren't discreet, were you, Jas?' her father pointed out sardonically. 'You made your disdain for the woman as clear as a bell. And now she's been murdered. And what motive do you think anyone else has for killing her except you and me?'

'You, Dad?'

Inside, Hillary could imagine the older man shaking his head wearily. 'Naturally I'm in the frame too. To protect you. You know I'd do anything to keep you safe, right? Well, you can bet your boots that Inspector Jones is thinking much the same thing right now. He might even be thinking we're in it together.'

'That's just stupid. Nobody in their right mind would think that.'

'Why not, Jas? It's as good a theory as any. You distract everybody, and I do the deed. Or vice versa. It makes a lot of sense, from their point of view.'

Again there was a long moment of silence. Hillary shot Jones another speculative glance. What the American was saying did, indeed, make sense. Even given the somewhat unique circumstances of that train journey, it would still have been as risky as hell to kill a fellow passenger in such a confined space and with three other witnesses in such proximity to both victim and perpetrator. It would surely lengthen your chances of success if you had a partner to help shield what you were doing. And if one of the Van Paulens had stood in front of the other as they leaned over the old lady and knifed her, it would cut the chances of being spotted significantly.

And there was no doubt father and daughter were a tight-knit unit and unlikely to fall apart or turn on each other. Even Jasmine could be relied upon to keep silent in such circumstances, because her father in prison was no use to her at all.

'But, Dad . . . I didn't kill her,' Jasmine said. 'And I know you didn't. So they can't prove anything, can they, because there's nothing to prove.'

'You think innocent people don't get convicted, Jas?' Jasper said dryly.

'Then what do we do?' Jasmine asked, and this time Hillary was sure there was real fear in her voice.

Which meant nothing of course.

For a start, this whole set-up could be just that — a set-up. She and Jones had been sitting out in the garden in clear view of anyone who might have been watching them through the lounge window, which was the next room along from the dining room. Father and daughter could have seen them return to the building, and with all the doors and windows open because of the heat, would know that their voices would carry. And any cop worth his or her salt would take the opportunity to eavesdrop on a conversation between two prime suspects.

What they'd heard could have been nothing more than a well-scripted play, meant just for an audience of two.

Alternatively, one or the other of the Van Paulens could have killed Imogen without conspiring with each other. Jasmine was certainly reckless and brazenly self-confident enough to assume she could pull off a murder without being caught. And the older, wiser, stronger and considerably more measured and in-control Jasper had the mental resources necessary to weigh up all the options then carefully plan and carry out the crime.

The real question was — had they? In Jasper's case, Hillary was not at all sure. His motive just didn't strike her as being strong enough. It was not even as if drugs *had* been found on his precious daughter. Nor had Imogen Muir been all set to testify about what she'd seen, as a court case — or the possibility of one — wasn't even in the offing. And even if the old lady *had* been the letter writer, and was keeping an eye on someone she'd come to detest and thus represented some vague threat in the future, it was all too piffling to require such a drastic solution as murder.

The worst-case scenario, *if* Imogen had managed to provide further positive proof of Jasmine's illegal activities, would see his daughter being charged with a minor drugs offence. So what? He could afford the best lawyers and the charges were hardly earth-shattering. A suspended sentence and a deportation order would be the likely outcome. And he was worldly wise enough to know as much.

She gave a mental headshake. No, unless there was something *else* going on that they didn't yet know about, she couldn't see Jasper killing Imogen.

But who was to say that there *wasn't* something else going on? Perhaps the mutual antagonism between the two women had its roots in something much deeper and darker that Jasper was desperately afraid might come to light?

On the other hand, she could *just about* see Jasmine killing Imogen out of nothing more than sheer spite or thwarted frustration. But was the spoilt brat really *that* spoilt? She supposed that would depend on just how deep-rooted Jasmine's sense of entitlement went. But, on the evidence so far, she hadn't seen anything that indicated to her that Jasmine was so mentally off-kilter that she would kill an old woman for writing an anonymous note dobbing her in it to the police.

But Hillary had only known Jasmine for a matter of hours.

'We hold tight.' The sound of Jasper's voice, answering his daughter's question, abruptly put a stop to her mental maunderings. 'We keep our heads down, we answer their questions — *truthfully* mind, Jas — but *only* answer their questions and nothing more. Don't elaborate. Never volunteer anything. And most of all, you behave yourself for once. No getting drunk. No more snide comments to Bel or anyone else for that matter. And most of all — no more meeting up with young men in cafés and buying little packages of what-the-hell ever. Do you hear me?'

'Yes, Dad.'

'All right.'

'You can trust me.'

'Good.'

'So there's no need to cut off my allowance.'

'Jas!'

'No, Daddy, I mean it. I need some money, after all. I can't not have any!'

'Sure you can.'

'But what if I need clothes? Or make-up, or new shoes or . . . oh, Dad, you can see I can't go around flat broke!'

'You need anything, ask me. I'll pay for it.'

'Fine!' she yelled. 'In that case, you can start by going down to the chemist and buying me some tampons then! See how you feel about that!'

Sudden movement had both Hillary and Ian scarpering quickly back out into the hall and nipping through to the bar — the nearest hiding place. They were just in time to see Jasmine stomping off in the opposite direction, her shoulders stiff and her back ramrod straight, all but quivering in indignation.

A moment later, her father, far less dramatically, also appeared and headed towards the open front door. Presumably, to walk to the shops to buy some tampons.

'Well, what did you make of all that?' Ian wanted to know.

Hillary shrugged. Her thoughts and theories were her own, and not yet for sharing. At least, not until she had something more concrete to go on that she thought worthwhile discussing. But there were practicalities to think of. 'Did any of the other passengers mention either Jasper or Jasmine doing something that grabbed their attention?'

'Creating a diversion, you mean? No, they didn't. So the conspiracy theory is out.'

Hillary wasn't so sure about that. But she let it slide.

'You need to follow up on that letter. Get all the experts on it. If it can be proved that Imogen did indeed write it, that'll prove something at least.'

'And if she didn't?' Ian asked curiously.

'Then that'll prove something else,' Hillary said with a grin.

'Gee thanks. I knew you'd prove useful!'

Hillary's smile slowly vanished. 'If I were you, I'd also get a proper mental assessment done of Jasmine. If she'll cooperate, fine. Get her head shrunk. If not, get a profiler in to sit in on the follow-up interviews. But it wouldn't surprise me if it turns out that she's all too familiar with spilling her guts to a therapist and will see it as an opportunity to impress upon us all what a good girl she is, deep down.'

Ian grunted. 'Far as I can make out, all rich Americans have them on speed dial! And given that young lady's problems . . .'

'Right. But ask them to pay special attention to her mental age and development. Is she really still a teenager at heart or is it all an act. You know the drill.'

Ian didn't, not really — he'd never had a murder case that required a psychological evaluation before, but there was no way he was going to let on to that in front of this impressive veteran.

'Anything else?' he asked casually.

'Yes. Timeline. You must have tried to work out exactly when Imogen was killed. Any luck?'

Ian sighed. 'Ever tried to herd cats?' he asked wryly. 'Nobody was paying attention to time, everyone was milling around, nobody was interested in the old lady, et cetera, et cetera. Best I can do — she was alive for the first twenty minutes of the journey — but once the train began to really climb, it was all about what was happening outside. We know she was dead when the train pulled in. And that's about it.'

It was what Hillary had expected. 'Well, all you can do is make sure that you cover the basics properly.' It would keep his immediate superiors happy and cut down on the chances of making any embarrassing mistakes this early on in the investigation. 'Always remember the golden rule.'

'What? Means, motive, opportunity, you mean?'

Hillary gave him a gentle smile. 'No. Always cover your arse.'

CHAPTER SIX

Jasmine sat in the café stirring her coffee angrily with a plastic spoon and silently fuming. Although her recent conversation with her father had frightened her, some of the shock and panic was already wearing off. Now that she'd had time to calm down — and the walk into town had cleared her head somewhat — she was inclined to think that he was just being his usual, super-cautious self.

What were the chances, really, that she was going to be arrested for murder? The thought made her giggle a little, and she noticed a teenage couple in one corner shoot her bemused looks. She pretended she'd seen something to amuse her on the screen of her phone which was on the table beside her, albeit turned off.

She'd already sent a short text to the number Peter Hardiman had given her and had been in no mood for social media. Although, come to think of it, posting that she might be arrested for murder in foreign climes would definitely increase her following.

Maybe later.

Right now, she was still too antsy to concentrate on boosting her online brand. Although she was sure she was in no danger from the cops that didn't mean that she wanted the hassle of being caught up in anything that would put her so firmly in the spotlight.

She was sure Peter wouldn't like it, for one thing — and his boss certainly wouldn't. Drug dealers liked to keep a low profile — every idiot knew that. Although Peter didn't talk about his boss much, she sure as hell didn't press him about it, needing, as she did, to keep him sweet. But she'd always been good at picking up on what people were thinking and feeling, and his body language fairly screamed fear and respect whenever Peter had to refer to him — which he never did by name, of course.

But as she sat and waited for her supplier to arrive, her thoughts returned again and again to her father. Was he really worried that they might get dragged into the old cow's murder, or was he just using it as yet one more excuse to try and frighten her and control her life? He was always doing it, Jasmine thought sourly. Her being in this stupid little rinky-dink town in the first place was a case in point. He'd only insisted on her coming away with him on this holiday to get her away from Claus.

Claus, the rich son of a once-famous racing driver, who had money to burn and tastes even more exotic than her own. She was seriously missing Claus and his wild antics.

She sighed and glanced at her watch, then fidgeted nervously. She was going to have to play Peter just right. But she could handle him. He was just a small-town player, trusted only to do the jobs that existed right at the bottom end of his lord and master's distribution ladder. How smart could he be?

Just then she saw him walk into the café and glance around. He spotted her almost instantly and headed for the counter where he bought some fancy coffee concoction that he thought made him look impressive, and brought it to the table. 'Hey, babe,' he said, giving her a very public kiss.

Jasmine always allowed this because it secretly amused her.

He'd told her it was necessary whenever they met in order to maintain their 'cover' and give the impression that theirs was just an innocent boyfriend/girlfriend meet-up during a coffee or lunch break. In reality she knew he did it only because he'd never get a girl to kiss him otherwise.

Around twenty years old, he was a tall, stick-thin lad with a shaven head and very unfortunate skin, riddled with acne. His ears and teeth reminded her of a donkey, and even his best feature — his large brown eyes — were usually bloodshot and caked in the corners with greenish crud.

He also didn't shower as often as he should. She was grateful that at least he'd avoided the cliché of multiple facial and body piercings.

Today he was wearing too-new jeans and a T-shirt advocating saving the planet.

Jasmine waited for him to settle before starting her campaign. 'Petey, I've got some bad news,' she began, and watched with satisfaction as he suddenly sat up straight and went a trifle pale. Instantly, she could feel the fear emanating from him. To Peter, bad news was to be avoided at all costs.

On her short walk to the café, she'd already begun to map out what she needed to do. Despite her father cutting off her cash flow, she had no intention of cutting back on her fun. Which meant she'd need Peter's cooperation, and she had every intention of getting it. She'd have to handle him just right.

'Oh? What?' he asked bluntly, his eyes darting nervously around the room.

'My old man's cut off my allowance,' she sighed forlornly, giving her own coffee another angry stir with her spoon. 'And for once I'm not going to be able to talk him around. I'm telling you, he's totally flipped out this time.'

'Why?'

Peter was beginning to sweat in earnest now. Already he could tell this was going to be a bad day for him. Marvin wasn't going to like hearing that there was a problem with the American girl, because he knew his boss had big plans for her. He had no idea what they were of course, but sometimes he'd come into a room and hear tail ends of conversations between Marvin and his lieutenants, and he picked up the odd hint or two here and there.

'Oh, the usual,' Jasmine shrugged. She had no intention of telling him about the cops. That was sure to send him running off in a panic and taking her connection with him. 'I swear he's got some inner radar as far as I'm concerned. He knows when I'm, er, happy and just has to ruin things for me.' This time her petulance was real, as was her scowl.

Peter shot another nervous look around the café, though nobody was paying them the slightest attention.

'So, does this mean you don't want any more *chocolate*?' Peter asked. 'You on a diet now?'

Jasmine sighed. 'Of course I still want my chocolates, Petey,' she reassured him, using her little-girl voice that always seemed to tickle him. 'It's just that I need a bit of help.' It always amused her that the man never referred to his wares in any terms other than confectionery. No doubt, at some point, some idiot or other had told him that if he was ever recorded by the cops, so long as he never spoke the names of drugs out loud, he could never be convicted.

The moron.

Peter felt a moment of panic hit him. He had strict instructions about what to do if their clients started wheedling about payment. Never give credit. Never let them get away with it. Cut them off at the knees. Get aggressive and violent if need be. No money, no drugs. No exceptions.

Except . . . he knew Marvin wanted this girl kept sweet. He didn't know why, but Marvin had told him to treat her well. And to keep his hands off her. Some of the others, he knew, used their positions of power to get the ones they fancied to sleep with them, threatening to cut off their supply if they didn't.

But Peter had never been able to do that. Well, not yet anyway.

'Petey?' Jasmine put a finger on the back of his hand and tapped it. 'Earth to Peter, Earth to Peter,' she mocked. 'You zoned out on me a bit there, didn't you?'

'Yeah. Sorry. It's just . . . I got instructions that chocolate needs to be paid for — no exceptions.' But even as he tried to sound tough, Peter wasn't sure if he was doing the right thing. That was the trouble with working for Marvin — he was so touchy and volatile that you never knew where you were with him.

If he gave in and handed over the gear to her without payment, Marvin could go mental on him. And trying to tell his boss that he thought he'd only been following his pre-standing orders to keep her sweet would count for nothing. He'd get a bashing. On the other hand, if he *did* refuse to give her what she wanted and came back and reported to the boss what had happened, he'd probably get a bashing for *not* keeping her sweet.

Some days you just couldn't win.

'Oh, it'll be paid for, don't be silly,' Jasmine said, watching the poor sucker wilt with relief. 'It's just that you'll have to accept gold instead of cash,' she slipped in the kicker smoothly.

'Eh?' Peter said, caught off guard. 'Gold?'

'Hmmm. I've brought some jewellery with me, see. Not too much, but enough for emergency purposes. Now, if I was back in the States and Daddy cut me off, I'd know all the best places to go to where I could pawn the stuff or sell it for the best price, but over here . . .' She glanced around, trying to look helpless. 'I'd just get ripped off. But I know you're smart, Petey,' she once again tapped the back of his hand with one peach-painted nail, inwardly laughing herself sick at the thought of this specimen having the brains of even a gnat. 'You'll know how to get a good price, right?'

'Right. Course,' Pete said automatically.

'So, we'll settle it on the current price of gold, yes?' Jasmine said casually. She was pretty sure this bumpkin had no idea that any pawnbroker or fence wouldn't give him anything like the going rate for precious metals but there you go. Jasmine only wished she could be around to see his face when he found out. What a scream! He'd probably make up the difference himself so that nobody would know he'd been suckered.

'Huh? Yeah, sure,' Pete said, not really paying her much attention now, even though, in the back of his mind, a vague alarm bell was ringing. It always rang that way when he suspected he was being played, but right now he wasn't so much concerned with that.

Because just when he thought he was caught between a rock and a hard place, he was being given a way out. And he was grabbing it, for all it was worth.

Now he wouldn't have to go back to Marvin completely empty-handed. And he was keeping this 'special client' sweet as well. Which was a win-win for little Petey! 'So, what you got then?' he all but whispered, leaning forward a little. 'Pass it under the table.'

Much amused, Jasmine pulled a slender gold-link bracelet from her wrist and passed it over. When she'd put it on that morning she hadn't known that she would be returning without it, but what the hell? It was worth it, just for the sordid thrill of this moment.

She felt a sense of satisfaction as a smooth, plastic-wrapped square was placed into her palm, then she slowly withdrew her hand and slipped it into her bag. On the other side of her, under the cover of the table, Peter dropped the slender chain into his jeans pocket.

'Right, babe, I've gotta get back to work,' Peter said, standing up and giving her another kiss. But this time, now that she'd got her stash, Jasmine decided to punish him by biting his tongue. As he drew back sharply, she smiled at him sweetly and blew him a kiss.

Peter grinned at her uncertainly and headed for the door.

Jasmine watched him go and giggled.

* * *

Hillary decided to lunch at the hotel, as she wanted to be around in case any of her fellow guests emerged from their morning naps. She was anxious to interview them all as soon as possible without, of course, them being aware that she was doing any such thing. Luckily for her, she was fairly confident that they would find it only natural for her to be curious about the fatal train journey. It was only human nature, after all, which meant that she should be able to get good accounts from most of her fellow guests without arousing their suspicion.

The first one to appear in the bar was Barry Kirk, who hesitated visibly at seeing her sitting on a barstool, but then approached and nodded amiably first at her and then at the barman, who looked suspiciously enough like Judith Pringwell to be a relative. He asked for a half of shandy.

Hillary, suspecting that this reticent young man was about to take his unspectacular drink and skedaddle with it, stopped him in his tracks by giving him a kind smile and immediately beginning a conversation. 'So, you've decided to resist the temptation of catching up on lost sleep then?'

Barry shrugged and took a small sip of his drink. 'I've found that it doesn't pay to interfere with your body clock too much. It's like giving in to jet lag — once you sleep away a day, by night-time you're awake and then you can't sleep again, and so it goes on. Far better, I've found, to bite the bullet and just stay awake for the day and then go to bed early.'

Hillary nodded. So, he'd travelled abroad a lot. Which was interesting. She'd have thought he was more of a homebody. 'Very sensible, I do that too,' she said, truthfully enough. Although the last time she'd had jet lag she'd still been married to Ronnie. 'But you must have had a really rough time of it last night. It can't be much fun spending so long in a police station?'

'No. I've never been in one before. It would have been rather interesting if the circumstances had been different.'

'I only knew Imogen for a matter of hours. But you must have known her longer — for a few days or so?'

'Yes.'

'She seemed a nice lady,' Hillary persisted gamely. 'It must have been such a shock for everyone.'

'Yes. It was awful.'

Hillary shook her head. 'I just can't believe that someone killed her. It seems so . . . I don't know. Surreal. You hear about these things on the news but you never think something like murder will ever have an impact on you, do you? I felt quite shaken up about it. But then, I expect it was far worse for you, being so close to it all?'

'Yes. I suppose it wouldn't be very gallant for me to say that I wished I'd offered to find a seat in another carriage instead of you, but . . .' He shrugged and gave her a shamefaced grimace.

'Oh, I don't blame you,' Hillary said, again truthfully enough. 'That sort of thing is bound to haunt you for a long time. And please, don't take this the wrong way, but were you surprised that the police let you all go? I mean, I wouldn't have thought it could be that hard for them to find out exactly what happened to Imogen?'

She had decided that the oblique approach would be a waste of time on a man as reticent as this and opted for shock tactics instead. And she was interested to see how he would react to her bluntness. She had all but stated out loud that one of her fellow guests must be a killer so there weren't that many options for him to choose from — anger, sarcastic humour, hurt feelings or stony silence (or variations thereof) were about his lot.

She saw him pale slightly, and instinctively draw back a little, but he didn't actually turn his back on her and walk away. Instead, for what felt like a long while he seemed to consider her words, and when he did speak, his tone of voice hadn't changed.

'I can see why you might think that. But in actual fact, things aren't as straightforward as they might appear to someone who wasn't in that carriage.' He then went on to describe to her that fatal journey, in pretty much exactly the way as she had already pictured it.

Everyone had left their seats almost constantly throughout the trip, either going from window to window or from the front to the back in the carriage trying to record the best view. 'So you see,' he concluded, staring down into his barely touched drink, 'any one of us could have been responsible.'

'That's awkward,' Hillary said, in massive understatement.

At this, even the very self-controlled Barry Kirk managed a wan smile and a grimace. 'Yes, you might say so.'

'But surely someone can remember the last time Imogen actually spoke to one of you?' she persisted. 'Did *you* speak to her, for instance?'

'Yes, but only fairly early on when we first started out, during the ride over the flat bit before the train began to climb. Once it did, like everyone else, I was bedazzled by the view.'

Bedazzled. Hillary wondered how many people nowadays even knew that word, let alone used it. It was something an academic would say, or a show-off, or someone who preferred to live as if they were still in Edwardian times. She had seen no previous evidence that this very self-contained man liked to show off, and although he dressed like a college professor about thirty years his senior, she somehow didn't see him playing a role in education. Which left her with a witness who seemed as though he was born out of his proper time.

And somehow, that felt right. She would have to ask Ian Jones, when the background checks became available, what this man did for a living.

'And did you get a good recording of it?'

'Oh, I do hope so. Not that I'm very good on a smartphone. I tell people I'm not smart enough for one. But I wanted to show the footage to my mother. She would have come here with me, but she had a bridge tournament set up months ago and didn't want to let anyone down.'

Bridge tournament? No wonder Hillary got the sense this man lived on a different planet from the rest of them — he'd obviously been brought up by a mother who had certain ideas. Which gave Hillary ideas of her own.

'She sounds a very formidable woman. I've always found bridge way too complicated to learn,' she lied. 'You sound very close to her though. I think it's nice when parents and children are close don't you? Are you an only child by any chance?'

'As a matter of fact, yes.'

Hillary mentally nodded. And what was the betting that, when Jones provided her with his details, she discovered he still lived with his mother? Not that that, in this day and age, would be all that unusual. The astronomical cost of living and the almost impossible task of buying your own home meant that many children were forced to stay on in the family home for longer and longer, or return to it periodically if they found themselves out of a job and unable to pay rent or mortgages.

Even so, she would have been prepared to bet a good portion of her salary that this man had never left home. And that 'home' would be some kind of smart mid-Victorian or Edwardian terrace, in some pleasant market town. And that Mrs Kirk would be fairly wealthy and comfortably upper middle class.

And if she was the domineering sort, or had just become accustomed to ruling over her one and only child's life with beneficent determination, what were the chances that Barry Kirk was relishing this holiday away from her? Given the chance for a rare taste of freedom, it could have gone to his head. And then, what if on arriving at the Riverside Inn, he'd found a replica of his mother waiting for him in the guise of Imogen Muir? They would have been of much the same age and ilk.

Had he come to suspect, whenever he found her eye on him, that she was watching him with maternal disapproval? Had he grown uncomfortable around her, and then quickly became angry and resentful?

With a small inner sigh, she warned herself not to get carried away. It was all well and good imagining all sorts of things that *might* have happened. But that didn't mean they had.

It was frustrating that she knew so little about what had gone on between these people before she'd arrived at the inn.

So before she started speculating about what-ifs, she needed to get a better picture of the set-up here.

And the only way she was going to find that out was by talking to them. Which meant concentrating on the here and now and saving the theorising until later.

'With her nervousness about heights, I imagine Imogen herself didn't pay that much attention to the view?' She got the conversation back on track.

'Oh, I'm sure she did,' he contradicted her at once. 'She seemed to be as impressed with it as everyone else. But it's true she didn't try to film it. I'm not sure if she had a phone.'

Hillary gave a mental nod. 'Yes, modern technology isn't the be all and end all, is it? You know, on the way up, I got a little tense about how high we were going, and how close to the edge the train seemed to be. Did any of the others feel the same?'

'I don't think so. Although, now you mention it, I believe Belinda did go rather pale, and towards the end, when we got to the highest point, I think she went back to her seat and stopped filming. So perhaps she did.'

'You're very observant,' Hillary complimented him. 'I'd be willing to bet that you would be the one to notice anything odd that might have taken place, if anything did.'

At this, the man with the receding hairline turned his face away from her and took another careful sip of his drink. 'Alas, I saw nothing at all odd. We were just a happy, excited group of people enjoying the day and the experience.'

Except for Imogen Muir, Hillary added silently to herself. Hillary was pretty sure that *she* hadn't enjoyed the train journey much.

'You and Patrick seemed to get on well with Imogen,' she changed tack carefully. 'But I would have said that Belinda was the closest to her, with them dining together and all. Now, I might be wrong, but I got the feeling there was some friction between Imogen and Jasmine? I noticed it the day I got here.'

But inviting him to gossip was clearly going a step too far, for Barry gave the briefest of shrugs and shook his head.

'I prefer to mind my own business wherever I can, Mrs Greene,' he murmured mildly. 'I usually find that's best, in the long run. Don't you?'

As an exit line, Hillary had to admit it took some beating, and she was forced to watch him saunter out of the door and head towards the dining room, leaving her with the distinct feeling that she had come out of that encounter second best.

It wasn't something she felt all that often, and she knew she'd have to be careful not to let it interfere with her thinking. Personal likes and dislikes had no place in a murder investigation. How often had she had to drum that into some green constable's thick noggin?

Picking up her glass of white wine spritzer, she followed Barry Kirk's path to the dining room, pleased to see Belinda's solitary form sitting at her usual table.

The chic Canadian looked up as Hillary approached her, and flashed her a brief, meaningless smile of acknowledgement. But in the tiny fraction of a second before Belinda John-Jacques had employed it, Hillary had seen the mixture of tiredness and anger in her eyes at the interruption.

A sensitive woman would have murmured a few words of condolence or sympathy and moved on. But Hillary drew out the chair opposite and returned Belinda's meaningless smile with one of her own.

'It must feel strange to eat alone here,' Hillary said gently. 'I thought you might like some company.'

'Oh bless you, yes,' Belinda John-Jacques lied.

CHAPTER SEVEN

As Hillary Greene prepared to delicately interview her next reluctant witness at the Riverside Inn, less than a mile away, Marvin Bodicote was conducting an interrogation of his own. And like most drug-dealing entrepreneurs, he couldn't have cared less about such niceties as gentle handling and cautious probing.

Bodicote was twenty-eight but strived to look older, believing that this somehow raised his profile and status with the other big fish who swam with him in what he felt to be an increasingly small pond. His ambition was excessive and his only obsession. He enjoyed the more theatrical elements of his chosen path, and if everyone from his suppliers to his customers to his own minions thought this both alarming and yet almost funny, nobody ever said so to his face. His minions didn't dare, since his explosive and unpredictable temper and love of violence was legendary. His customers were too afraid they'd be cut off if they didn't fawn over him in the way that he liked. And his suppliers valued his custom too much, since his buying steadily increased year on year.

In front of him, Peter Hardiman hopped nervously from foot to foot, trying to read from his boss's face and body language what kind of mood he was in. Which was never easy.

He could be joking and generous one moment, then fly into a rage for no discernible reason the next.

Today, Bodicote was, as ever, dressed in a proper business suit of navy blue, with a shiny silk tie, today the colour of rich cream. Spending hours in a converted gym in his double garage, he was a lean individual, with short brown hair and pale blue eyes. For some reason he disliked facial hair and made sure that any potential underling shaved off their beards or moustaches before approaching him for employment.

It was rumoured he had all *The Godfather* films on reels in his private cinema in the basement of his house and watched them almost religiously. Nobody was quite sure whether this was actually true or not, but at times he certainly acted as if he thought he was some sort of criminal overlord, instead of a mid-level drugs dealer in a rural catchment area.

This lunchtime, he was to be found in the house of his second-in-command, who had ordered in a Chinese take-away. The lieutenant had transferred the dishes to his best china and his girlfriend had set an impeccable table, complete with a small floral posy in the middle.

He'd learned his lesson after the last time he'd handed Bodicote his food in the small cardboard containers it came in, along with only a fork and a spoon. Peter had been told by one of the lads who'd been there at the time that the boss had made him eat it off the floor of his kitchen, since he couldn't be bothered to learn good table etiquette.

Now, however, the remains of the meal merely loitered harmlessly on the table as Marvin thoughtfully surveyed his unhappy underling. He was leaning back in his chair, one arm dangling negligently across the chair next to him.

'Let me get this straight. You bring me this,' he nudged the piece of jewellery that Peter had handed over to him a minute ago and which he'd dropped onto the table beside his plate, 'instead of cash? Have I got that right?'

The homeowner and lieutenant, a short, stocky blond man who for some reason was known only as 'Moose,' shifted a little nervously at this opening gambit. He didn't like the ominous, quietly amused friendliness of Bodicote's tone. He'd just bought a new three-piece leather suite and he didn't want to get blood on it after owning it barely five minutes. His girlfriend would sulk for weeks.

'Yes, Mr Bodicote. But I only did it because you told me to keep her sweet, like, otherwise I would've insisted on cash up front, like you always say,' Peter got out in a rush.

At this, Marvin's fingers, which had been drumming lightly but ominously on the back of the chair, stilled. It was, like so many of the drug dealer's habits, an ostentatious and faintly ridiculous gesture. But nevertheless effective.

Peter Hardiman gulped noisily, his Adam's apple bobbing comically in his throat as he swallowed hard.

'Sweet? Who are you talking about?' Marvin asked sharply.

'You know, that American bird staying in town with her old man.'

'Van Paulen?'

'Right, that's the one. That's her.'

Marvin sat forward a little on the chair, a frown pulling his dark but sparse eyebrows closer together. 'She paid up all right before though?'

'Oh yes, boss, good as gold. But today she told me her old man had cut her off. I reckon he's got wise to the fact that she's found a supply of happy pills, and he doesn't like it. But she told me it wasn't a real problem, like, as she's got a lot of jewellery with her — good-quality stuff that she can use as payment instead. Normally, I'd tell her she was having a laugh, and to come back when she had the readies. But I said I'd do it just this once, like, since you said to keep her on side, and that I'd check and see if it was OK with you. I thought that was the best thing to do, otherwise she might have tried to find someone else or . . .'

He trailed off because he saw the boss was no longer listening. He shot a quick look at Moose, hoping to see reassurance on his face that he'd done well, but Moose wasn't willing to commit himself either way just yet, and merely gave a shrug. He knew as well as Peter that trying to guess which way Bodicote would jump was impossible.

At least, Peter thought hopefully, the fact that he wasn't foaming at the mouth, or talking all quiet and sarcastic, were good signs. It made him feel like worms were gnawing at his guts when his boss got all quiet and pale.

'Is that a fact?' Marvin finally said mildly, leaning back once more in his chair and resuming his finger-drumming. 'Now whilst I find that very interesting, it seems to me that her rich daddy is getting a bit too cocky for my liking. I think it's time I go to phase two.'

Neither Moose nor Peter asked what he was talking about, since Marvin never discussed his plans with anyone. That he always *had* a plan had slowly become evident to anyone watching his inexorable rise to somewhere near the top of the food chain.

'Now, Pete,' he smiled inwardly as Hardiman jumped like a kicked dog at the use of his name and almost stood to attention, 'do you know this dad of hers by sight?'

'Yeah, I think so. I saw her walking around a bookshop with an older geezer a couple of days ago and they looked sort of alike.'

'Fine. But park up for a bit near that old-fashioned hotel she's staying at and make sure. Then, when you get the opportunity, I want you to rough the old man up a bit. Be clever about it, mind,' he added sharply, aware that this particular goon wasn't the brightest lightbulb in the lightbulb factory. 'Make it look like a common or garden mugging. A few punches and maybe a kick or two — nothing to really cause him any damage. Goose and golden eggs and all that.'

Peter had no idea where geese came into it, but he nodded quickly. 'Right. You actually want me to take his wallet and stuff then?'

Marvin sighed heavily. 'Yes, Pete, I want you to take his wallet and stuff,' he repeated with exaggerated patience. 'And his watch if he's wearing one. And anything else bling. But whilst you're doing it, you warn him to let his daughter roam loose and with a nice full purse — or next time, he might get a knife in his ribs. Got it?'

Peter nodded quickly, trying to hide his dismay. Although he'd been in on a few 'punishment beatings' in the past, that had always been as part of a gang. He'd never been asked to go solo before. And although it sounded simple enough, it seemed to him that the potential for mucking it up was far higher than he'd have liked.

What if someone came to the old geezer's rescue, for instance? Some have-a-go hero would be a right pain. Or what if he accidentally hit his mark too hard and ruptured something? He might even croak on him! Old geezers were always having heart attacks and whatnot, weren't they? Or, on the other hand, what if he hit too soft, and the old sod got away. Or worse — what if the old bloke clocked *him* one? He wasn't *that* old. Not doddering-with-a-walker old. And didn't Yanks carry guns? What if . . .

'Think you can manage that, Pete?' Marvin's silky voice interrupted his unhappy musings, and when he looked his boss in the eye he saw that Marvin was smiling — that shark-like smile that always gave him the shivers. It was as if Marvin could read his mind.

'Course, boss,' he muttered unhappily.

'Right then, off you go. Make sure of your man, watch him for a bit, and when the time's right, put the boot in. No need to rush — sometime tomorrow will do it.'

At this, Moose began to smile as well, and Pete wondered if the boss had cracked a joke and he just wasn't getting it. But as Marvin raised an eyebrow at him, he suddenly realised that he was being told to sod off and get on with it, and with a sort of ducking-head motion he shuffled off.

Marvin watched him go and sighed.

* * *

'Sounds like you and she got on really well,' Hillary said, as Judith Pringwell placed a dish of Dover sole in front of her, and a Caesar salad in front of Belinda.

Both women nodded their thanks, and the hotel owner left with a murmured hope that they enjoyed their meal.

'Yes, I suppose we did. I think she was lonely, underneath that facade she put up. Between you and me, I don't think she ever really felt comfortable in her own skin. She seemed . . . I don't know. Sort of tense.'

'Oh? How do you mean exactly?' Hillary asked, pouring out a glass of water for herself, and then one for Belinda, who had nodded when Hillary indicated the jug she was holding.

'I don't quite know how to put it. On the surface, she looked and talked and behaved like a proper Brit, you know? A little reserved and stiff-upper-lip, like a lot of her generation and class. She acted as if nothing could faze her, and she had the world just where she wanted it — politely but firmly under her thumb. But underneath it all, I'm not convinced she was so self-assured. And I did begin to wonder . . . well, if she might be struggling a bit — you know, moneywise.'

Belinda paused to spear a piece of lettuce and regarded it without much favour. 'It was just little things that she sometimes let slip without realising it. She gave the impression, for instance, that her husband was a wealthy industrialist, but after a while, I realised that he was nothing more than a scrap metal merchant. Oh, I'm not saying he didn't make a mint out of it, but he was hardly a Rockefeller.'

'A self-made man then,' Hillary said with a nod. 'Nothing wrong with that.'

'Exactly. But I got the feeling her husband dying had meant a slow drop in her income that was beginning to affect her way of living . . . Maybe she was worried that people might realise it and would look down on her. Or worse, pity her. And that made her angry, maybe? I sometimes got the feeling that she was displeased about something. I don't know — I'm not a psychologist.'

'Doesn't mean you're wrong though,' Hillary said flatly. 'Most of us live complicated lives — and we can't all be forced into neat little pigeonholes.'

'Ain't that the truth?' Belinda shot back with feeling.

Then, catching Hillary looking at her curiously, she quickly shifted the attention back to the dead woman. 'Imogen told me once that "her Derek" — that's how she always referred to him — was born here in Wales, and when he was first building up his business used to travel a lot around here, on the lookout for new sources of scrap and making useful contacts. It made me wonder; with a job like that, a man on the road and away from home a lot . . . Well! Most men would jump at the chance to play around a little, wouldn't they? And I wouldn't have put it past him. Her Derek didn't sound like the sort to ration himself, if you ask me.'

Hillary shrugged. She doubted whether Belinda, with three divorces behind her, was exactly unbiased when it came to marital fidelity and the trustworthiness of husbands (unless she was the one who'd been doing the cheating?) and gave a non-committal smile. 'Mostly, she just struck me as lonely. She told us her only child was living on the other side of the world.'

'Yes, she told me the same,' the Canadian admitted sadly. 'I wondered if that's why she took to Patrick so much — and to a certain extent, Barry. They must both be around about the same age as her own son.'

'Did she try to mother them then?'

'Oh no. Not really. I mean Barry hardly says boo to a goose, does he? But Patrick, I think, played up to her more. Teased her a bit, I mean. I often found them talking, and Patrick would laugh, and Imogen would look sort of flushed and pretend to be annoyed with him.'

'Annoyed? You think they argued?'

'No, I don't think so. I think he just liked jollying her along and I think she liked pretending to put him in his place.'

She put down the lettuce leaf that she'd been contemplating without eating it and reached instead for her glass of white wine. She'd ordered a bottle — and, having offered some to Hillary, who had declined it — poured a single glass for herself. Now she took several dainty sips that nevertheless reduced the level in her glass significantly. Not that Hillary blamed her. She must have found the last twenty-four hours exhausting and frightening.

'I hope the police aren't being too hard on you,' she said gently. 'That inspector seems a decent sort to me though?'

'Oh I'm sure he is. But . . . it's just I can't get my head around things,' Belinda wailed softly. 'Who would want to *kill Imogen* of all people? And right under our noses like that! I tell you, I don't . . .' She suddenly lowered her voice and looked around quickly. But the only people in the dining room apart from Barry Kirk, who was sitting at his usual table, were a few tourists who had wandered in just to eat. 'I really wish I could go back home. But the police have my passport. I know it sounds silly, but I just don't feel safe anymore. Here, I mean,' she added, indicating the room around her.

'I don't think that's silly at all,' Hillary said, and meant it. 'Not when you take into account that someone here must be responsible for what happened to Imogen.'

Belinda almost choked on her wine, making her eyes water a little, but after a pause, she simply nodded her head. 'That's why I don't mind talking to you. *You* weren't in the carriage. But I don't want any of the others getting too close to me. You need to watch out too! We all do. Well, all but one of us anyway.'

Hillary wondered if her attractive companion really thought she might be next on the killer's hit list or had jumped to the conclusion that they were dealing with a lunatic who might strike anyone at random. Hillary thought a crazed would-be serial killer was unlikely but wasn't ruling it out either.

She assured Belinda that she had no objections to sharing a table whenever Belinda felt the need of company and would take care of herself. 'But don't you have *any* idea who might have done it? After all, if you can help the police catch whoever was responsible, you might be going home sooner than you think.'

'I wish I could, but honestly, I had no idea anything at all had happened. And yes, I know how stupid that sounds — you shouldn't be able to kill someone like that, in such a small space, and not be found out. But . . .' She spread her hands helplessly.

'Did Imogen seem nervy to you at all, in the train I mean? When you first started off?'

'No, I can't say as she did.'

'And she never seemed to be afraid of anyone here before that day? She never said someone was making her feel uncomfortable or anything?'

'Not to me, she didn't,' Belinda said firmly, and took another quaff of wine.

Hillary reluctantly took the hint that it was time to change the subject, and asked Belinda about the article she was writing on Hay-on-Wye instead. She even listened with vague interest as the Canadian advised her about the various bookshops that she, as a debut novelist, should cultivate first.

* * *

Judith Pringwell stacked the empty dinner plates in the dishwasher and then stood in the kitchen, absently staring out of the window at the view of the river as her small number of staff bustled busily around her.

The police had warned her that the news of the murder had leaked out and would probably make the local press overnight, and she could only hope that it wouldn't be taken up nationally. Although she suspected that the strange circumstances of Imogen Muir's death were bound to catch the media's eye.

Imogen's identity was also being released, now that her son overseas had been informed, but Judith had been assured that the name of the hotel where the victim had been staying wouldn't be supplied. But how long would it take the press to find out? Perhaps they might assume Imogen had been staying in Aberystwyth though, since that was the departure point of the train journey into the mountains? That might delay them a bit.

She wasn't looking forward to having to fend off reporters and curiosity-seekers, and she'd already warned her small staff not to talk about Imogen or anyone else staying at the inn to anyone. Some of them seemed to find it exciting, whilst others were more subdued. But all of them were expecting an influx of off-the-street diners sooner or later, and she supposed she should set about ordering in extra food to meet the expected demand.

But she found herself too listless and nervy to bother with that just now.

If only she could be sure that Imogen coming here to stay at *her* hotel, of all places, really *was* just one of those freak coincidences that sometimes happened in life, she'd feel easier about things. The one-in-a-million chance that seemed impossible, but nevertheless sometimes happened, she could cope with. But the alternative . . . especially now . . .

She mentally shook her head.

She hadn't known what to make of it when Imogen had first arrived, and she still didn't now.

Although she'd been the one to take the telephone call from Imogen arranging the booking, she hadn't recognised the other woman's voice; but then, why should she? She'd never spoken to Imogen before in her life. And Muir was a common enough surname not to ring any real alarm bells. She might have been forewarned if Imogen had given her first name, but she'd used her initials — I.M. And even that warning sign had passed her by. After all, it had all been so long ago, in what felt like another lifetime now.

So it wasn't until Imogen had shown up with her cases that she finally realised just who it was who was coming to stay. For of course, Judith *had* seen a photograph of her. Her curiosity had made sure of that!

'Do you think we should start doing cream teas? It wouldn't be hard to set them up, and it would probably bring in a fair bit.'

Judith gave a slight start and turned to look at her brother, Lloyd. He liked working part time behind the bar, since after retiring from his job at a large electrical store it got him out of his house and provided a welcome boost to his pension. But he was always offering her unwanted advice on how to run her small enterprise. Normally she indulged him, but today she was too on edge.

'Cream teas? What on earth for?'

'Well, you know. It's bound to get out sooner or later about Mrs Muir staying here, and then we'll have tourists coming out of our ears. If we offer cream tea in the afternoons we're sure to make a small fortune. Make hay while the sun shines, and all that.'

Judith sighed. 'Right now I don't fancy batch-baking hundreds of scones, thank you very much. Isn't it time you got back to the bar?'

Lloyd looked ready to argue, so she literally turned her back on him and continued to stare out of the window, and after a moment, she heard him reluctantly move away.

As he did so, her conscience tickled her. Come to think of it, cream teas would be a good income boost, if they got inundated with the interest. And she needn't bake herself—she could have a word with one of the bakers in town. They'd be happy to take on a large order. And she could buy some best-quality supermarket jam and clotted cream. The garden was large enough for . . .

But it was no use. She couldn't keep her business brain to the forefront of her mind.

Because, what if Imogen turning up here *hadn't* been a coincidence after all?

For the first two days of her stay, Judith had waited nervously for Imogen to approach her, not sure how to tackle the situation should there be a confrontation. Even when that didn't happen, she still kept a wary eye on the other woman in case she should say something, oh-so-casually in passing. Or give some sly sign or hint that she . . . *knew*.

But nothing at all untoward had happened. And when the time came for Imogen to set out with all the others on that fatal train journey, Judith had been all but convinced that she'd been worrying for nothing.

But now? Well . . . now *what*? she asked herself angrily. What had happened all those years ago couldn't conceivably be connected in any way to what had happened to the poor woman now, could it?

And yet, she still felt uneasy.

* * *

If she had but known it, the owner of the Riverside Inn was not the only one in the handsome Georgian building who was feeling deeply uneasy.

In his room, Barry Kirk sat on his bed, his back propped up comfortably against the headboard with plenty of pillows, and scrolled down on his phone. When he stopped, he was looking at a ten-year-old newspaper photograph of a familiar face and nodded to himself.

So, Hillary Greene was a police officer. Or, according to what he'd been learning so far, she had been one once. Retired at the rank of DI. Now working as civilian consultant at Thames Valley Police HQ. Barry had no idea what that meant or entailed, although he could easily find out, if he was willing to put in the time and the effort. It was amazing what information there was to be had online, and this, coupled with his habit of wanting to know just who it was that he had around him, meant that he was now aware he had to be wary of her. He'd been a little suspicious of her right from the start. There'd been something about the way she reacted and behaved so coolly and efficiently after finding Imogen dead that just hadn't sat well with him. Now, he knew why.

The question now was: should he tell the others that they had a police spy in their midst?

He was fairly confident that her presence at the inn had begun innocently enough and was just one of those things that you had to put down to life being bloody-minded. The alternative was to believe that the woman was psychic and could predict murders, which was just plain daft. His mother might believe in all that stuff, but he definitely didn't. No. It was just an unhappy trick of fate that she was here. And the bit about her having her first book published was all true enough (he'd checked that too), so the reason she'd given for her presence in Hay was probably genuine too.

But that didn't answer his self-imposed question.

Should he keep his knowledge to himself, or share it? It was obvious why neither she nor Inspector Jones were anxious to divulge what she did for a living to the others. Having a murder dropped in her lap, there was no way either she or Jones could be expected not to take advantage of her presence here at the Riverside, right in the midst of their suspect list, to help gather intelligence on them.

But would it be a good thing — or not — to tell the others? Which would be likely to benefit him the most? As a small child who'd never fit in at school, he'd been a prime target for the bullies, and he'd become very adept at using his brains to keep himself safe and stay one step ahead. And as an adult, he saw no reason to change his habit of never poking his head above a parapet or letting down his guard. So much so that it had now become second nature to him to make like a mouse and fade into the wainscotting. Being quiet and cautious had never failed him yet. And life could be so tricky.

For a long while, Barry Kirk carefully weighed up the pros and cons, and decided, on the whole, it would be best to keep silent. At least for the time being. Later on . . . well, who knew? Also, he might just find it very useful indeed to know that he could let things drop in a certain ear and be confident that it would get passed on to the man in charge of the investigation immediately, and with none of his fellow train passengers any the wiser.

But if he was going to play that game, he would have to be careful, he warned himself, and make very sure that nothing he did or said could backfire on him.

It was a pity they weren't letting them leave the town. He really wanted to get home, where he'd feel safer.

He wasn't ashamed of being afraid. Only the stupid wouldn't be afraid at a time like this.

* * *

Somebody who was *not* feeling afraid was DI Ian Jones, who was currently searching Imogen Muir's room. It had been gone over before, of course, by Sergeant Soames the previous evening. And, according to his report, nothing of significance had been found. But it never hurt to double-check, and besides, Jones always liked to see things for himself.

Sometimes he'd catch himself daydreaming about his wife and the life he used to have, and he worried that his work might suffer because of being distracted. As a consequence, he knew that on occasion he went too far the other way and pushed himself too hard over every little detail of the case he was working on.

It reassured him somewhat to see that Hillary Greene also liked to immerse herself in work, for when they'd run into each other in the hall, and he'd told her what he was about to do, she'd asked if she could come along.

Now the two worked alongside each other in companionable silence.

Hillary wished she could go through the dead woman's handbag. But that, along with every item it had contained, would have been bagged separately and logged into evidence by one of Jones's trained officers and was probably now in the evidence locker back in the local police station.

With a sigh, she turned her attention to the vanity unit. Again, most of the items that had once been on it had been bagged and tagged, but a photograph of the dead woman and a man — presumably her husband — stood to one side of the mirror. Judging by the clothes, the Polaroid quality of the tint and the younger version of Imogen's face, Hillary guessed that it must have been taken more than twenty-five or even thirty years ago.

The image was small and somewhat blurry, but Mr Muir looked, at the time of the photograph being taken, to be a rather chunky man with bluff, hearty features that had probably been a lot more handsome when he'd been younger. They were standing on a bridge somewhere, and he had his arm around her. He looked smug. But she looked happy.

With a small sigh, Hillary put the photo back down again.

'Anything?' Jones asked.

'Afraid not. What do you know about her husband? You are doing a background check on him?'

Jones shrugged. 'Sure, but it's way down on some constable's to-do list. He's been dead nearly five years. Why?'

Hillary shrugged. 'Either someone killed Imogen over something that happened very recently — maybe only since she'd come here to stay — or they killed her over something that happened in the past. And since we don't know which yet, my advice is not to overlook anything. The more we know about the backgrounds of everyone here, the better. Even long-deceased spouses.'

Jones nodded. 'OK — thanks. I'll ask my team to prioritise that,' he said, genuinely grateful for the input. 'Mind you — I know, statistically speaking, that most women are likely to have been killed by their husbands, but in this case, I think we can safely rule him out, don't you?'

'Ah, statistics,' Hillary responded, equally dryly. 'Did you know, if you laid every cigarette smoker end-to-end around the world, more than 67 per cent of them would drown?'

It took a second before the Welshman began to sputter with laughter.

CHAPTER EIGHT

The next morning, Hillary thought she detected something slightly sheepish in Ian's manner when he joined her for breakfast at the inn. She had just returned to her table from the buffet bar with a pot of apricot yoghurt and a bowl of muesli and found him filching a cup of coffee from her pot.

'Help yourself,' she told him breezily as she took her seat, and he grinned weakly in apology. He looked a bit dark under the eyes and she had no trouble diagnosing an all-nighter. These were often par for the course during the first forty-eight hours or so of any murder investigation and having done the same herself, many a time, she knew the symptoms well.

'Want some toast?' she offered. 'I can order extra.'

'Thanks.'

She watched him stir his coffee for a moment, and then when he found himself under scrutiny, he gave her an abashed grin. 'You were right about those deep background checks. I've dug a bit more under the surface of all our contenders, and whilst I'm still waiting for results on some of them, I've already discovered something interesting.'

Hillary poured some milk onto her muesli and raised an eyebrow. 'Which one?'

'Our Canadian minor celeb.'

'Not a celeb?'

'Not a Canadian,' Jones corrected with a grin. 'Turns out the lady with the fetching transatlantic drawl spent her first seventeen years right here in the UK. Luton, to be precise.'

'Ah yes, glamorous Luton,' Hillary said. 'Can't imagine why she would want to emigrate and reinvent herself.'

'All right, all right,' Ian said, holding out his hands in mock surrender. 'Just saying.'

'I know you said that none of them has a criminal record, but in this case, that might only apply to her life in Canada. You'll no doubt have asked someone in Luton to check out any possible juvenile record but do you know the reason behind the move? If she was only seventeen, I'm presuming she went out along with her parents?'

Jones nodded. 'Yeah, it was a work thing, it seems. The father got offered a promotion. The parents returned here when he retired, but by then she was on to her second marriage and stayed put. Got residency, got almost-famous. Got Botox. Whatever. Now she walks the walk and talks the talk. I'd have thought, though, that living here for the formative years of her life, she'd still show some signs of being a Brit.'

'Makes you suspicious that she hasn't volunteered the information?'

'Yeah, a bit.'

Hillary nodded. 'Me too. Imogen Muir never lived in Bedfordshire during the years Belinda was growing up, did she?'

'I've already got someone checking on that, but it seems unlikely.'

'Well, we can always just ask her,' she said as, looking over Ian's shoulder, she saw that the lady herself was entering the dining room.

Today, the fashionable younger woman was wearing a tawny-coloured one-piece trouser suit with patches of gold and black that showed off her slender figure to advantage, and her cap of dark, geometrically cut hair to perfection.

Modest black heels and a single piece of jewellery, a chunky hand-beaten gold chain, completed the ensemble.

Belinda noticed her at the same moment, and Hillary saw her eyes go to the man seated opposite her. Hillary took mental note of the involuntary way in which Belinda's footsteps were checked as she instinctively hesitated. Was she contemplating turning tail and heading for the proverbial hills, perhaps?

Hillary smiled. 'Hello, Belinda,' she called out gaily. 'Want to come and join us for a tick? I think DI Jones wants to see everyone again today. Just some follow-up questions, he said. I've told him I can't think of anything I can add, but he's nothing if not persistent. Why don't you pull up a chair and get it over and done with? Then you can relax for the rest of the day.'

As well as maintaining the fiction that she was a witness herself and explaining away Ian's presence at her table, the impromptu speech was also a good way of ensuring that she could listen and watch Belinda's reactions without causing more suspicion.

She didn't miss the look of admiration for her quick thinking that Jones gave her, but she was careful not to acknowledge it.

With some reluctance Belinda came abreast of them and pulled over a third chair. 'No, I won't join you for breakfast, I wouldn't want to impose, but I'm happy to chat for a bit.'

Call her suspicious, but somehow Hillary doubted her sincerity. She made a show of peeling back the top from her yoghurt pot, picked up a spoon, and pretended to politely ignore them as Jones took the initiative.

'Thank you, Ms John-Jacques,' he began politely. 'I take it that's a professional name, by the way? It's not your last husband's surname, is it? And you were born Belinda Corker, I believe?'

At this, the elegant woman winced. 'So you've rumbled me at last,' she gave a little laugh. 'Well, can you blame me for using a pseudonym? I mean, just imagine growing up with a name like that! Bel Corker!' She gave a false shudder.

'Yes, I can imagine your school days might have been a bit fraught,' Ian said with a vague smile. 'But why didn't you mention that you were born over here in the UK, Ms John-Jacques?'

'It just never occurred to me, I suppose,' she said, with a casual shrug of her shoulder. 'After all, I've lived longer as a Canadian than as a Brit, and my life is over there now. I hardly ever give Luton much thought — believe me.'

'Did you ever meet Imogen Muir when you were growing up?'

'Imogen? Good grief, no,' Belinda said, looking and sounding genuinely amazed. 'Why, should I have?'

It was a good question, and Ian was too canny to let it just sit there. 'Mrs Greene here has nothing to add to her statement, but do you? Now that the worst of the shock has passed, and you've had a night to get some proper sleep and think things over, have you remembered anything else — any little detail at all about the train journey that you forgot to mention?'

'I don't think so, no. To be honest, I'm trying not to think about it at all. It's just too awful.'

Ian nodded. 'All right. Well, either myself or my sergeant will be around for some time to come. Don't hesitate to get in touch if anything occurs to you.'

Belinda nodded, rose and left, trying not to look as relieved as she probably felt.

'What do you think?' Ian asked, when she was safely out of earshot.

Hillary shrugged. 'I think it's about time I started to visit some bookshops and do what I originally came here to do,' she said reluctantly. 'If I don't make a start introducing myself and my book to the town's booksellers, I'll have my editor on my jacksy. And that, believe me, wouldn't be a pretty sight.'

And until more data started coming in, there was realistically very little she could do here at the inn. She'd already been seen talking to Ian by Belinda, and if she kept on quizzing her fellow guests, chances were, they'd start to wonder about her. She'd noticed that there was already an oppressive and paranoid atmosphere stealing over the place, as the reality of their situation began to seep in.

'But for what it's worth, I think she was holding something back,' Hillary said, giving the slightest of nods in Belinda's direction. 'And she must have gone to some trouble to skirt letting on about her true origin of birth when giving her original statement. You know as well as I do how admin like to dot the I's and cross the T's.'

'You're not buying her claim that she didn't want her real name getting into the public domain, then?' he asked with a wry smile.

* * *

After an hour of getting her bearings wandering around such charmingly named byways as Lion Street, Bear Street, High Town, Castle Street (which did indeed have an actual castle) and the very Regency-sounding Belmont Road, Hillary finally paused at a bookshop called Murder and Mayhem.

It sounded just her kind of bookshop.

With advance copies of her novel tucked away in her sturdy canvas bag, she entered the world of old, second-hand and new books, the aroma of vanilla and dust being given off by the stock instantly welcoming her like a long-lost friend.

After making the acquaintance of the lovely woman sitting behind an ancient dark wood desk so piled high with books that she almost had to stand to peer over them, Hillary spent the first hour stocking up on Penguin crime classics for her own private reading, before getting down to 'business'.

When she finally left, minus one copy of her book, it was with sincere promises ringing in her ears that orders for six copies 'in the first instance' of her novel would be winging their way to her publishers by the end of the week at the latest.

Feeling like she'd earned a treat, she stopped off at an ice cream parlour to enjoy a three-scoop tub of butterscotch, toffee and chocolate (well, she was on her *holiday*), then headed back towards the Riverside. Slowly leaving the tourist-laden centre of town behind her as she made her way from the shops towards the river and the quiet, more residential thoroughfares of the town, she felt relaxed and happy.

She made her way onto Wye End Road and walked for about five minutes before turning off down the single-track lane that terminated at the inn and the river beyond. Here the tarmac ended and gravel began, which was fine, since only those who had business at the inn actually used it.

Lined by a row of cottages that stood way back from the lane with large front gardens, the roadside was somewhat overgrown with bushes and shrubs, before terminating in the wider opening leading in to the car park of the inn itself.

As the Welsh slate roof of the bijou hotel became visible beyond a variegated laurel hedge, Hillary — who had been enjoying the sound of birdsong and the honeysuckle-scented air — stopped dead in her tracks.

There had been no one in sight for the past few minutes, and tucked away out of the mainstream down here, even the sound of the small market town's scarce traffic was all but indistinguishable; so the sudden and furious sound of scuffling and shaking greenery just around a curve in the lane ahead of her had her pulse rate suddenly rocketing.

As did the anger-and-pain-filled yelp that almost instantaneously followed on from it.

Without thinking, Hillary took off in a sprint. It took her only seconds to gain the bend in the lane, and once there she came to a dead stop and quickly put her head around the corner whilst keeping the rest of her body out of sight. Running headlong into an unknown situation might be brave and look heroic, but it was also extremely stupid. A painful lesson she'd only had to learn once, whilst walking the beat as a green youngster.

It took her less than half a second to assess what she was seeing. Two figures were struggling with each other — a taller figure with the white hair of an older person, and a skinhead, who was getting in several punishing punches in rapid succession. The older man was trying his best to fight back and managed to land a few kicks, but he was obviously fading fast. They were both grunting with concentration and effort and as they spun around, grappling for dominance, Hillary recognised Jasper Van Paulen as one of the combatants.

She took the other half a second to gauge her enemy, then stepped onto the grass verge to mask any sound of her approach, dropped her bag at her feet and walked three quick, silent paces, bringing her within striking distance. Without hesitating, she viciously and strategically kicked the back of the skinhead's left knee at a downward angle, which pitched him forward and brought him to the ground.

In doing so, he almost knocked Jasper off his feet as well, but since the American was pushed backwards, the laurel bush prevented the older man from joining his assailant in the dirt. There were several sharp cracks as the snapping twigs took most of Jasper's weight, then the skinhead began to spew forth gutter language, howls of pain and blood-curdling threats in no particular order.

Putting his hands down on either side of his head in order to lever himself back to his feet, he began to get up. Hillary watched tensely as he quickly created a gap between himself and the ground until he was almost in the downward-dog position — which was the only yoga exercise she knew.

Now, it was a commonly held and very British belief that you never kicked a man when he was down. Boy Scouts, comic book heroes and readers of *Boy's Own* would consider such a thing to be scandalously uncalled for, and definitely 'not cricket'.

Hillary however, never having been a Boy Scout nor a subscriber to comics (let alone lofted a cricket bat), lost no time in taking a backwards step in order to redistribute her weight more evenly, and administered a second (this time upwardly aimed) kick, catching the thug right under his ribcage. This lifted him clear off the ground for a second, winding him so badly that he didn't even have the breath to yell. When he face-planted for a second time, he curled into a foetal position, almost at Jasper's feet, and began to retch.

As he began the process of trying to suck in air, Hillary turned to check out Jasper for damage and said sharply, 'Are you all right?'

The American was bleeding from a cut lip, and the top of his left cheekbone looked sore and was set to come up in a spectacular bruise a little later on. He also looked pale and shaken, and for a moment simply stared at her without understanding, as if she had been speaking Swahili.

'Hillary? Mrs Greene?' he muttered, dazed. 'What on earth are you . . . *look out!*'

His last few shouted words of warning weren't really needed, for Hillary had already seen for herself the skinhead's hand reach out to make a swiping motion at her ankles, and she was leaping backwards like a demented ballerina on steroids. For she knew full well the meaning of that particular sweeping motion, and although she didn't have time to register the glint of sunlight on an actual blade, she was already stamping down heavily on the back of the skinhead's hand. It was only then that she saw and heard the flick knife clatter onto the gravel and skitter away.

She shifted her weight again, expecting him to make a lunge for it and preparing to beat him to it, but that turned out to be a mistake, for instead of moving away from her, he made a lunge *towards* her, headbutting her in her stomach before she could react.

This time, it was *her* breath that left her in a pain-wracked 'whoosh' and she instinctively folded over. As she did so, she felt, rather than saw, the skinhead gain his feet at last.

Which was not good news for her.

Ignoring her brain's screaming insistence that she remain bent over and protect her stomach with her arms, she forced her abdominal muscles to straighten up instead and face the imminent threat. And for the first time, she got her first — if fleeting — look at him, full-face.

She only had time, however, to register an impression of bad skin, bad teeth and a bad attitude as he promptly aimed an elbow at her face. She'd been in enough fights in her time to know that if she let it connect with her nose it would break it, and she snarled something pithy to herself as she managed to turn her face just in time to avoid the worst of the blow's impetus.

Unfortunately, his bony elbow caught her a glancing blow on the vulnerable part of her temple, and for a second, her vision went white, receded, then came back again. And an instant later, she realised that she was on the ground herself now. Fighting off incipient panic, she instinctively tried to stagger to her feet. As she did so, she felt a hand under her armpit and was about to deliver an elbow-to-the-face of her own when she realised, just in time, that it was Jasper and not the skinhead who had a hold of her and was helping her to get up.

Out of her now-clearing peripheral vision she caught a shifting pattern of rapid movement and turned to see the skinhead legging it around the corner of the lane and disappearing out of sight.

If she'd been twenty years younger, she'd have taken off after the little sod, but after taking one, compulsive step in pursuit, common sense took over, and she reluctantly let her fight-or-flight reflexes relax.

'Are you all right, ma'am?' The concerned American voice coupled with the old-fashioned title of respect for some reason made her smile.

She turned to Jasper and nodded. 'I'm fine,' she gasped. Well, apart from the fact that her stomach might never forgive her, and her throbbing head seemed convinced that a band of campanologists had taken up residence inside her skull. 'How about you? Do you need a doctor?'

'Don't think so. I'm a bit stiff and biffed up, but I reckon it's my pride that's been hurt most of all. The little bastard took my watch and my wallet,' Jasper complained. 'I don't mind about the cash in the wallet so much, but that was my daddy's watch.'

Hillary, obeying her stomach's continued insistence that she fold herself back over on it, slowly did so, holding onto the front of her shins with her hands for stability and letting her head fall forward so that she could take several slow, steady breaths. After a moment, the ringing in her head faded.

'Ma'am, you want me to call for an ambulance?'

She looked up to see Jasper holding his mobile phone and waving it at her. 'The swine never got this, at least.'

Hillary smiled and shook her head. 'No. I'm just a bit winded, that's all. The inn is right here — what say we head back there and pay the bar a visit? I don't know about you, but I could do with a stiff drink.'

Jasper Van Paulen grinned widely. 'Now that sounds like a pretty damned good idea to me. And can I just say, thanks for helping me out there? You came in like the cavalry, that's for sure.'

As they slowly and gingerly made their way the remaining distance to the inn, Hillary began to think in earnest.

'I'm just amazed that you got mugged *here*, of all places,' she said, shaking her head in a good impression of disbelief. 'I feel as if I should apologise for my country. Or on Wales's behalf. Or something.'

'Aw, forget it. There's wrong 'uns everywhere you go nowadays,' Jasper said bitterly, taking out a handkerchief and wiping his lip cautiously. 'And I should have been paying more attention myself, I guess,' he conceded ruefully. 'Fact is, I just didn't see him hiding in the bushes there. And it's so quaint and peaceful here, I forgot to be wary, you know?'

Hillary nodded. But it didn't make sense. Muggers didn't usually choose to hang around dead-end little byways like this. How often could they expect a victim to pass by here? And could it be just a coincidence that a prime suspect in a murder gets 'jumped' within a day or two of witnessing someone being killed?

'Did he say anything to you at all?' she asked.

The movement of the handkerchief on Jasper Van Paulen's face halted for a fraction of a second, before recommencing its dabbing motion. 'Say anything? No, ma'am, not a word.'

Hillary saw him glance at her quickly and then away again. She sighed, then winced at the pain it caused her stomach. 'Ah, right. Still, I don't suppose, when you think about it, that there was much for you two to chat about.'

'Don't suppose there was at that,' he agreed gratefully.

* * *

'And you think he was lying?' Ian Jones said, a short while later, after Hillary had related her latest adventures.

They were now in her room, and she'd just made them each a mug of coffee. She'd asked Judith to track the inspector down and send him up to her, too uptight to worry about what the others might make of her entertaining the policeman in her room.

'Oh yes, he was lying,' she said. She sat down gingerly on the side of her bed and took a sip of much-needed coffee. 'If that was a common or garden mugging then I'll eat my hat. If I'd brought it with me, which I didn't. No, for starters, most muggers snatch and run, you know that. At most, they might give a thump or two to get their mark to let go of the phone, or wallet, or whatever. But their top priority is to get in and out with the goods as quick as lightning. But this little hooligan was intent on delivering a beating.'

'A punishment beating?'

'Perhaps,' Hillary mused. 'Or a warning off? Either way, it begs the question — what's our American friend done to deserve either? I'll be interested to see whether he reports it to you or decides to keep schtum.'

Jones thought for a moment. Then he tapped his phone and a few seconds later, brought up an image to show her. 'That him?'

Hillary looked at the face on the screen and nodded. 'Yeah, that's him. Who is he?'

'Peter Hardiman — one of Bodicote's toerags. You know, the one who was seen selling to Jasmine, according to our anonymous letter writer.'

Hillary nodded. 'Well, that makes sense. We heard Jasper ourselves derailing his daughter's money train — if you'll pardon the reference. She must have passed on the bad news to her supplier and now your local friendly neighbourhood drug dealer isn't feeling all that friendly towards our Jasper.'

Ian nodded. 'I'll pass it along the food chain. But I doubt, even if they pick him up, that Peter Hardiman will implicate his boss.'

'Hmmm. What's more, Jasper probably won't willingly testify against him anyway. The last thing he wants is more hassle and potential publicity concerning his daughter's drug habit. He'll probably spin some line about not getting a proper look at his attacker.'

'You could always testify to the attack,' Jones pointed out.

'My pleasure. But right now, we've got bigger priorities, so it might be a good idea to shelve any action on that front just now. Even granted that Jasper or his daughter suspected Imogen Muir of writing the letter about Jasmine's drug habit, I can't really see how this latest attack gets us any further forward in zeroing in on Imogen's murderer, do you?'

The inspector thought about it in silence for a while, then shrugged over his coffee mug. 'Can't say as I do.'

'No. Me neither,' Hillary concurred gloomily. 'So, let's not get too sidetracked by this Van Paulen/drug angle thing. Especially since Hardiman will probably back off now that he's delivered his message to Daddy dearest.'

'Let's hope so,' Ian grunted. 'The last thing we need is the likes of Marvin Bodicote getting under our feet whilst we're trying to track down our killer. With a bit of luck though, even that maniac will have enough sense to keep off our radar from now on.'

* * *

Marvin Bodicote's dead-eyed stare had the usual effect on Peter Hardiman, and the skinhead began to shuffle his feet nervously.

'I *did* do what you wanted, boss,' he whined. 'I took the old man's money and told him that he needed to let his daughter get what she wanted or next time he'd get a knife to the ribs. And I gave him a good thumping, just like you said. It's just that this other crazy woman jumped me. Out of nowhere! It weren't my fault, honest it weren't. I never saw her coming, did I, what with giving the old man the boot, and being half in the bushes myself, and—'

His words came to an abrupt halt as Bodicote held up an imperious hand for silence. They were meeting once again in Moose's kitchen, and it was to his second-in-command that Marvin directed a knowing look. On cue, Moose gave a little snicker in response.

'So, let's get this straight. A middle-aged lady beat you up,' Marvin drawled, as Hardiman flushed bright red with shame. 'Did she get a good look at your face?' he demanded.

'No, boss, I swear she didn't,' Peter lied instantly. 'She couldn't have. I took off, didn't I? I'd done what you asked, and you never said nothin' about putting in the boot to bystanders. I never do nothin' you don't tell me to do, you know that, boss.'

Marvin's face twitched with distaste at the sycophantic whine, and again he turned to the grinning Moose. 'Get that young kid — what's his name . . . Daniel Rhys to find out just who this old bat is. She was in her fifties, you say, a red-head?' he glanced at Hardiman questioningly.

'Yeah. Quite a looker for a wrinkly,' Peter said. 'I seen her before going into and out of the hotel, when I was putting the eye on Jas's old man. I reckon she's a guest there. But I can—'

'You can get lost, that's what you can do,' Marvin told him in disgust. 'Go on, get out of my sight. Now.'

After Hardiman had swiftly left, Moose shifted restlessly. 'Does it really matter, boss? Some have-a-go heroine comes to the old man's rescue. So what?'

'So I want to know what's going on, that's what,' Marvin shot back. 'I don't like any of this funny business. I don't like it that our American cash-cow has got mixed up with this murder business. I don't like it that her daddy seems to have acquired a mysterious bodyguard. And most of all, I don't like all these coppers interfering on my patch.'

'Perhaps we should back off for a bit?' Moose asked hopefully. 'I mean,' he added hastily, as Marvin shot him a warning look, 'just until all this weird train-murder stuff dies down.' Like his boss, he'd read the latest about it online, and had no doubt that it was brewing up into a big media circus. Which meant the cops would be frantic to get it done and dusted. 'I know you've got plans for the American bird, but this is murder she's got herself mixed up in . . . Do we really need to put ourselves in their crosshairs? The cops were already sniffing around her because of that anonymous letter business anyway. Isn't she getting to be more trouble than she's worth?'

'No,' Marvin Bodicote said shortly. He was determined that Jasmine was going to become his stepping stone to setting himself up in the good ol' USA, and nothing and no one was going to be allowed to baulk him. Millionaire heiresses were hardly two-a-penny, and what were the chances of a second one virtually falling into his lap like a ripe plum? Bloody zero, that's what.

Which meant he'd be all kinds of a mug not to take full advantage of his good luck whilst he had the chance. Jasmine, once back in the States, would have all kinds of rich friends who'd be only too happy to have a safe and reliable dealer to supply their needs. And with his brains, he'd need only the smallest of footholds on which to start building himself a nice little empire over there.

Why settle for this poxy backwater when, in ten years, say, he could retire to Florida and live on a yacht for six months a year. Or maybe go to California and mix with the film stars — maybe even produce one or two?

Right from a kid, he'd known he was born for bigger and better things. And why shouldn't he be someone? He had the looks, the brains, and now he had enough money to start to make the big plays. If others did it, so could he.

He just had to keep his eyes on the prize.

'Tell Rhys I want to know the name of Jasper's good Samaritan. And tell him to keep a general eye on the comings and goings at that bloody inn and report back. I don't want Jasmine getting arrested for no murder. She's no good to me in jail. Tell Rhys he'd better keep me informed what the cops are up to.'

'Right,' Moose said, a shade reluctantly. He only hoped that his boss wasn't biting off more than he could chew this time.

CHAPTER NINE

Patrick checked the clock in the lounge and decided that, since it was nearly four o'clock, it was too late to do anything worthwhile further afield, and so carried on into the bar and ordered a pint of Guinness. He was just about halfway down the glass when he felt someone join him and turned to smile at Hillary.

'And what can I get for the hero of the hour?' he asked. It had been inevitable that the news of Jasper's mugging would rapidly become a minor sensation amongst the small hotel's inhabitants, but Hillary hoped that it would be short-lived. She didn't feel comfortable in the limelight. When she asked for a white wine spritzer, it was promptly produced by the barman.

She had got herself comfortable on the bar stool next to him, and was raising her glass to him in appreciation, when she noticed his eyes move beyond her to a point just over her shoulder.

She didn't need to turn around, for she knew who was joining them; Ian had told her only a few minutes ago that he wanted to reinterview Patrick next, and they'd decided that this 'accidental' meeting in the bar was the best way of allowing that to take place in a way that seemed natural for her to be in on the proceedings.

'Ah, Mr Unwin, I'm glad I ran into you again. I've one or two follow-up questions for you. Nothing too alarming — just some background information on you this time,' she heard Ian say as he passed by her and took the stool on the other side of Patrick. 'I've been learning all about your misspent youth. I'll have a tonic with ice please,' he added to the barman.

Judith's brother Lloyd nodded and diplomatically went out to the kitchen just off the bar, ostensibly to fetch more ice.

'Uh-oh, that sounds ominous,' Patrick grinned. 'Whatever it is you've been learning, I'm guilty as charged, your honour!'

He turned a little on the bar stool so that he could fully face the policeman, presenting Hillary with his half-turned shoulder and left side profile. Dressed in casual jeans and a short-sleeved cream-coloured T-shirt that revealed his thin but wiry tanned arms, Hillary was reminded of his former profession as a jockey. Although short at only five feet four or so, she reminded herself that this man, whilst he might look almost elfin with his curly brown hair and blue eyes, was probably, physically, the fittest of all their suspects.

Not that it needed a lot of muscle to slip a very sharp blade into someone, she reminded herself.

Ian grinned. 'Oh, I don't doubt it,' he agreed. 'I've had the chance now to talk to some of my colleagues in the racing game, and although I was sure I already had a good idea about how murky it could be, I've had my eyes well and truly opened, I can tell you.'

Although Ian, after discussing the ins-and-outs of the Van Paulen situation with her had gone on to relay the gist of the intel coming in on the former jockey, Hillary was interested to see how Patrick Unwin would react to his past misdeeds coming back to haunt him. It was a pity his back was now turned to her, but she would be able to tell a lot from his body language.

'Ah, sad but true, I'm afraid,' Patrick said sorrowfully, shaking his head and making his curls bounce. 'When gambling's involved and fortunes can be made and lost, human nature can get very dark indeed. The tales some of the lads told me made me shudder.'

Jones nodded. 'You yourself were never really top flight, were you? Sorry, I don't want to sound judgemental, only accur—'

'Ah, that's no matter,' Patrick interrupted, waving a hand in the air before picking up his glass and taking a gulp. 'Me ego's not so fragile as all that! And you're quite right,' he said, having swallowed heartily. 'When I started out I had all the usual daft dreams of being a new Frankie Dettori. Didn't we all? As a lad I dreamed of winning the Cheltenham Gold Cup and riding the new Red Rum to consecutive Grand National wins.' He gave what sounded to Hillary like a genuinely self-effacing laugh. 'But then, what's the point of dreaming if you don't dream big? That's what I always say.'

He took another mouthful of his drink and then shrugged as he put the glass back on the bar. 'Reality was a bit different though. And after riding a series of no-hoper nags on cold November days at Newmarket with just a handful of spectators to cheer you on and some over-ambitious sod trying to deliberately ride you into the rails on the bends, it soon knocks that sort of nonsense out of you.'

'Oh, it wasn't as bad as all that, surely? My source says you had a few winners. That must have made up for it?' Ian coaxed.

'Oh sure. Nothing's so grand as flying past the finishing post first on a 31-0 outsider and seeing that one punter who bet on you in the stands shouting and screaming their lungs out . . .' He laughed again. 'But there were never enough of them.'

'Is that why you quit to work in the oil industry? A bit of a leap, that, wasn't it?'

'No, it wasn't the disappointments so much as all the injuries,' Patrick corrected him. 'I spent almost as much time in A&E as I did on the racecourse. And no, it's not because I was useless as a jockey, or at least, no more useless than 90 per cent of my fellow riders.' Here, Hillary could imagine him flashing that charming grin of his again. 'It's just that, over the jumps especially, you're bound to fall occasionally. And having a horse fall on top of you is no joke. Not to mention getting kicked by the other horses following on, unless you can manage to roll out of the way. I must have broken practically every bone in my body at some point. Or at least, it felt as if I did. My mother said getting kicked in the head so often should have knocked some sense into me. And maybe it finally did.'

He laughed again, and reached for his now much-depleted drink, but instead of lifting it, he just turned it around and around on its place mat. 'Funny thing is, once I put it all behind me and got a "proper" job, earning a decent and regular wage for once . . .' He trailed off and shrugged.

'You missed it?' Ian prompted.

Patrick sighed. 'Oh, don't get me wrong. I enjoy having a decent car to drive around in now, courtesy of my company. And the nice penthouse flat in Aberdeen. And being able to eat what I want, and never minding putting on an ounce or two and all of that . . . But yeah. Sometimes, when I'm placing an order for a million quid in drilling equipment whilst wearing a snazzy suit . . . Yeah, I suppose I'd rather be covered in mud and wearing garish silks and freezing to death on some windswept course in Norfolk somewhere. Mad, ain't it?'

'Not really. But are you being a little, shall we say, disingenuous? My sources tell me that your departure from the world of horseracing had a little more to do with throwing races than being forced out due to injury. There was that little matter of the disciplinary hearing in front of the Jockey Club, I understand.'

At this, Patrick burst into laughter and nodded. 'Like I said before — guilty, your honour.'

Hillary saw his shoulders tense then relax again as he reached for his drink and this time nearly drained it. Then he sighed heavily and shook his head.

'Ah, what's the use, eh? You're quite right. I got nobbled by this bent bastard who had a nasty habit of breaking your kneecaps if you didn't knuckle under and do what his bully boys suggested. And by then I was getting too old for all that malarkey. And of living hand to mouth . . . Ah, what the hell, I could come up with excuses 'til Doomsday. The truth is, yeah, I took some backhanders to hold back a few nags.'

Ian nodded. 'Dope a few horses, did you?'

'Not dope, no,' he denied instantly. 'There's lots of things you can do to slow a horse down besides drugs you know. Giving a horse a bucket of water to drink just before a race can nobble it just as well and there's no trace of anything to show up in a blood test. Some bastards did far worse though,' he said, his voice turning dark and ugly, 'things that lamed a horse for life, or worse. But I wouldn't have nothing to do with that. I love horses, always have.' His voice seemed to crack a little and he cleared his throat. 'That's what got me into racing in the first place. No, it's heartbreaking to see one suffer — or worse, die on the racetrack. It rips the guts right out of you.'

Ian nodded. Hillary could see that he thought the Irishman was probably quite sincere in what he was saying, and now that he'd owned up to his past bad choices, delicately changed the subject. 'Quite a switch from horse- riding to a high-flying career in big business though. Just how did that come about, exactly?'

Again, Patrick laughed, his mercurial mood swings catching Ian a little off guard, Hillary could tell.

'Ah, no need to sound so suspicious, officer, I promise you! Besides, it sounds far more glamorous than it is. I got lucky, that's all. I had an old mate who was working for one of the big oil companies in Scotland, and he got me a junior job in the office, as a favour, like. Never having done business studies or gone to uni, I was never going to rise high though — not high, high — but it's all relative, ain't it? Anyway, I left the money-end of it well alone and let the city sharks fight it out amongst themselves, and turned my attention more to the technical side of it. Took some night courses. Got to understand the machinery and manufacturing and sourcing end of things. You know — get out of the office and get a bit of dirt under my fingernails — the kind of work that none of the pen-pushers were interested in.'

'Ah, you specialised. That was bright of you.'

'That's it. Pretty soon they were sending me overseas to find new suppliers, and there I was, Patrick Unwin, former also-ran jockey, and now a proper jetsetter! How they laughed back in Ireland. Well, you've got to laugh at life, haven't you? Otherwise you'd go doolally. Now I'm either being "entertained" by manufacturers, eager to get me to sign deals with their company, being plied with champagne in fancy five-star restaurants and getting flown first class here and there — or, right on the end of the scale of things, I'm on-site overseeing installation of gear, dressed in manky oilskin coats and wellies and reeking of petrol.'

'Sounds an interesting life,' Ian said. 'And now here you are, in Hay-on-Wye of all places,' he finished suggestively.

'So I am,' he agreed cheerfully. 'And you can thank my old ma for that. She told me it was time I visited family in this area before either they popped their clogs or I did. She's convinced, you understand, that sea helicopters are about as safe as nitroglycerine and that one day I'm going to head off in one to an oil rig in stormy weather and end up in Davy Jones's locker. Keeps praying to the saints to keep me safe, she does. So I thought I'd give her a break from it. Not even she thinks I can come to any harm in a town full of bookshops.'

And then, cocking his head, he looked at DI Jones ruefully. 'And now here I am, about to have my collar felt in a murder case. Just goes to show, don't it?'

'Oh, your collar is safe enough for the moment, Mr Unwin,' Ian said enigmatically.

At this, the Irishman burst out in what sounded like genuine laughter. 'And very relieved I am to be hearin' it, Inspector. Long may it continue. Anything else?'

'Not for the moment, sir.'

'Ah, in that case, I'm going to finish my Guinness and take a stroll up to the hills. At least there's plenty of *them* around hereabouts.'

And so saying he drained his glass, nodded and winked at Hillary and sauntered away.

As if on cue, Lloyd came back to the bar with a bag of ice and gave Ian his drink.

'Thanks. I think I'll take this outside in the garden,' Ian murmured, rattling the ice cubes in his glass.

Hillary, as prearranged, stayed on in the bar until she'd finished her own drink, then left herself. A few minutes later, she joined Ian under the shade of a laburnum tree.

'So, what do you think?' he asked immediately.

'About our Irish friend?' Hillary shrugged. 'I think he enjoys deliberately overdoing the national stereotype and is as crooked as a penny that's been run over in the road. And I wouldn't be at all surprised, if you sent someone to that oil company of his to dig around a bit, that they'd discover some inventory irregularities amongst all that expensive machinery he oversees.'

'What? A few bits and bobs going missing off the back of lorries in out-of-the-way laybys? Yes, I was wondering the same thing,' Ian agreed. 'And is it my imagination, or does his Irish brogue get stronger every time we speak to him?'

Hillary laughed. 'Why not? That sort of charming, fickle joker is usually liked by one and all. He's probably a hit with the ladies too.'

Ian sighed. 'But he's never been caught red-handed.'

'Too wily,' Hillary said with a twitch of her lips. 'That sort knows how to look after his own skin.'

'So, we're agreed he's not exactly lily white,' Ian sighed. 'But I still don't see why he should have any reason to kill a woman he's never met before, let alone do it in a train carriage with five potential witnesses.'

'You're not coming up with any connection at all between Imogen and any of the suspects?'

'Not so far. The Van Paulens have never been in the UK before, so any contact with the victim had to have been very recent.'

'And Barry Kirk?'

Something in her voice must have alerted him, because Ian glanced at her thoughtfully. 'You got a feeling about Kirk?'

Hillary shrugged. 'Not that I can quite put my finger on, no. He just . . . makes my skin itch a little, that's all.'

Ian blinked. 'Interesting. But so far, we've got nothing that says he and Imogen ever met either. And nobody around here has anything to say about them clashing since they booked into the inn or anything like that. The only thing the staff noticed was the chilly atmosphere around Imogen and Jasmine. And we know what's behind that.'

Hillary nodded, then glanced behind her at the inn. A lovely Georgian house, with lovely gardens, surrounded by lovely scenery. 'Something's rotten in there,' Hillary Greene said slowly. 'I can feel it. Smell it. Almost taste it. And it's only going to get worse as time goes by. They're in an impossible situation — one of them a killer and being forced to wait to see if they've got away with it — whilst the others are innocent, all suspecting each other in turn. Nerves will get stretched to breaking point and inevitably, they'll start to turn on one another.'

Ian shot her a worried look. 'You don't think we're in for anything . . . else, do you?'

He was clearly hoping she would say something reassuring, but to his dismay, Hillary merely shrugged. 'I wouldn't be surprised,' she said quietly.

* * *

Leaving a now thoroughly unsettled DI Jones to return to his station to hold a team meeting, Hillary made her way back inside. Choosing at random a crime novel from her recent purchases, she made her way to the lounge.

There she settled down with *The Sunshine Corpse*, by an unknown (to her) Australian author writing in the 1950s called Max Murray. She hadn't made much headway into Chapter One, however, before she became aware of voices.

She recognised the male voice as that belonging to the barman Lloyd, Judith's brother. Although she didn't know the younger, female voice, it soon became apparent that she was one of the three young women who worked part time for the hotel owner.

'You haven't seen the furniture polish have you?' the young woman was saying. 'I just put it down a minute ago and now it's vanished.'

'That'll be the resident ghost,' Lloyd replied. He sounded as if he was serious, but Hillary suspected he was just being deadpan. And although she couldn't see them, since they were out of sight beyond the open lounge door, Hillary could well imagine the look of scorn being sent his way.

'I'm serious — I'm always losing the dratted thing. I swear it deliberately hides itself from me.'

'It'll be just where you left it,' Lloyd said, unhelpfully. 'Where were you using it last?'

'In Mr Kirk's room — his room's always the final one on my list. I can't find it anywhere in there, but I know I had it. Do you think he'll complain to Judith if he comes across it?'

'Doubt it,' Lloyd reassured her. 'And don't worry — my sister won't bite your head off if he does. She'll be more likely to volunteer to go to his room and smooth things over. She'll be good at that.'

There was enough of a smirk in his voice that it was clear even to Hillary (who wasn't able to see the man's facial expressions) just what he was implying.

'What? *Judith!*' The response was typical — a shade shocked, a shade impressed, a shade gleeful. 'No, go on!'

'Oh, don't let her ladylike ways fool you. She was a proper goer in her day, my little sister,' Lloyd said, with a chuckle.

'You're pulling my leg.'

'No, honest. There was this fella who used to come here back in the old days, who managed to find a bed here even when all the guest rooms were taken, if you get what I mean.'

'Back in the old days, huh,' the young voice repeated scornfully. 'You make it sound as if she was living in Victorian times. Good on her, I say.'

As the two voices, still joshing each other good-naturedly, moved away and faded into silence, Hillary, with a smile, returned to her chapter.

Good on her, indeed.

* * *

Unaware that her past private life was being salaciously discussed by her brother and a member of her admiring staff, Judith was resting in her small, private study. It was at the side of the house, overlooking nothing more exciting than a narrow path and a privet hedge that bordered her neighbour. For this reason, she'd decided it wasn't good enough for her guests, and had claimed it for her private hideaway.

It was a small but pleasant room, with an open fireplace and one wall given over to bookshelves. There were two armchairs, a coffee table and a small television in one corner which she seldom bothered to watch.

In front of her, on the coffee table, lay an open black papier-mâché box, highly decorated with white and red flowers. In it, she kept her precious odds and ends that she'd accumulated over the years. A pearl ring of her mother's, some postcards from her first boyfriend, a dog collar for a beloved pet who'd been dead for nearly twenty years now.

And the letters.

She lifted these out and held them in her hand. They weren't tied up with ribbon or anything fancy like that, but they were yellowing with age, and were well worn. Not surprising, given the number of times over the years that she'd taken them out and read them.

They were not from her husband — the man she'd married before he buggered off with a curvaceous traffic warden. No — she'd divorced *him* without a qualm.

The letters were from *a* husband, all right — just not her own.

As she felt the familiar sensation of the thick paper, the nap softened over the years of handling to an almost velvet-like texture, Judith felt tears prick her eyes. She missed him still, even now.

She was confident (wrongly, if she had but known it) that nobody had ever known about her 'fancy man'. It was a term that reached back into another generation. Nowadays, she supposed she would be applauded for moving on and finding someone else to love. But back then . . .

They'd taken so much care to keep their relationship private. It had helped that he was a travelling man, but was often in the area on business. And if the neighbours saw him come and go — well, what of it? She was running a hotel — that was the beauty of it.

She sighed as she spread the letters, still in their envelopes, out into a fan shape. Should she destroy them? She didn't want to. Her secret lover had been dead for some time now, and these were nearly all she had left of him. And she certainly couldn't bear to destroy his photograph.

Could anything of his pose a danger to her now? Or was she just overreacting? Just because she had police in the house, there was nothing to say they'd ever find these. Why should they? They had no interest in her or looking through her things. On the other hand . . . Imogen *was* dead. And not just dead — *murdered.* And this latest attack on poor Jasper Van Paulen. Where was it all going to end?

For a moment, a cold chill shuddered its way through her.

When she'd first heard the news about Imogen's death, she'd been numb and disbelieving. And then, when it finally began to really sink in that the police believed one of her current guests was responsible, she'd felt mortified. But never, until now, really afraid.

Perhaps because it had just seemed so unreal. So, well, almost *silly*. She simply couldn't imagine any of them being a killer. That vain and shallow girl Jasmine? Never. Just a pampered princess with too much entitlement and not enough brains. And her father was a gentleman in the true meaning of the word, if ever Judith had met one. So who then? Belinda, the mildly famous elegant woman, with far too much to lose by ever doing something so stupid? The affable, probably roguish but surely harmless Irishman? Barry Kirk? That little mummy's boy?

No, Judith simply couldn't bring herself to feel afraid of any of them. And with the house full of police like it was (she was even 'putting up' a constable overnight, every night, on the large sofa in the lounge) she felt reasonably safe. She normally locked her bedroom door every night anyway.

But maybe she should have a word with that nice Inspector Jones? Tell him she didn't want any of her current guests in her hotel anymore? Well, apart from Mrs Greene of course. Judith was sure she'd be safe enough letting Hillary stay on — she hadn't been in the train carriage, had she? Except it wouldn't do her or the Riverside's reputation much good if she got a name for being inhospitable. Surely it was better to carry on treating them all as if they were still welcome here?

Judith sighed. If only it wasn't all so confusing.

But there was no getting away from it — just now, as she'd been holding her precious letters in her hand and wondering if she should destroy them after all, a nightmarish thought had come to her.

Since somebody had killed Imogen, they must have had a good reason for doing it; but *what* reason? Until now, Judith had been almost serene in the certainty that this affair didn't really touch her at all.

But what if she was wrong? Foolishly, *dangerously* wrong?

As she sat in her lonely hideaway, torn between the growing conviction that destroying her precious love letters was the wise thing to do, or that she need do nothing of the sort, Judith Pringwell began to softly weep.

But, after a little while, she pulled herself together and returned the letters, unburnt, back into their box and hugged it possessively to her chest. She told herself firmly to calm down. She was just letting nerves get the better of her, that was all. She'd let herself become overwrought and got spooked.

The death of Imogen couldn't have anything to do with her.

* * *

That evening Daniel Rhys came back to his master, looking as pleased as the proverbial dog with two tails. It hadn't surprised him that that prat Pete Hardiman had screwed up his latest job. The man was a total loser. But not him. And now that Marvin was finally trusting him with more high-level tasks, he'd been determined to come up trumps. And after barely a few hours on the job, he'd done just that.

'Mr Bodicote, sir,' he said, approaching the great man as he sat out in Moose's back garden. 'I've found out who she is.'

Moose, who was barbecuing steaks at the far end of the lawn, watched as the youngster handed over his smartphone to the boss, who presumably studied the image captured there.

'Nice. You're sure she's staying at the Riverside?' Marvin said shortly.

'Yes, sir, positive. I took a picture of her car too — a crappy Volkswagen Golf. I'll send the screenshots of both her and the car to your phone shall I?' he said, taking his phone back.

Marvin nodded and regarded him approvingly. 'Initiative. I like it. You said you've found out who she is too?'

'Yes, sir. I've got this hacker mate who can do amazing stuff. All I had to do was text him the number plate, and he came back with a name. Hillary Greene.'

Something in the way the youngster delivered the line made Moose put the steaks to one side so that they didn't burn, then ambled on over. It also made Bodicote glance at him sharply. 'And?'

'She used to be a copper, sir. A DI no less. From Thames Valley.'

'You better be kidding me . . .' Marvin ground out between his teeth.

The youngster paled a little and clamped his mouth shut.

Moose, though, knew that the boss's sudden bad temper had nothing to do with the young lad's performance. It was just that Marvin simply hated coppers. And the more senior they were, the more he hated them. Even though he'd never been convicted of a thing, he seemed to take it personally — as if every single one of them was out to get him.

Moose was feeling antsy. Wasn't Thames Valley one of the biggest police forces outside the Met? And a former DI would have been a big deal. 'But she's retired or something, yeah?' Moose asked, hoping it might appease the boss a little.

'Yes, Mr Moose,' the young Rhys said, seemingly finding nothing odd in the words. The fact was, he didn't actually know Moose's given name — either forename or surname.

Marvin grunted. 'Look up her career. I want more details.'

'I already have, sir,' Rhys said, hoping that, once more, his initiative would be noted and appreciated. 'She was something of a star in her day. She worked mostly murder inquiries, but did other stuff as well. Got a medal for bravery, saving one of her fellow pigs from getting shot and taking the bullet herself. Now she works out of something called the CRT, as a civilian consultant. I googled it — CRT stands for Crime Review Team. So I reckon she solves cold cases, like they did in that old telly series.'

'I don't like this,' Marvin said. 'What's she doing here? The timing stinks.' He took out his phone and looked her up for himself. 'Shit. It says here she's been on a few high-profile drug busts. Broken a ring that was using the canal system and boats. And she was shacked up with some fella who brought down . . . Bloody hell! One of the really big boys.'

'Maybe she's only here about that funny business on the train?' Daniel Rhys dared to offer up his own thoughts. 'Her being a one-time big shot murder detective I mean.'

Marvin scowled at the screen, then, as if the youngster was suddenly irking him, viciously jerked his head. 'On your way then. I'll let you know if I want you again.'

'Yes, sir.'

'And, Rhys?'

'Sir?'

'You can take over Mickey's route from now on,' he said beneficently, his mercurial mood swinging him back the other way.

'*Thank you*, sir!'

Moose watched the delighted young thug depart, and supposed, grimly, that he'd have to be the one to break the bad news to Mickey that he was losing his prime patch. And dissuade him from trying to get in some retaliation on the sly.

'I'm off,' Marvin declared suddenly, surprising Moose by getting up abruptly and retrieving his designer jacket from the back of the garden chair on which he'd been sitting.

'Don't you want your steak?'

Graphically, Marvin Bodicote told his second-in-command just what he could do with the steak. Which would have been very painful even if it hadn't already been sizzling hot.

On the short drive to his own home, from which he never conducted his business, Marvin brooded. Four days ago, things had been going his way as sweetly as he could ever have hoped. He'd hooked his American heiress, and with her had come all his big dreams for a golden future.

Now the silly cow had got herself mixed up in some weird murder case, her father was cutting up rough — or trying to — and to top it all, he now had some sort of semi-retired super-cop sniffing around on his patch.

It all had the smell of trouble — big trouble — if he didn't nip it neatly in the bud.

After parking his car in his triple garage, he headed inside and made his way to the large kitchen, which was barely used to cook food. There, he put on the expensive coffee-making machine that he liked so much. As he waited for the beloved beans to percolate, he prowled restlessly.

The trouble was, he didn't really have anybody of the right calibre at his beck and call that he could trust to off a cop. Moose was a good second lieutenant in his way and could be relied upon to keep the punters in line and deliver punishment beatings and all that general stuff. But pull off a clean hit? One that had to be executed flawlessly, and with no possible trace back to himself? No way.

He supposed he could call in a specialist from the smoke. But they were expensive, and besides, things like that had a nasty habit of getting around. How long would it be before his rivals got wind of it, and started wondering if he was somehow vulnerable? Or worse yet — even contract killers had been known to get caught and then throw their employers under the wheels to get a lighter sentence.

No. If he wanted something like this doing, he'd just have to do it himself.

He took off his tie, folded it carefully, and put it in one of the drawers meant for cutlery. In this drawer there were also several sets of cufflinks, tie pins, a Rolex watch and numerous other ties, all made from imported silk.

He strolled to the kitchen window and looked over his landscaped garden without seeing it.

He had mixed feelings about the task that lay ahead of him. There were always risks involved in getting your own hands dirty, which is why he'd avoided it so far. But there was no denying — the thought of it was deliciously exciting.

And all his life he'd fantasised about killing a cop.

Reaching into his inside jacket pocket for his phone, he again selected the email attachment sent by Rhys and opened it. Within seconds he was staring at the woman again. It had probably been snapped by a newspaperman at some crime scene or other. It was likely years old, but if she'd come even close to keeping some of her good looks . . .

She was attractive. No doubt about it. Which only added to the excitement.

Hillary Greene.

'Hello, Hillary Greene,' he murmured, almost lovingly, at the screen. 'Looking forward to meeting you.'

And he began to smile.

CHAPTER TEN

The next morning was as sunny as all the others, but Judith woke up with a slight sense of depression. After rising and going through the usual chores of showering, dressing and overseeing the breakfast routine, she finally forced herself to snap out of it. She had decided that she was going to make the best of the situation, and not be so feeble.

Passing through the reception hall, she saw Jasmine and Jasper coming down the stairs, and seeing them reminded her of something she needed to get sorted out. Putting on her usual friendly smile she waited for them to reach her.

'Good morning. I hope you slept well?'

'Oh yes, thank you, Judith,' Jasper spoke for them both. 'I'm still feeling a bit stiff and sore though. I must say, I'm mighty glad Hillary turned up when she did. She was amazing. She was telling me she'd taken some self-defence classes recently and had had no idea they'd come in handy so soon. I must get her a bottle of something to say a proper thank you. That lady sure has some spunk.'

Judith nodded. 'I'm sure she'll appreciate that. I wondered if I might have a word? I know you're both due to leave on Monday, but I understand, er . . . that you might be having some difficulties concerning your departure date?'

She had heard talk amongst the guests that the Van Paulens had had to surrender their passports to the police, so the chances of them flying back to the States any time soon had to be slim. But she didn't want to be so tactless as to just blurt it out.

She saw Jasmine's face twist in resentment and was unsure whether it was aimed at the police for their impertinence, or herself for daring to bring it up, but again it was Jasper who answered, and quickly, before his daughter could make the target of her wrath known. 'I'm afraid we are going to have to stay on in the UK longer than we thought,' he admitted.

'Ah, I wondered if that was the case. I just wanted to let you know, if you want to, I'd be happy to extend your booking here. At least until you can make alternative arrangements to find somewhere more, er . . . long term.'

'That's mighty generous of you, Judith. I take it that our rooms aren't booked from next week then?'

'Oh, yes, I'm afraid they both are,' she admitted, a little pensively. 'But I can bunk down in my private study down here and free up my own suite for the duration. And there's a pleasant attic room I can convert for the second guest.'

'That sounds like you're going to have to go to an awful lot of trouble on our account. Can I help at all?' Jasper immediately offered.

'Oh no, no, I wouldn't dream of it,' she said, just as Patrick Unwin and, following close behind him, Barry Kirk came out from the dining room, having just finished their breakfasts. 'I'll manage — and I'm sure my brother will help me out,' she added, a shade doubtfully. Nowadays Lloyd didn't appreciate manual labour. And, in truth, she wasn't looking forward to all the added upheaval. Clearing out all her things from her room and transferring them downstairs wouldn't be so bad, but getting the attic room ready would take her some time and effort. And she'd definitely need help shifting the furniture about . . .

'What's up? Trouble in paradise?' Patrick teased, catching the tail end of the conversation.

'I'll say. We're putting Judith out something awful,' Jasper said, and explained the problem. And before Judith knew what was happening, she found Patrick volunteering the services of both himself and Barry to help her. Flustered, and feeling wrong-footed, she tried to dissuade them, but without success.

Jasper, caught up in the spirit of things, escalated his daughter's silent wrath by saying that he was sure Jasmine would be happy to help too, since they were the cause of all the trouble, and insisted that he wasn't so stiff and sore that he couldn't be put to work doing something useful.

And so it came about that this mismatched group made their way to the top of the house, and thence up a rather bare and patently seldom-used staircase that Jasper insisted on calling 'atmospheric', which led to a wide space under the eaves.

Judith had had it cleared out when she took possession of the house, and it now looked cavernous and daunting. At least it had working electricity and plain but new carpeting throughout. The walls she'd had painted a neutral magnolia, and the series of dormer windows let in plenty of light. But it hardly resembled a bedroom. Yet.

'I can have a bed delivered by the end of the day, but there's a spare wardrobe and dressing table in the garage,' she admitted nervously. 'I was going to sell them on at some point and never got around to it. And I can take two of the occasional tables from the lounge to use as bedside tables here.'

'What about curtains?' Jasmine said, and hastily added, 'I can go into Ross-on-Wye and get some for you. What colour would you like?' That the girl only wanted an excuse to get out of doing some actual cleaning or hard work was obvious to everyone, and Jasper went a little red in the face, but Judith was happy to accept her offer. Especially when Jasper insisted that he'd pay for them.

For a moment, Jasmine's face lit up at the thought of getting her hands on Daddy's credit card, but quickly fell when he made it clear that he'd make the payment over the phone to the homeware store in question.

'Right then, let's get started,' Patrick said, rubbing his hands together. 'What do we do first, Mrs P?'

Judith smiled and shook her head. 'First, I need to do a thorough clean, but I'll get Mandy and Janette to help me with that. I really can't ask you to do the hoovering and dusting and washing down the woodwork. As it is, I'm pretty sure I'm breaking no end of hospitality rules by letting you help me out at all. But I have to admit, I could do with your help getting the furniture up here, once I've got it up to standard.'

Luckily, there was a 'general' bathroom that she'd left intact on the floor below, simply because the cost of taking it out had made it unviable, and she only hoped that the new tenant, come Monday, wouldn't object too much to not having an en suite. Perhaps she'd be lucky and it would be an American like Jasper who would consider it 'atmospheric'. The one bright spot was that the Van Paulens' rooms were both singles, so at least she would only have one guest to pacify.

* * *

A few hours later, Hillary stood in the reception hall and watched with interest as Barry and Patrick set off up the main staircase carrying a small table each, followed by a sullen-looking Jasmine who was also laden, but in her case with some bulky plastic-wrapped, teal-coloured material which she hugged angrily to her chest.

Intrigued, she followed them all the way up to the attic, where she could hear Judith and Jasper's cheerful voices. When she was informed of the transformation taking place, she instantly volunteered her own services. Although, like Jasper, she'd woken up with her own fair share of stiffness and soreness, she wasn't about to pass up this chance to learn more about her suspects. And sharing adversity was one sure way to strike up some camaraderie.

'What can I do?' she offered the room generally.

'You can help me put these up,' Jasmine said immediately. She was sitting on a newly pilfered chair from one of the lounges and was threading curtain hooks through the tops of a set of curtains. The look on her face suggested that she might as well be cleaning out a cesspit. 'There are three windows to do, and hanging the first one up made my arms ache like mad.'

Hillary smiled internally but endeavoured to put a sympathetic look on her face as she joined her. She sat on the only available stool and reached for one of the curtains and a packet of hooks and began to thread. 'It's nice to see people all pulling together to help someone out,' she began brightly. 'I know why you and your father are doing it, but Pat and Barry could be off by the river fishing or something.'

The two men in question had left to tackle the wardrobe in the garage, whilst over in the corner, Judith and Jasper were checking out where all the power points were and setting up a bedside lamp next to where the bed would have to go.

'Oh you know Pat. That man likes to be the centre of attention,' Jasmine dismissed the magnanimity of her fellow helpers with a shrug.

Hillary grinned. 'I know what you mean. But I'd have said Barry was just the opposite. He prefers his own company, and even when our paths cross, I can't seem to get a word out of him.'

At this, Jasmine gave an unladylike snort. 'Oh, him! He's a loser of the first order if you ask me. When I pushed him on what he did for a living he told me that he owned his own company — Kirk & Kirk Interiors. I thought for sure he was just conning me, so I googled it, but sure enough, he had a website and stuff.'

'Interiors? He's a decorator?' Hillary asked, surprised.

'Nah, just a provider of stuff. You know — for people who want statement pieces for their dreary little bedsit or whatever. But when I checked it out a bit further, it turns out the other Kirk in Kirk & Kirk Interiors is actually his mother!

I ask you. How lame is that? And if you think that's hilarious — get this. I finally got some drinks into him one night and he admitted that it was his mother who went around tatty shops, snaffling up the vases and paintings and cutesy little collectables while he provided "speciality" items.'

Hillary continued placidly placing curtain hooks in the top of the curtain's ribbing and cocked her head to one side. Shooting the girl a knowing smile, she couldn't help but wonder why Jasmine had bothered looking up their fellow guest in the first place. Could it be that she resented the fact that Barry Kirk didn't automatically fancy her and pay court to her?

'Uh-oh, that sounds a little bit dodgy,' she obliged the American girl with the response that she was clearly waiting for. 'In my experience, "speciality" can cover a multitude of sins.'

Jasmine again let rip with an unladylike snort. 'You're telling me. And do you want to know what his particular speciality is?' She paused to let the drama build, then screwed up her face in disgust. 'Stuffing dead animals.'

From all the build-up, Hillary had been expecting something far worse, and again hid her internal smile carefully. 'You mean he's a taxidermist?' she asked, matter-of-factly.

'Is that what they call it? Plain disgusting is what I call it. I expect he tours the country around here looking for roadkill! And what's someone like that doing in a classy place like this, that's what I want to know,' she added maliciously.

Hillary, who was finding a little of Jasmine Van Paulen went a long way, schooled herself in the art of patience. 'I understand taxidermy has become popular again in certain circles,' she mused, although she suspected that trying to educate Jasmine about anything other than popular culture was a waste of time and effort. 'It had its heyday back in Victorian times when everyone wanted exotic specimens for their display cases. But like virtually everything that goes out of fashion, it seems to have come around again. Nowadays, interior decorators are often on the lookout for good examples, and even modern specimens can fetch good prices. It's not as if there can be that many Victorian pieces to go around, after all.'

'Well, I still think it's gross,' Jasmine said firmly. Then she fell silent as they became aware of a clambering and clunking disturbance on the stairs outside. Accompanied by some amiable cursing and mutual jeering, the man in question, along with his Irish companion, backed into the room, a large art-deco style wardrobe lodged between them.

'You've got all the upper-body strength of cold custard,' Patrick was informing his friend cheerfully, whilst the sweating and red-faced Barry grimaced.

'You're a one to talk! Did you think I didn't notice you tip this monstrosity at an angle towards me, so that I was taking at least two-thirds of its weight up all those stairs, you flea-bitten pipsqueak of an ex-jockey?' he shot back.

'Damn, I thought I'd got away with that,' Patrick mourned, puffing a little himself now. 'Ah, Judith my lovely, where do you want this awful mahogany behemoth?'

'Oh, put it down against that wall please. And once it's there, I'll never have it moved again!'

'Music to our ears,' Patrick said. 'And may I be struck by lightning for being a mug if I ever do anyone a good turn again,' he added.

Judith, anxiously trotting alongside the struggling men to make sure that the wardrobe didn't get dinged (it was a period piece after all) shot him a genuinely fond smile. 'Who are you trying to kid?' she demanded playfully. 'You know you'll take in the next lame dog that comes along. You're just a soft-hearted charlatan, and that's all there is to it.'

'Shush, woman,' Patrick pleaded, pretending to be scandalised. 'You'll ruin my reputation, that you will. Everyone knows I'm a wrong 'un.'

With the wardrobe finally safely housed, the two men stood panting for a bit, amiably trading the odd insult or two. As they got their breath back, Judith said anxiously, 'I'll go downstairs and bring back coffee and cake for everyone. Or does anyone prefer tea?'

Only Barry did, which set him up for more goading from Patrick. But soon they were sitting on the window ledges of two of the dormer windows to get their strength back for their return journey with the dressing table and contemplating the growing transformation of the room.

Hillary, realising that Jasmine had no intention of making her arms ache again by putting up a second set of curtains, took her own pair to the window not currently in use as a makeshift seat, and stepped up on the stool. Stretching up and raising her arms towards the curtain rail, however, set off the soreness in her limbs from where she'd hit the ground yesterday, and she couldn't help but wince.

Noticing it, Jasper quickly sidled over to her. 'Can I help, Hillary?'

She glanced down at him and smiled. 'Just make sure I don't fall off the stool, will you?' The last thing she needed was to repeat her pratfall of yesterday!

She felt the gentle pressure of his hand on the small of her back and nodded her thanks over her shoulder. 'You have any idea when the police will give you your passports back?' she wondered aloud.

'No, but I can't see it happening until they make an arrest,' he said quietly. 'I'll have to scout around for somewhere else to stay long term. We can't put Judith out like this for long. Cheltenham maybe. It's a nice-looking town,' he said vaguely. Then shook his head. 'You know, I just can't get my head around things here, I really can't.' He lowered his voice to a bare whisper. 'I know that either of those two fellows over there, or Belinda, must have killed Imogen, but I just can't make myself believe it.'

Hillary said nothing about him leaving his daughter out of the suspect pool.

'I can't see Bel wanting Imogen dead,' he continued quietly. 'Those two got along just fine as far as I could see. And as for Patrick?' He turned so that he could observe the Irishman, who was currently checking his phone for messages. 'You can see for yourself what he's like, offering to help out right away when Judith needed him.'

Hillary, intrigued by where he was going with this, paused on the last hook to be fitted and looked down at him. 'That just seems to leave Barry Kirk,' she pointed out quietly.

A small frown flickered across the American's face. 'I suppose it does,' he agreed.

'Your daughter doesn't like him,' she goaded, just a little. Stirring the pot was always a useful tactic, and every now and then succeeded in bringing something nasty floating to the surface. 'I think she objects to what he does for a living. Although I can't see how that would qualify him as a prime suspect.'

'Huh? I thought he ran an antiques business?' Jasper said, looking confused. Obviously Jasmine hadn't shared Barry's 'disgusting' speciality with her father, then.

'I think . . .' She broke off her explanation as Judith came back laden with walnut cake and pots of coffee and tea. She set it on a small table and began to pour.

Jasmine, naturally, turned down the cake but accepted some coffee and sidled out of the door with it and disappeared. Everyone noticed, but diplomatically pretended not to.

Hillary murmured something about taking a quick trip to the loo and used the opportunity to return to her room. Once there, she promptly phoned Jones.

He picked up at once, and as he answered, she could easily picture the scene, with him back at his desk in the busy office. It would be piled high with incoming reports, empty cardboard cups from the dispensing machine, and, if he was lucky, a photograph of a dog or a cat that loved him.

'DI Jones.'

'It's Hillary Greene.' She gave him the news that the Van Paulens were staying on at the inn after Monday but were likely to decamp to Cheltenham thereafter, and listened as he filled her in with the latest reports. Nothing really stood out for either of them though, and when he'd finished, she put in her own request for information.

'Do you know what Barry Kirk does for a living?' It was a more or less rhetorical question, for she could remember him giving her a folder of all the basic background information on their suspects. Over the phone she could hear the rustle of papers as he searched through his desk for the right file.

'Uh, just a mo . . . yeah. Here it is. He runs an online business where you can buy *objets d'art* for the home.'

'Hmm. Apparently, his mother does all the general stuff, but he specialises. In taxidermy.'

'Taxidermy? Not my taste but . . . oh.' Hillary smiled. It hadn't taken him long to get the point. 'I'd imagine a taxidermist would have at his disposal all sorts of interesting implements,' Ian's voice came over the airwaves thoughtfully. 'Sharp, pointed, delicate instruments.'

'Made of fairly strong stainless steel, or something like it,' Hillary agreed.

'I'll get someone on it. Have them take over a taxidermy kit to pathology and see if anything matches Imogen's wound. Thanks for this,' Ian said, meaning it.

Hillary told him it was no problem and to stick at it, and then hung up thoughtfully.

But she wasn't thinking so much about the murder weapon as something else.

And she felt her heartbeat pick up just a little.

* * *

Daniel Rhys was sitting on a low wall with a good view of the lane that led to the Riverside Inn. He'd been there about an hour when he spotted his mark appear and begin walking briskly towards the town. She had a heavy-looking canvas bag looped over one shoulder and he was careful to let her get a good head start before taking off after her.

It wasn't as if he was in much danger of losing sight of her, since the direction she was heading only led to the centre of town. Even so, he felt a bit like one of the PIs you saw on the telly and was feeling chuffed that Marvin Bodicote had given him the assignment of keeping tabs on the cop from Thames Valley.

Today, she was wearing a longish lilac-coloured skirt and cream lacy top, which even he — no fashion connoisseur — could see set off her auburn hair well.

Back when he'd been a teenager still at school, he knew a lot of lads who boasted about sleeping with their fellow classmates' more attractive mothers, but he knew most of them had only done it to rile the son or daughter of the mother in question. He didn't think that any of them (well, maybe with the exception of that dirty sod Adam Sillicoe) had ever tried it on for real though.

But as he followed the attractive middle-aged woman from one bookshop to another, he didn't doubt that she'd have set the tongues wagging if she'd ever appeared at the school gates.

Marvin's brief to him had been specific — he just wanted to know where she went and who she spoke to. But after nearly an hour of watching her go in and out of the bookshops, Daniel decided that it wouldn't hurt if he overstepped his instructions just a little. After all, showing initiative had earned him brownie points before.

So, after he'd loitered for some fifteen minutes outside a particular bookshop that she'd visited in Back Fold, and he saw her entering yet another bloody bookshop just a few yards down the little cut-through to Castle Street, he promptly nipped into the place she'd just left and approached the desk.

A girl was sitting on a chair reading. She was pretty, but looked the toffee-nosed sort, probably a student with a well-off mummy and daddy who was slumming it working in a shop during the summer break. 'Excuse me, but was that a famous author I just saw leave?' he asked. 'A woman with reddish-brown hair and a cream top? Only I thought I recognised her from an article I read in the *Bookseller*?'

He hadn't grown up in a town like Hay without learning something about the industry and had opted for the opening line as the best way of finding out what the Oxford cop was doing. Was she looking for a particular book maybe? If so, he wanted to know what it was. For he'd noticed that her bag never seemed to get fuller — if anything it seemed to be diminishing, which made no sense.

So he was really surprised when the girl went ahead and actually nodded. 'Yeah, she's got a book just come out. Some crime novel that she's promoting and handing out.'

Daniel, although taken aback, kept his head. 'Yeah? What's the title?'

'Hold on . . .' The girl checked the various books that were scattered about on the desk, and finally picked one up. 'It's called *The Farringdon Conundrum*.'

Confident that his boss would want it, he reached into his jeans pocket for his wallet. 'I'll take it.'

'Sorry, can't sell this — it's a promotional copy. We'll have to go through the usual channels and order it from our supplier. I promised her we'd order in a couple of copies though — do you want me to place an order for you? We can have it for you by tomorrow.'

'Yeah, do that. Hold it for me, will you?'

A few minutes later, he walked quickly past the tiny shop that Hillary Greene had entered earlier and turned around the corner, out of sight. Now that he knew what she was up to, some of the pressure he felt to keep tabs on her was waning.

He was sure that Marvin would be pleased with him when he reported back later on though. And if the boss asked him to get a copy of the book, he could tell him that he'd already put in an order for it.

Confidently expecting another complimentary pat on the back from his master in due course, Daniel Rhys found a shady spot near the castle and sat down to watch the exit to Back Fold.

He might not have been feeling quite so cocky, however, if he knew what his mark was doing right at that moment.

For, within the small independent bookshop, Hillary Greene was sending his photo to Ian Jones, accompanied by a brief message.

Ian — do you know this joker? He's been following me around all afternoon.

CHAPTER ELEVEN

That afternoon, Hillary wasn't the only one with things on her mind.

Belinda stared out over the magnificent view from Symonds Yat but barely saw it. She'd taken plenty of pictures for her blog, but the actual beauty of where she was had totally passed her by. Instead, she was too busy wondering why nobody had yet told the police about the near tumble that she'd taken into Imogen's lap during that last train journey.

She knew why *she* hadn't mentioned it, naturally. Early on in life she'd learned it was best to steer shy of cops. But why had nobody else spoken out about it? With every hour that passed the question nagged at her more and more.

Was it really possible that nobody had seen it happen? True, the train had been going around a sharp bend at the time, and everyone was trying to get a shot of the actual steam engine in front of them as it made the turn. But surely not everyone could have been so distracted?

She was fairly confident that Jasmine hadn't noticed, or she was sure the spiteful cat would have gone out of her way to mention it to that DI Jones — especially since she herself had to be the prime suspect. Everyone knew that Imogen must have written that note to the police about her drug buys, and that the young American woman had hated her ever since.

And if Jasper had noticed her put her hand on Imogen's chest to prevent herself from falling, he would also have said so, and for much the same reason. Oh, he probably wouldn't have been so gleeful about it as his daughter, but it was clear that the man would do anything to keep that spoilt brat of his out of trouble. So, although he'd have been more reluctant about it, he would still have blabbed.

Which meant she was left with only the two men to worry about. And as she contemplated her fellow male guests at the Riverside, she was almost sure that Patrick would have teased her about it by now if he'd seen the incident happen. He wasn't the sort who could be discreet about anything. And he had that puckish sense of humour that wouldn't allow him to pass up a chance to make mischief, even about something so serious.

But she was by no means so sure about Barry Kirk. Several times now she was sure she'd seen him watching her out of the corner of his eye, and thought she detected a reticence about him whenever their paths crossed.

But if he'd seen her that day, why was he keeping quiet about it?

Uneasily, the word 'blackmail' came to mind. Which was worrying in more ways than one. Would she pay him to keep quiet about that very incriminating lurch and the hand she had to put on Imogen's chest? And if she refused . . . what would he do about it?

* * *

As Belinda contemplated a future that was looking more and more perilous, Patrick was driving back from a visit to his cousin's place, where he'd spent most of his time giving piggyback rides to her two youngest sons — non-identical twins. And a right handful they had been.

It had been good to get away from the inn and the growing sense of tension there, he acknowledged to himself. For although that morning had passed pleasantly enough, with everyone doing their bit to help Judith out with the new room arrangements and what have you, he couldn't deny that he was growing more and more antsy with every minute that passed.

It was never going to be a walk in the park, knowing that every now and then his fellow guests were looking at him and wondering if he was a killer. What's more, he was beginning to have misgivings about the writer in their midst. Hillary Greene's superhero act saving Jasper from the mystery mugger was giving him certain vibes. He didn't think there were that many ordinary members of the public who would have known how to handle that situation with such competence. And didn't she seem to be just a bit too pally with the investigating officer?

On the other hand, he knew all that stuff she'd told them about her having written a book was genuine enough — he'd gone into one of the bookshops before heading out to town and ordered a copy. So maybe he was becoming paranoid. Or maybe not.

And then there was Jasmine.

No doubt about it, the situation with Jasmine worried him.

When would the police stop messing around, pull their finger out and arrest her? What were they waiting for? That's what he really wanted to know.

* * *

Nor was Patrick the only one worrying about the American girl. Her father, at that moment, was standing in her room and staring down forlornly into her jewellery box.

She was supposed to be in town searching for a book on Cheltenham and the Cotswolds. He'd hoped that the idea of having to stay in a different location would distract her, and he'd heard much about the charm and beauty of that area. Mostly, of course, once the police gave them permission to leave, he just wanted to get her away from here and her latest dealer.

But he suspected she would buy the very first book she could find and then be off in search of more thrilling forms of entertainment. And since he could not see several items of the jewellery that he knew she'd brought with her — and hadn't been wearing when she went out — he strongly suspected that she now had the money with which to buy them.

He closed the drawer carefully, making sure that he left no traces behind him that she might notice, and moved over to the window to stare out over the River Wye and the fields beyond.

He'd promised his wife he'd look after their daughter. Even on her deathbed, when cancer was only days away from taking her, Cherie's thoughts had all been on their only child. *'She's fragile, Jasper. She'll need you.' 'She's not like you, my darling, she's not strong.' 'Sometimes I think she'll self-destruct.' 'Jasper, promise me you'll keep her safe.'*

And he *had* promised. How could he not? And he had been true to that deathbed pledge all these years. But he was beginning to feel more and more tired and not up to the challenge anymore, and the admission only added to the weight he could feel pressing down on his shoulders. Just how much more guilt could he bear before it crushed him?

His reflection in the window glass showed a man who looked all of his years and then more. The bruise on his cheek stood out, and dark circles under his eyes didn't help, but how could he sleep? Imogen had seemed to be such a nice, ordinary woman. But, like many of her generation, she had strong views and principles. And principles, moreover, that she lived by.

He sighed heavily. Like Jasmine, he too strongly suspected that she was the author of that letter to the cops. If only she'd been like so many people nowadays and had just minded her own business!

Turning away from the window, he put a hand up to cover his face as a creeping sense of helplessness washed over him. 'I'm so sorry, Cher,' he whispered to the empty room. 'I've tried. You know I have, if you've been watching over us. But I think this time I may have failed you.'

* * *

If Jasper Van Paulen was in despair, at that moment Barry Kirk, walking in the hills, was feeling quietly content. He had found the fresh corpse of a buzzard which was such a beautiful bird, and it would have made a wonderful specimen, but he was on holiday, with none of his tools or chemicals at hand.

So, reluctantly he left it where it was for the local foxes to find and devour and continued walking. The trail he was on skirted the more arduous mountain paths, which suited him just fine. He was perfectly content to merely stroll and enjoy the sunshine and scenery — and not wander too far from where he'd left the car, either. He was not one of these keep-fit fanatics who passed him now and then, jogging or lugging rucksacks on their backs, their feet encased in proper walking boots.

Barry liked to live pleasantly. He liked decent food and a superior wine, and good books. He was happy with the life he'd arranged for himself and had no desire whatsoever to change it. Or have it changed for him.

This break had started off so well. The town had been as picturesque as he'd hoped, the bookshops were wonderful, the inn delightful. Who could have guessed it would take the turn it had?

But as he walked, he couldn't help but contemplate the current, sorry state of affairs; and all in all, he didn't like the look of them. Not one little bit. In fact, he might have to give things a nudge . . . But who to throw under the wheels? Belinda was vulnerable because of that little trip he'd seen her take in the railway carriage. Patrick was a possibility too — the cops, he was sure, were bearing it in mind that he wasn't exactly squeaky clean. But Jasmine had to be the favourite . . .

* * *

Jasmine had no idea that her father was at that moment rifling through her things and wouldn't have cared much if she had. Oh, it would have been annoying that he'd cottoned on to her jewellery-selling solution to her immediate problems, but she would have been confident that she could sweet-talk him into a better mood.

She might have been a little less sanguine to know that Patrick Unwin — and probably all her fellow guests — were secretly just waiting for her to be arrested so that they could leave this tiny Welsh town and get on with the rest of their lives. But she was not so self-absorbed (quite) to the extent that she didn't realise she had to be top of the suspect list with the police.

They'd made that quite clear. For all that she'd pretended that that long night of questioning after the discovery of Imogen's body hadn't fazed her, in private, she could admit to herself that it had shaken her considerably.

They had first started to put the pressure on with that anonymous letter, of course, and her 'association' with a local drug dealer. Naturally, she'd flatly denied everything for after she'd been stopped and searched, Peter Hardiman had been quick to assure her that the cops were just fishing. Allegations meant nothing, he'd sneered. Cops had to have proof — and what proof did they have? Even if the old bag had seen them, he'd snorted disgustedly, it was just her word against theirs.

No, it was not the drugs angle that worried Jasmine that afternoon, as she drifted impatiently through the open-air 'honesty bookshop' waiting for her contact to arrive. All she had to do was keep her mouth shut, keep her eyes open for cops in plain clothes, and be very careful at times like this, when she was making a purchase.

She looked around regularly, but saw nothing to worry her. The castle loomed above her, overlooking the little park where rows of second-hand books were lined up on bookshelves with a deep overhang, to keep the books out of the worst of the elements. At either end of the bookshelves were the honesty boxes where readers were asked to leave their money. Of course, if you were totally skint you just didn't bother — hence the concept of 'honesty'.

It was a concept that amused Jasmine greatly, and every time she saw somebody fastidiously drop coins into the box it made her want to laugh out loud.

She watched a young guy in clean jeans and T-shirt browsing the bookshelf furthest away from her, but instantly dismissed him as being a threat. If that Inspector Jones had someone following her, he wouldn't have picked someone so obvious. No. Jasmine thought she'd be wiser to keep her eye out for harmless-looking middle-aged biddies or some girl who was trying too hard to look like a student.

She glanced at her phone. Pete was late, but then the bastard was well aware that she wouldn't be going anywhere until he showed up. Which pissed her off even more. She was already feeling antsy, having used the last of her little pills last night, and imminent panic was in danger of setting in.

If all this hassle with the cops scared Pete's boss away, where did that leave her? She'd have to find another connection, and with the situation like it was, that would be almost impossible. The news of Imogen's murder was out now, and although the press hadn't yet tracked down the 'people in the carriage' it would only be a matter of time. And finding a connection with reporters dogging her every step . . .

Jasmine gave a little shudder.

Not for the first time, she cursed the moment Imogen Muir had arrived at the Riverside Inn. Looking all sweet-little-old-lady, with all her refined ways and airs and graces. And her, nothing but the widow of some rag-and-bone merchant! If the harpy wasn't already dead . . .

* * *

Ian Jones pulled up in front of the Riverside Inn and sighed. He hadn't been sleeping particularly well ever since the break-up of his marriage. There was something so comforting about sleeping next to a warm body at night and then waking up to start the day with another human being. Nowadays he had to make do with the noise of the radio whilst eating breakfast alone.

Making a determined effort to shuck off his blues, he quickly tracked Hillary down to their favourite spot in the back garden. She was sitting under the laburnum tree again, drinking something that looked suspiciously as if it might involve alcohol. She also seemed to be deeply engrossed in reading a crime novel.

Stifling a vague feeling of resentment over her leisurely ways, he sidled up to her. 'It's all right for some,' he drawled. 'Sitting by the river, sipping pina coladas and idling away the hours. Some of us poor souls have to work for a living.'

'It's a white wine spritzer, and I'm doing research.'

Ian grinned and made a show of turning his head like an owl in order to read the title of the book. 'Will you write another crime novel then?' he asked, genuinely curious.

Hillary shrugged and obligingly put a bookmark in her tome and put it down. In truth, she had no idea how to answer that. Would she? She didn't think it would be possible to keep on doing her full-time job and write as well; once, maybe, when she'd been younger and had energy to spare. But there was no denying that the prospect of taking it easier and writing another book or two was appealing. On the other hand, could she see herself resigning from the CRT and her team?

'So, what's the latest?' Feeling oddly uncomfortable in her own skin, she firmly changed the subject.

'I've been showing around the photo you sent me. Turns out he's one of Bodicote's boys. Daniel Rhys.'

She nodded. It didn't surprise her. 'Any form?'

'Not this one. Probably because he's too young and too new. And, word has it, he has more than the usual amount of brain cells than most of Bodicote's underlings. Which means the drug squad haven't been able to feel his collar yet.'

Hillary shrugged. 'Can you send me a picture of this Bodicote character?'

'Sure. I'll do it now.'

As he got busy tapping his phone, Hillary contemplated a hanging yellow laburnum flowerhead and gave a small, internal sigh. She had hoped Jasmine's drug dealer would back off, but it didn't look as if he was going to. Still, right now she had other priorities. 'Can you show me that list of items found in Imogen's room again?' She'd left her phone in her room deliberately, enjoying the feeling of being disconnected from the outside world for a while.

Jones obliged by handing over his own phone, and she skimmed through the list thoughtfully. She was beginning to develop a theory about their case and wanted to test one of her premises.

As Jones watched her and realised that she was searching for something specific, he felt a frisson of excitement stir his blood. 'What are you looking for?' he demanded. Was it possible he'd missed something? It wouldn't be surprising if he had — a murder investigation threw up reams and reams of data, and it was all but impossible for one person to process it all. Even so, the thought that he might have slipped up somewhere put his teeth on edge.

Hillary held up a hand indicating he should be patient, and after a few minutes, nodded and said, 'Huh.'

'Care to share?'

But to his considerable annoyance, she only leaned back in her chair and slowly tapped a finger against her chin. 'Not really. No, wait,' she said quickly, as she saw him open his mouth to argue. 'It's nothing earth-shattering, I promise you. Nothing that would set the hearts of CPS lawyers pounding. Nothing that you can take back to your boss, like a good doggy with a juicy bone. It's just . . . suggestive, that's all. To me, anyway.'

'Suggest away,' Ian said flatly. Whilst he was genuinely glad to have someone with her experience to call upon, that didn't mean he liked feeling out of the loop.

But Hillary merely smiled. 'I'd rather not just yet.' Then, seeing that the SIO was feeling seriously pissed off with her, she turned a little in her chair and fixed her sherry-coloured eyes on him firmly. 'Having theories are all very well, Ian, but without evidence to back them up, they can end up putting blinkers on your thinking. And that can be catastrophic. Believe me — I've seen it happen. Killers walk when the man in charge has tunnel vision. And since you're the SIO, one of the worst things I could do at this point would be to send you off on what could be a wild goose chase. Especially when all I have is a hunch and a suggestive smidgen to go on.'

'But you have someone in mind now, don't you?' he challenged her, unwilling to let it go.

Hillary nodded slowly. 'Yes. I think so. But like I just said, it's far too tenuous to be of any use to you just yet. Me — I'm second fiddle in all this. So let me chase down the wildfowl, whilst you keep yourself firmly focused on the good stuff — facts, physical evidence, witness statements. OK?'

Ian reluctantly nodded. It wasn't as if she wasn't saying anything that his own superintendent hadn't already told him. And he knew it made sense. Even so, the moment he had some free time, he'd go over that list of Imogen's possessions and see if he could see for himself what it was that had tweaked her investigator's nose.

'OK, if you want me to keep on the straight and narrow,' he drawled, 'let me recap. As for witness statements, you've seen and heard for yourself what we've got. And so far there's no sign of the weapon, though over 60 per cent of the railway tracks have now been searched. For what that's worth. As for physical evidence, the forensics on the railway carriage are about as you'd expect, given that half of Wales seems to have travelled in the damned thing this season. I just don't think science is going to help us out much on this one.'

Hillary not only felt for him, she was also inclined to agree with him. But she had had one thought which might prove useful. 'I've been thinking about that. We're agreed that the murder must have been premeditated, yes?'

'Agreed. Unless the murder weapon was some common or garden item that the killer just happened to have on him or her. Which is about as likely as me backing the Derby winner three times in a row,' Jones grumbled.

'So, unless the killer had some sort of medical training — which I take it you're now sure none of them has . . . ?'

Ian quickly shook his head. 'I wish!'

'Right. Then, if I was an average layman intent on stabbing someone in the chest, I would expect to get blood on my hands. And since I couldn't very well wear gloves in the middle of summer without attracting attention, I'd want to improvise something to help mitigate the risk of contamination. A scarf perhaps, covering my hand when I made the incision.'

'Belinda?' Ian said, already shaking his head. 'No, I'd already considered that, and rejected it. We asked everyone to describe the clothes their fellow passengers were wearing, and nearly all agreed on the basics. Plus, we have your own statement to rely on as to what everyone was wearing. And Belinda wasn't wearing a scarf when she was picked up at Beggar's Leap. Neither was Jasmine for that matter.'

Hillary already knew that. One of the first things she had done, whilst guarding the carriage and waiting for her local colleagues to arrive, was to mentally go over everyone's attire. 'But did you ask if anyone had brought a newspaper with them that morning? Either of the women could have had one folded up in their tote bags, or the men might have had something rolled up and stuck in their back pocket.'

Ian shook his head doubtfully. 'Do people still buy newspapers nowadays? Doesn't everyone read them online?'

'I don't,' she said truthfully.

'OK, I'll ask,' he said, but it was clear he didn't think anything would come of it. 'But no newspaper was logged into evidence.'

'Well, if the killer used it to keep their hands or clothes free of even the smallest amount of blood spatter, there wouldn't be, would there?' she pointed out dryly. 'They'd have got rid of it PDQ.'

'You're just trying to distract me from what you've spotted amongst Imogen's possessions,' he growled, still sore about her aggravating reticence.

'Cheer up,' she advised him. 'You're just at that stage of the investigation when you begin to feel as if everything is bogging you down and you're getting nowhere fast. But it's not true, so don't let it get to you. And always bear in mind — at any point some small, seemingly insignificant fact can come to light, which, when added to some other small insignificant fact, adds up to something much bigger.'

Ian grunted, not one whit placated. 'You will let me know if that wild goose you're chasing turns out to be one of those magical insignificant facts, right?'

'You'll be the first to know,' she promised, crossing her heart with an index finger. 'And don't stress. I wouldn't be at all surprised if the case doesn't break soon.'

'You really think so?' he asked quickly. Then, a shade more suspiciously, '*What* makes you think so?'

But Hillary wasn't ready to be drawn just yet. 'Just a feeling I have. You get them sometimes. So, what are you doing tonight?' she deftly distracted him.

'Tonight?' he echoed blankly.

'It's Friday night. When was the last time you relaxed and allowed yourself to unwind a little?'

'Hah. Chance would be a fine thing.'

She nodded knowingly. 'Well, why don't we go out somewhere for a drink? Maybe grab a meal? The food here is good, but I could do with a change. Can you recommend anywhere?'

Ian shrugged, but then realised she was probably right. He could do with spending some time away from his desk. 'I hear the Old Black Lion has a good reputation for food. I'll see if I can get us a table.'

Hillary knew they'd only end up talking shop but was content that she would have at least winkled him out of his office for a few hours. With her good deed done for the day, she reached once again for her book.

She was, after all, on her holidays. Well. Sort of.

* * *

That evening Hillary showered and put on a long black skirt with a magenta floral motif and teamed it with a plain black scoop-necked top. Never one for high heels, she was happy enough with her pair of black, flat, ballet-style shoes. A quick spritz of a perfume she'd once bought on impulse from an independent perfumier shop in Bourton-on-the-Water and she was ready.

As she passed the reception desk, Judith, not seeing her in time, walked straight out from behind the desk and bumped into her. Luckily, Hillary made it a habit to wear her bag crosswise over her shoulder and underarm, so it could never be snatched off her by a purse thief. Judith, however, had just slung her bag loosely over one shoulder.

The owner of the hotel was also dressed up to go out, and her face suffused with embarrassed colour as she hit Hillary and dropped her handbag, spilling its contents all over the tiled floor. 'Oh, Mrs Greene, I'm so sorry. I just didn't see you coming,' she huffed.

'I'm as much to blame as you,' Hillary lied, and bent down to help the flustered woman retrieve her scattered bits and pieces. She diplomatically left it to Judith to collect her purse and gold-encased lipstick tube and reached instead for the less personal items like a packet of tissues, hairbrush and a small notebook. On the floor was a photograph, face up, that from the creases in it was clearly years old. The man in it looked vaguely familiar.

Judith, still blushing furiously, hastily picked it up, along with a packet of aspirin, and shoved everything back into her bag. 'I hope I didn't hurt you?' she asked anxiously.

'No, not at all,' Hillary assured her, standing up and handing over her own contributions. 'I hope you have a nice evening. Going anywhere nice?'

'Oh, just to a little bistro here in town with some friends of mine. A girls' night out — the four of us have been doing it for ages — meeting up once every month for a meal and a catch-up. But I'm not looking forward to this one. The inspector's just warned me that an enterprising reporter has found out where Imogen was staying and predicts we'll be under siege any time now. When my friends find out how close I've been to this case, they're bound to be shirty with me for not letting them know all about it. But the inspector told me not to talk to anyone, so . . .' She shrugged graphically.

Hillary nodded. 'He's quite right. It's best to keep silent — especially when you don't really have anything worth saying,' she added casually. 'I don't suppose you *have* thought of anything since DI Jones spoke to you last?'

'Hmmm? Oh, about Imogen you mean, and anything odd that happened that day? No, not really. Well, nothing useful anyway. I could have told him that she was almost a vegetarian and had a soft spot for animals. Which may be why she was a little frosty to poor Barry Kirk. You know he's a taxidermist?'

'I found out just recently,' Hillary nodded. 'But what makes you think that she and Barry didn't get along?'

'Oh nothing really,' Judith said hastily. She glanced ostentatiously at her watch. 'I really need to get going or I'll be late.'

Hillary smiled and let her get a few yards ahead before following her outside into the pleasant evening sunshine. It wasn't far to walk to the pub, but on impulse she decided to take Puff instead. He'd been sitting in the car park for a few days now without being used, and he could do with a bit of a run.

Naturally, he wouldn't start. Naturally she cursed and threatened him with what would happen if he didn't oblige. And naturally, eventually he chugged into life and took her without any more fuss or bother to the narrow street where the Old Black Lion resided. And since she'd already been told that there were no parking restrictions in the town during the evening hours, she parked without a qualm on a double yellow line almost right outside the former coaching inn's door.

Inside, she found Ian was already waiting for her at the table in one of the front windows. He looked somehow lonely to her, like a man who was used to sitting beside someone else, and it flashed through her mind that he was either newly divorced, or else had not long come out of a long-term relationship.

Which was, of course, no business of hers.

She took her seat opposite him with a brief smile and asked for a white wine spritzer when the waitress arrived promptly with the menu.

'So, the results have come back from the handwriting expert about the anonymous drug-deal note,' Ian said without much ado, once she was settled. Hillary raised an eyebrow in query. 'The report starts off on how difficult it is to be definite with printed block capitals, et cetera, et cetera, but after a few false starts and bits about stuff that went over my head . . .'

'Let me guess,' she said. 'They don't think Imogen wrote it.'

Ian's lips twisted. 'Good job I don't make any bets with you! I was pretty sure myself that it *would* confirm she was the informant.'

Hillary gave him a reassuring smile. 'Well, she *was* the first choice of culprit amongst the others at Riverside.'

'But not in your eyes apparently?' he pressed. 'Is that why you advised going the extra mile to get the writing assessed? And by the way, thanks for that. The super was impressed. Although neither of us is quite sure where it leaves us,' he added despondently.

Hillary perused the menu thoughtfully. 'It leaves us with an obvious question, surely?'

'Who did write it, you mean? And why?'

But it was neither of those that had been uppermost in Hillary's mind. She leaned back to accept her wine glass as the waitress brought it, and for a few minutes, shop talk was banned as they made their dinner choices. It wasn't until the waitress had left that Hillary got back down to it.

'Two snippets for you. Judith seems to think that Imogen and Barry Kirk weren't on the best of terms, but she isn't prepared to say why to me. You should have better luck, though. I have a feeling she thought it was to do with Barry making "art" out of animals. Which may or may not be the case.'

'Either way, he never went out of his way to mention any frostiness between them,' Ian said dryly. 'I think I'll have another little word in his ear tomorrow. My super is amping up the pressure on me to tighten the squeeze on our suspect pool.'

Hillary could well imagine, and one look at the SIO's drawn face told her he was beginning to feel beleaguered. 'He just doesn't buy it that no one in that railway carriage saw the murder happen,' Ian swept on. 'Hillary — they can't *all* be in on it, can they?' he asked anxiously.

'No,' Hillary said shortly. 'And here's something else. I know you're concentrating on the people in the carriage that day, but I'm beginning to think that our hostess, Judith Pringwell, has been keeping secrets as well.'

'What?' he spluttered, staring at her over his glass of lager. 'Don't tell me that! *She* can't have anything to do with it — she wasn't there when Imogen died. Unless you're going to tell me something outlandish, like Imogen was stabbed *before* she left the inn! I read one of those golden-age murder mysteries once where a victim was stabbed with such a thin instrument that he didn't even know he'd been stabbed and didn't bleed out for quite some time. Apparently, the author based this on some real-life historical assassination or other. But it seemed far-fetched to me.'

'I know the case you mean. A European empress or something, in Austria or Switzerland, I think. Back in those days, she'd have had tight stays in her dress, keeping her bound up so tightly it acted as a sort of bandage or something, preventing too much blood loss all at once.' She grinned at the look on Ian's face. 'Don't worry, nothing like that could have happened to Imogen. Death was all but instantaneous, remember?'

'Yes, of course. I knew that. I need to get more sleep.' He slumped back against his chair. 'So what's this about Judith exactly?'

Hillary explained about their collision and her spilled handbag. 'And that's when I saw the photograph that had fallen out on the floor. It must have been taken a few decades ago, I would guess, given the old-fashioned colouration and from the style of clothes the man was wearing. The thing is — I'd seen a photograph of the same man before. Amongst Imogen's things.'

Ian frowned. 'What do you mean? The only photograph she had was one of her . . . oh . . . her husband. And you say Judith Pringwell is carrying around a photo of the same man?'

Hillary told him about the conversation she'd overheard between Judith's brother and one of the staff, about Judith's wilder side.

'So you reckon they were lovers then?' Ian nodded slowly. 'In the dim and distant past?'

Hillary shrugged. 'I think it was probably a bit more substantial than that. You don't keep a photograph of a man in your handbag, especially one who's been dead a few years, if you'd just been ships that passed in the night. I think Imogen's husband travelled a lot, and what's more, he did so for many years — who's to say how long he and Judith had been getting together before he died?'

Ian's frown became a scowl. 'And then, lo and behold, his widow just happens to turn up at the same small inn run by her now? And dies within days?'

Hillary smiled. 'Interesting, isn't it? But before you get all hot under the collar, remember what you quite rightly said — Judith was never in that railway carriage.'

'But she could have paid someone to do it for her,' he argued, beginning to sound excited. 'I haven't been checking *her* out properly because she was never a suspect before.

Hillary, this is great. This could be the break we've been hoping for!'

Hillary shook her head. 'Hold on, Ian,' she warned him. 'Just think about it for a minute or two. For a start, why would she want to kill Imogen? If it's a case of a woman scorned, shouldn't it be the other way around? Wouldn't Imogen want the mistress dead?'

Ian thoughtfully swirled the lager around in his glass. 'Hmmm. Do you think Imogen found out about the affair — say, she found something that made her suspicious in her husband's things — and decided to come here to check out Judith for herself?'

'Why? Her husband's been dead a few years now.'

'Even so,' he put in, reluctant to let go of such a promising new lead. 'There could well be things going on that we don't know about. Our financial team has had a look into Imogen's finances and it does seem that she's not quite as wealthy as everybody probably imagined.'

So, Belinda had been spot on when she'd suspected that her friend wasn't quite as well off as she had been. But had she seriously underestimated the situation?

'Don't tell me she was actually broke?' Hillary asked sharply. Now this was what she called interesting news.

'No, nothing like that,' Ian admitted, waving a hand vaguely in the air. 'But she'd been living in a big house with big overheads, and times are getting tighter and tighter. The money she got from her husband's life insurance wouldn't have lasted for much longer.' He shrugged. 'To you and me she was wealthy, but by her own standards, I can well imagine she was beginning to feel the onset of a cold draught. She'd have had to curb her standard of living before much longer — and forget all those expensive trips to the other side of the world every year to see her son and grandchildren.'

'So she comes to Wales to find out if her husband's long-term mistress is sitting on some assets that should belong to her?' Hillary asked sceptically.

'Why not? Some people are convinced the world owes them a living. So, say she confronted Judith and told her she wanted her share of any largesse her husband had lavished out,' he took up the baton and ran with it, 'and when Judith told her to sling her hook, the old lady cut up nasty.'

'And how did she do that, exactly? By law, there's nothing that says a mistress has any obligation to pay back anything her dead lover left her. She could have told Imogen to go whistle in the wind.'

'Perhaps Imogen had something on her? Or just plain threatened her?' Ian persisted. 'She could have told Judith she'd get some high-price fancy lawyers involved. Not everybody knows their rights, and it's possible Judith didn't have the heart or guts for a full-on legal battle?'

But Hillary could tell he was losing his enthusiasm for the scenario.

'So, in order to get out from under, Judith asks one of her current guests if he or she wouldn't mind obliging her by stabbing her nemesis in a train carriage with everybody else looking on?' Hillary asked archly.

Ian gave a reluctant bark of laughter. 'Well, if you put it like that . . .'

Hillary toasted him with her glass then cocked her head a little to one side. 'Just out of interest — who would you pick for the hitman?'

'Barry Kirk,' Ian said instantly, then just as quickly changed his mind. 'No, Patrick. He's no physical coward, and we already know he's a bit of a chancer. Mind you, Kirk *is* one of the quiet ones — and you know what they say about *them*.'

Hillary smiled. 'You don't fancy either of the two women then? Or Jasper?'

'A rich American old man, his spoilt daughter, and a not-quite-so-rich but still well-off minor celebrity? None of them would have need of extra cash.'

'This is true,' Hillary agreed mock-seriously. Then she shrugged and got down to business in earnest. 'Tomorrow, I want to go back to Beggar's Leap and take a look around that railway station. I never did get a chance to see the waterfalls or check out the lay of the land the day Imogen died.'

'Then I'm coming with you,' Ian said at once. He couldn't have her finding something of interest that his own team might have missed — at least, not without being on hand himself to take charge. He was confident that he knew her well enough by now to know that she wouldn't be interested in claiming any glory for herself, but still. He didn't want to picture his super's face if it was a visiting, retired Thames Valley officer who cracked the case, and not a member of his own team.

'Before we go, it wouldn't hurt to rattle Barry's cage a little,' she mused.

'And Mrs Pringwell's.'

Hillary shook her head. 'No — I don't see any point in that. At least, not unless you get desperate.'

'I'm desperate now,' he whined.

'Drink your lager,' Hillary advised him crisply and without sympathy.

* * *

Outside the pub, parked in a flashy SUV with darkened windows, Marvin Bodicote watched the pub patiently. He could clearly see Hillary Greene and her companion, backlit in the pub's dining-room window, eating and chatting like they hadn't a care in the world.

He had arrived shortly after Daniel Rhys had called him to update him on her trip to the pub, and on the spur of the moment had told the boy to get off home for the night and had come to continue the surveillance for himself.

He was hoping that she'd ditch her companion and walk back to the inn by herself — down all those dark, unlit, unpopulated narrow little lanes. He strongly suspected that the man she was dining with was the copper in charge of the murder case, and Marvin stared at him bitterly from behind the darkened glass. If Jasmine Van Paulen was arrested for the murder, bringing to nothing all the plans he had in mind for her . . . Just the thought of it made him want to shriek with rage and start banging his fists against the steering wheel.

But he must remain calm.

Besides, the man was not the real threat here, he reminded himself. He was still wet behind the ears. It was *her* — the woman from Thames Valley that he needed to eliminate. He'd done nothing but research her all day long, and some of her more successful cases had made him whistle between his teeth. She had a knack of getting her man — or woman — no doubt about it.

But she was never going to add one Marvin Bodicote to her list. Of that he was damned sure.

But luck was not with Marvin that night, for although at just gone half past ten, the two of them emerged from the Old Black Lion and immediately split up, Hillary Greene walked barely a few steps away from the door of the pub and then climbed into a dilapidated poxy silvery-green Volkswagen Golf. It coughed and spluttered and looked as if it wouldn't start for a minute, giving him the false hope that she'd have to walk after all, but then the damned thing started with a jaunty belch from its exhaust and pulled mockingly away.

He sneered in frustration as its taillights disappeared into the night.

But there was always tomorrow. Sooner or later, Marvin knew, he'd get his chance.

CHAPTER TWELVE

The following morning was a Saturday, although naturally DI Jones was in the office bright and early — but he was not the only one doing more than his fair share. The eager young detective constable he'd assigned to dig into Belinda John-Jacques' pre-Canadian life had come up trumps and he hustled into his office the moment Ian was settled.

He was a lanky lad with a closely shaved head and big brown eyes that wouldn't have looked out of place on a King Charles Spaniel. 'Sir. I reckon I know why Belinda and her family moved to Canada sharpish, and it had nothing to do with a better job for her dad!'

Ian leaned back in his chair and rubbed a hand across his face. 'Going to share it sometime today, Constable?' he asked, but there was no real bite in his voice, and the DC only smiled.

'Yes, sir. It seems the lady was something of a glamour model.'

'Huh?' He straightened up abruptly. 'When was this?'

The constable consulted his notes to remind himself of his data and nodded. 'Nearly twenty-three years ago, sir.'

Ian did a quick calculation and then swore under his breath. According to their records, the Canadian woman was thirty-eight years old. 'That would have made her, what, fifteen, sixteen at the oldest!'

'Yes, sir.'

'Why didn't the initial background check come up with this?' he demanded wrathfully, getting to his feet. But the youngster in front of him was unfazed.

'Sir, there were no criminal prosecutions, so there was no record of it. The photographer was strictly local and a small-time amateur who'd just started up. Getting teenagers to pose topless, that sort of thing. He legged it for parts unknown when Belinda's dad got wind of it. He couldn't figure out where his daughter was getting all her spending money from. I only hit paydirt when I was tracing the family's near-neighbours and found one who'd moved to Sennybridge, and on the off-chance, drove over and interviewed them in person.'

He had, in fact, simply been desperate to get out of the office for a couple of hours and had never expected anything to come of the visit at all, but, naturally, he decided the inspector didn't need to know all the petty details.

'Apparently,' he rushed on, 'it wasn't that much of a secret to those in the know in her neighbourhood, but everyone kept it hushed up. But the girl's dad thought that his daughter wouldn't have much of a chance in life with everyone looking at her and smirking, so he upped sticks and moved to Canada.'

Ian, by now, had slowly sunk back against his chair. A few quick mental gymnastics told him that, interesting though the information was, it was unlikely to be in any way relevant to his inquiry.

'Did you show Imogen's Muir photo to them?'

'Yes, sir, but neither recognised her.'

Ian sighed heavily. And why would they? The chances that Imogen and the prepubescent young Belinda had ever crossed paths had to be infinitesimal. And the chances that any of this might have anything to do with Imogen's murder all these years later had to be more infinitesimal still.

Nevertheless, he'd mention it to Hillary Greene when he met up with her at the Riverside. She was bound to be interested. And that reminded him — he had better get on over to Hay. If they were going up to Beggar's Leap later, he needed to get a head start on his interview with Barry Kirk — and perhaps Judith Pringwell. He glanced at his watch, thanked and dismissed the young constable, and hastily gulped down a cup of coffee.

* * *

Hillary was enjoying her breakfast when Ian joined her. Again, he availed himself of the breakfast buffet and joined her at the table, and this time all their suspects were there and none of them missed the rather obvious rapport between them. She could hear hurried whispered conversations starting up in a susurration all around her.

But she was no longer worried about being 'outed' as someone thoroughly on the side of law and order. She was confident that she'd learned all there was to learn from the residents of the inn, and subterfuge, at this late stage in the investigation, would only prove to be more of a hindrance than a help.

The way forward now was going to be dogged legwork on the part of Ian and his team to find the evidence needed for a conviction. Because Hillary was — in her own mind at least — fairly sure that she knew where he'd have to look and was optimistic that they'd be able to find it. The killer of Imogen Muir had been safe only for as long as their motive remained obscure. Once a full police investigation spotlight was shone on it, however, the proof of guilt would come, of that she had little doubt. Which meant Ian's superintendent would start to look on him far more favourably from here on in.

As she would tell him very soon.

Briefly, her conscience troubled her; had she delayed sharing her thoughts longer than was necessary? Had she been selfish, revelling in an active and ongoing investigation for the personal satisfaction it had given her, when she should have been openly discussing her thoughts and theories? She didn't like to think so, but then, she knew she was only human.

Unaware of his companion's inner angst, over a bowl of muesli, Ian blithely recounted the latest news about the less-than-salubrious background of their Canadian celebrity.

Hillary listened thoughtfully and at the end of it gave a small sigh. 'She must live with the constant worry that her past might come to light,' she mused. 'Her life and career could come tumbling down if it did.'

'Or not. Nowadays, she'd probably just gain a million more followers on social media and write a bestselling book,' Ian said cynically. 'At least it can't have anything to do with our murder case.'

Hillary grinned. 'Unless Imogen, who we now know was in need of refilling her coffers, somehow found out about it and was blackmailing her.'

Ian nearly choked on a raisin.

She was, she knew, being a bit disingenuous here, since she had her own reasons for thinking it highly unlikely that Imogen had been blackmailing the Canadian. But it wouldn't do any harm to teach the young inspector that in a murder case, you really needed to consider every angle.

'That would provide her with a solid motive,' Hillary added, reaching out to calmly refill her coffee cup. 'I suppose we'll have to ask her. So far, we've assumed that the friendship between the two women was impromptu and genuine, but perhaps we've misread the situation totally? It could be that Imogen was just keeping a close eye on her meal ticket.'

Ian, now getting over his choking fit, eyed her closely. Something in her tone made him think she wasn't taking her own words all that seriously. 'You don't sound very keen on the idea.'

But Hillary merely shrugged. 'As time goes on, Inspector Jones, you'll find that your *feelings* about things are really neither here nor there. Oh, you should listen to them — but never to the detriment of everything else. Follow every lead, no matter how tenuous. Trusting your gut is all fine and well, but using your brains is always better.'

'I'll remember that,' he promised.

* * *

Belinda looked up nervously as Hillary and Inspector Jones approached her table a few minutes later. Her artfully made-up dark chocolate eyes moved from Hillary to Jones and back again as if she couldn't quite put something together.

'Hello, Belinda, mind if we join you for a few minutes?' Hillary asked casually.

'Oh, sure,' she said, with a distinct lack of enthusiasm.

As Hillary grabbed a spare chair from one of the other tables, she noticed Jasper and his daughter hurriedly whisper a few words to each other, then rise and go, leaving half-full coffee cups behind them.

'I just wanted a quick word with you about your days as a teenager,' Ian said quietly. Belinda, not surprisingly, paled a little at this opening gambit and glanced around nervously. But the only other occupants of the dining room, Barry and Patrick, were seated on the other side of the room and were busy talking amongst themselves.

'I don't see why that should—' Belinda began to protest, but Ian quickly held up a hand to stop her.

'We know about the photos,' he warned her flatly.

Belinda went, if possible, paler still.

'There's no reason why anyone else should know,' Hillary put in quickly. 'Unless it turns out to be relevant.'

Belinda rallied a little and went on the offensive. 'I don't see why it should. It was ages ago, and really, no big deal. And just why are *you* here with the inspector anyway? What business is it of yours? You weren't even in the carriage with us,' she added bitterly.

Hillary shrugged. 'I work with the police back in Oxfordshire,' she said gently, and left it at that.

'So you're a police spy. Wonderful,' Belinda said. Then moved a wing of glossy black hair back from her cheek with a casual flick of her hand. 'Not that it worries me at all who you are. I've got nothing to hide. Well, not about Imogen,' she added hastily.

'So, she didn't know about your colourful past?' Ian demanded.

Belinda frowned. 'No. Why would she? We never met until we both ended up in this place,' she glanced around the perfectly pleasant dining room as if it were currently occupying some ring or other in Dante's Inferno. 'And I wish I'd never come here, I can tell you that much. It was a toss-up between here and the Norfolk Broads. To think, I might have been on a boat sailing down a river now, instead of . . . all this! Isn't it weird how one simple decision, that doesn't seem to matter at all, can suddenly change your whole life?'

'We've got people going over your old stomping grounds,' Ian swept on, riding roughshod over her brief philosophical interlude, 'and over Imogen's past residences too. If it turns out that your paths ever crossed . . .' He let his voice trail off, but the implied threat was wasted on Belinda, who merely gave him a polite sneer.

'Go ahead, dig around as much as you like.'

To Hillary's ear the woman's confidence sounded genuine, and she saw that Ian thought the same, for he quickly changed tack. 'Did Imogen ever say anything to you about Judith?'

'Judith?' Belinda blinked at him in surprise. 'You mean *our* Judith — the owner here?'

'Yes, that Judith,' Hillary put in.

'No. I mean . . . What exactly *do* you mean?'

'Did you get the impression that the two women knew each other? Before Imogen booked in here that is,' Ian pressed.

'No,' Belinda said at once and with conviction. 'At least, Imogen never said anything to me about it. Why?'

'No reason,' Ian said quickly.

Hillary shifted restlessly in her chair, and he took the hint at once and glanced across at her, giving her permission to continue the interview. 'Belinda, think back to the morning of the train journey. Did you have a paper that day? A newspaper?'

'No, if I want the news, I go online.'

'Do you know if anyone here regularly does take a newspaper?' she persisted.

Belinda frowned a little, then nodded. 'Yes, Barry does. At least, I saw him reading one not so long ago.'

Hillary nodded and glanced across the table towards the two men. Pushing back her chair she began to rise, and seeing that she had finished, Ian nodded at Belinda. 'All right, Ms John-Jacques. Is there anything else you want to add? Now would be a good time if there was.'

For a moment the chic woman seemed to hesitate, but then her chin came up a little and defiance flashed across her face. 'No, I don't believe there is,' she stated firmly. 'Now, if you don't mind, I have plans for today.' So saying, she got up and walked elegantly away.

'I think we rather rattled her cage,' Ian said dryly.

'No doubt,' Hillary agreed. 'Now let's go and do the same with the male contingent.'

* * *

Patrick saw their approach first, and — just like with Belinda — his gaze went speculatively from one to the other. Then he looked across the table. 'Hey up, Barry, looks like they've come to take you away, mate,' he said cheerfully, nodding his head in their direction. As Barry, startled, turned to look over his shoulder, Patrick leaned right back in his chair and half-turned, dangling one arm over the back, a picture of puckish nonchalance. 'Now, Hillary, my darlin', what's a nice lady like you doing looking so cosy with a flatfoot?'

Although the voice was teasing, she could tell, under the banter, that he was far more wary than he was trying to let on.

'Ah, confession time,' she said, as she reached the table to stand looking down on them. 'You only know me as an author, but my day job involves working at Thames Valley Police Headquarters. So when all this kicked off with Imogen, Inspector Jones here asked me to keep my eyes and ears open.'

Barry Kirk, Hillary saw at once, did not look at all surprised.

'Ah, now you've gone and broken me heart,' Patrick said woefully, clapping his non-dangling hand to that area of his chest. 'You've just shot to pieces my belief that I was a good judge of character.'

Hillary grinned back at him. 'You'll get over it,' she informed him briskly. 'We just wanted to clear up a few things.' She turned to look at Barry, who so far had yet to say a word. 'Barry, you read a newspaper every day, yes?'

'No,' he contradicted.

'No? Belinda's just told me that she's seen you reading one recently.'

'Ah now, that would probably be mine,' Patrick put in smoothly. 'I have . . .' he lowered his voice to a whisper and looked around in mock alarm, 'don't tell anyone . . . a *Daily Mail* addiction,' he finished dramatically. 'I've tried to give it up, honest I have, but to no avail.'

'Stop clowning around,' Ian advised him, in no mood for people who liked to play the fool. 'Do you have it delivered here?'

'No, I'm an early riser. Can't help it — it comes from all those early starts for the racecourses, and it carried over to my desk job. Even on holiday I still wake up at six or earlier. I usually take a stroll into town before breakfast and pick up a paper from the newsagents.' This time all banter had left his voice and he looked at Ian curiously.

'And you bring it back here?'

'Yep. I read some of it in my room, then bring it down here sometimes and finish it off after breakfast, over a cup of coffee. That's when this one here often pilfers it off me, after I've finished with it. Too tight to buy his own I reckon, hey, Barry?'

Barry Kirk smiled mirthlessly. 'Not everyone has just had a big promotion and can expect an astronomical rise in their salary.'

At this Patrick looked briefly annoyed, then bashful. 'Ah, that's true enough.' And seeing Hillary's enquiring look, spread his hands in mock modesty. 'What can I say? The big bosses like the cut of my jib and are about to honour me by doubling my workload and lumbering me with all sorts of challenges — not least about how to dispose of miles and miles of oily, sea-corroded pipelines. Do you know the cost of environmental clean-up jobs? And some people have the cheek to say it's because I'm Irish that I have all the luck!'

'Did you have a paper with you the morning of the train journey?' Hillary asked, ruthlessly bringing him back to the matter in hand.

Patrick looked at her and his eyes narrowed. 'Did I now?' He thought for a while, then shrugged. 'I probably did. I usually do. But I can't remember to say for sure. Sorry. Barry — do you remember?'

Barry Kirk nodded. 'Yes. You had one that morning. And you brought it down here with you too.'

'And did you pilfer it?' Hillary asked him with a smile.

'Not that day, no.' He sounded neither defensive nor particularly interested. He did, however, eye Patrick thoughtfully.

'Can you remember what you did with the paper that day, sir?' Ian asked, turning back to Patrick.

The Irishman's eyes narrowed again. 'I'm trying to . . . but after what happened that day, I was a bit knocked for six, and the old brainbox isn't as clear as it might be. Hold on now . . . let me try and reconstruct the day.'

Everyone waited in silence for a few moments, and then the Irishman began to nod. 'All right — I know I didn't have it with me when we left to go to Aberystwyth,' he said slowly. 'I'd have tossed it onto the back seat of the car normally, but that day the car was full. And I'm pretty sure it wasn't in my room when I finally got back to it. I know the maids here don't bin the papers until the next day, so they wouldn't have cleared it away. Which means I probably *did* leave it on the table — nine times out of ten, that's what I usually do when I'm finished with it. Does that help?' He looked from one to the other, his eyes more wary than ever. 'And what's the big interest in the *Daily Mail* anyway?'

Ignoring the final question, Hillary and Ian glanced at each other, both thinking the same thing. 'We can always ask the waitress if she remembers removing it and throwing it away,' Ian said.

Hillary nodded in agreement, but in truth, didn't hold out much hope that the girl would remember if she'd done so. Why would she? It would just have been a routine chore for her, probably done automatically and barely registering.

She turned back to Patrick. 'Can you remember who was still in here that morning when you left after breakfast?'

Patrick grinned. 'Now there I *can* help you,' he said, looking proud of himself. 'Usually, I'm one of the last to leave, but that morning I was the first one out. I was driving you all to the train station, remember, and I wanted to do some odd bits and bobs in my room before the off. So everyone was still at their tables. Right, Barry?'

Barry Kirk, after a moment's contemplation, slowly nodded. 'Yes. I agree with that.'

Ian sighed. Which meant that anyone on his suspect list could have waited until the room was empty and then retrieved the paper and — if Hillary's theory was correct — used it later as a shield against any blood spatter from Imogen's wound.

'All right, thanks,' Ian said to the two men.

When they turned to make their way to the alcove off the room where the buffet was now being cleared away they could feel two pairs of eyes watching their backs.

But when they found the regular waitress who worked the morning shift, Hillary's earlier pessimism proved to be only too warranted. She simply couldn't say whether or not she'd cleared any newspaper off the tables the morning that Imogen Muir was murdered.

'I know your team would have searched the railway station for any weapons or anything out of the ordinary,' Hillary said to Ian once they were back in the now deserted hall. And before she could add anything more, was promptly interrupted.

'And a bloodstained *Daily Mail* would definitely qualify,' Ian put in staunchly.

'Yes. If they'd seen it,' she agreed. 'But what if whoever killed Imogen hid it somewhere where it wouldn't be found easily? If you'd just killed someone, and even if the newspaper you'd been using didn't have much blood on it, would you have the nerve to put it in any old rubbish bin? Especially since you'd know damned well that the place was bound to be given a thorough once-over by the police.'

'No, I wouldn't. Hell, we need to send a veritable army back to Beggar's Leap again for a really detailed search,' Ian groaned. 'And I'm not sure the super is going to want to spend the budget on something like that.'

'Yes, I know. Especially since it's just a theory of mine,' Hillary agreed. 'But cheer up — since we're going up there now anyway, there's nothing to stop us from trying to reason out where the killer might have left it. You never know your luck.'

Ian snorted. 'Right.'

Hillary shrugged. 'It's a long shot, I agree. But . . .'

Ian sighed heavily then glanced at his watch. 'All right. I'm game if you are. It's more than a good hour's drive from here — want to set off right now?'

Hillary nodded. Why not?

But if she'd taken more heed of Belinda John-Jacques' recent comments about how one simple decision could change your life forever she might not have been so cavalier.

Outside, parked in a line of cars with a good view of the entrance to the narrow lane that led to and from the Riverside Inn, Marvin Bodicote waited patiently. He wasn't usually much good when it came to patience, but this time he was rather enjoying himself. He was finding the anticipation almost addictive. Would he be able to get her on her own — or not? Would he use the knife in the sheath he had strapped up his sleeve, or when the time came, would he prefer to strangle her?

Hillary Greene's book had arrived at the bookshop promptly that morning; one of his minions had delivered it to him only an hour ago, and he'd been reading it whilst he waited for her to finally put in an appearance. And the cat-and-mouse game that was starting to play out between a killer and a cop only added to his excitement.

But whilst he knew that in her poxy book the cops would inevitably win, he had a very different ending in mind for his own version of a *real* crime thriller.

CHAPTER THIRTEEN

As Hillary followed Inspector Jones out of the front door, she spotted Puff parked up neatly under the shade of a tree. To her mind he looked like a dog that hadn't been for a decent walk for quite a while and was looking at her with reproach and hope.

'Do you mind if we take my car?' she said to Jones, who merely shrugged.

Ian, unlike most male drivers he knew, had no objection to being driven by a woman. What's more, a male friend of his in Traffic was convinced that women made better and safer drivers — although that same friend would rather have his teeth pulled without anaesthetic than say as much to his wife or daughters.

Thinking of his own estranged wife brought Ian's mood down a notch, and he followed Hillary towards the Volkswagen Golf and got in without comment. Hillary, once settled, turned the key in the ignition, telepathically informing her car that if he showed her up now she'd trade him in for a moped once she was back home.

Puff started up first time and sounded good. She turned on the radio, which was permanently set to the station that played only 1960s tunes, wound the window handle to allow in the fresh air on yet another hot day (who needed fancy electronic switches?), and set off.

She noticed the impressive car with darkened windows parked on the road facing the entrance to the lane, but only to ascertain that it was stationary and therefore no obstacle to her pulling out into oncoming traffic.

'You might have to direct me when we get nearer to our destination,' she warned Ian as she negotiated the busy main road through the town. 'I know we'll be following the same route Patrick took for at least half of the way, but I've only ever been all the way up to Beggar's Leap via the train.'

'No problem. The mountain roads are always kept in good repair. Not nearly so many potholes as you have in England, let me tell you. And they only start to get really steep and twisty when we have to head up towards Devil's Bridge.'

Hillary swallowed hard, and hoped Puff hadn't heard him. The last thing she wanted to do was dent his confidence.

Jones seemed content to sit back and enjoy the scenery and the great (and some of the not-quite-so-great) tunes from the swinging sixties. Gene Pitney was singing his heart out about nobody's child an hour later as Hillary spotted the first signs for Devil's Bridge. *Come on, Puff,* she mentally encouraged her car, *show me there's life in the old dog yet.*

As they began to climb, gently at first, and then, after a while, more radically, Hillary kept her eyes firmly away from the drops at the side of the road and concentrated on taking the bends at a steady pace and in a low gear. Eventually the tops of the trees were level with her view out of the window, and then began falling away below. At some point, her ears popped.

Puff (probably mindful of the moped) responded like a dream to every gentle press of the accelerator or change of gear, and she could hear his engine rev defiantly. Only towards the end, when they had to be within hearing distance of the waterfalls themselves, did she detect any sign of strain on the old car. By then, though, they'd made it to a level part where a hotel had been built, and further along, the train station itself, and the old boy could safely rest on his laurels or his tyres.

As she pulled off onto the side of the road that had been specially widened to take parked cars, she sat back, maybe sweating just a little, and with a sigh of relief and satisfaction, turned the key in the ignition and looked around.

Ahead of her she could see only forests of dark trees, with various deeply shadowed paths cutting their way through them. A black car with darkened windows that looked remarkably similar to the one she'd seen parked outside the entrance to the hotel overtook her and indicated to turn off into a small car park that looked as if it serviced the steam-train terminus. She watched it thoughtfully, then gave a shrug. She only hoped whoever was inside had a head for heights, because once you were on the train there was no getting off.

She sobered as she reminded herself that for Imogen Muir that had been only too true.

As she opened the door and stepped out onto the traffic-free road, she could immediately feel the cool dampness in the air and hear rushing water in the distance. And this was no gentle tinkling or burbling sound, but rather the roaring of a significant body of water falling heavily onto rocks far below.

'I never actually got this far on the day Imogen died,' Hillary mused, looking around. She could see railings lining the road on the other side, and here and there, brighter dots of colour, presumably belonging to the clothing worn by other visitors to the site, disappearing and reappearing in the trees.

A large notice attached on the railings stated that there was no internet connection in the area, due to the rock formations, waterfalls and the nature and location of the site.

'Well since you are supposed to be on holiday, why don't you go and explore the place properly — maybe take a few photos? I'll meet you back at the station when you're finished.'

'All right,' she agreed amiably, and after shutting and locking the car door, couldn't resist giving a very smug-looking Puff a congratulatory pat on his bonnet. 'You enjoyed that, old boy, didn't you?' she said warmly, causing Jones to give her an astonished look, before turning his head quickly to hide his wide grin.

Wisely though — *very* wisely — he made no comment.

* * *

Marvin had parked his car not far from the café that catered to the steam-train passengers and then got out to position himself half under the canopy that covered the next-door shop selling all the usual tourist tat that you would expect of a place like this. Beside a stand of postcards that glorified steam trains, the Welsh scenery, and cute dogs and cats, he took a half step behind it as he spotted Hillary Greene's dinner partner of last night walk through the entrance to the car park and stroll casually his way.

Although his gaze went immediately behind the policeman, he could see no sign of Hillary Greene herself. He waited patiently for a few moments, but it wasn't until Jones had almost passed his hiding place that he realised that she wasn't just trailing a little behind but wasn't about to show any time soon.

So where the hell was she? He scowled, not liking the fact that he didn't know what she was up to.

He'd begun to guess their ultimate destination when they'd taken the turning to Devil's Bridge and had been anticipating a boring day watching them questioning people or sniffing around and looking for clues or whatever the hell it was that cops did all day long.

Once Jones was safely past him, he headed towards the exit of the car park and cautiously peered around the bend in the wall to look back towards the poxy Volkswagen that had been parked about a hundred yards further down.

There was no sign of Hillary Greene. She was neither in the car, nor walking this way.

Where the hell had the woman disappeared to?

He began to walk rapidly back down the hill, aware vaguely of the sound of rushing water somewhere off in the distance. It was cooler and darker here under the shade of so many forest trees, and he began to jog a little as he bobbed his head about, trying to catch sight of that now familiar figure with its bell-shaped head of auburn hair.

A sign with a helpful arrow on it pointing the way 'To the Falls' loomed up around the next bend and he saw a small booth set into the railings. It cost £5 to get in to see the waterfalls, and at first he went right past it, checking that the road ahead was empty of any pedestrians first, before trotting back and fishing out his wallet.

He was now confident that the woman from Thames Valley must have gone sightseeing. So much for the presumed dedication of coppers on murder cases; not that he was complaining about her lack of work ethic — the thought of her here and wandering about alone was enough to make his heart beat faster with excitement.

Because, looking around, there didn't seem to be exactly hordes of people all around him. In fact, as he jogged down some steps and investigated further, there seemed to be various trails through the woods to choose from, and although he could see some people, and hear voices emanating from various dark and mysterious pathways, it was obvious the place wasn't overrun with tourists just yet.

Which meant he might well be in with a shot at tracking her down and finding her alone. And under the cover of all these sheltering trees, his chances of not being seen by any witnesses had to be better than average, right?

And who knew — he might not have to use the knife at all. If she was anywhere near the edge of one of the many cliffs overlooking the valley below, just one good push should do it. Naturally, in a health-and-safety-conscious world there were barriers and fences everywhere, but they shouldn't present a problem. If they looked too high for a straightforward shove, he could always beat her senseless and lift her over the top.

There might not even need to be any murder investigation at all. He could make it look like just another tragic accident. If only she didn't stick to whatever were the most popular viewing points he was in with a chance. In any case, there were sure to be lesser-known tracks, with lesser views, where he might be able to take her without being seen. Drag her into the trees off the path and deal with her, then scout around for a likely-looking spot where someone careless might accidentally trip and slither down a slope and out into the void.

Now wouldn't that be just too delicious for words? And wouldn't it piss off the famous murder detective if she herself was murdered and nobody ever knew it? Perhaps he shouldn't knock her out after all. It might be much more fun to keep her aware of what was happening.

The thought of her fuming all the way down until she was broken on the rocks made him laugh out loud.

* * *

Everything about the small railway station looked just as Jones remembered it, and he headed straight for the wooden sleepers that made up the set of steps leading to the platform itself. He'd passed the café and small shop with the wooden picnic tables scattered around when he paused to take in an overview of the area, and it was then, looking back, that he noticed the dark car with the darkened windows.

There was no real reason why it should have attracted his attention, except that the car park was not yet full and something about the vehicle made him pause. It was gleamingly clean and imposing and had probably cost a mint. Was that it? Nearly all of the other cars around it were more mid-range and far less impressive.

But there was nothing to say that rich tourists might not fancy a steam-train ride as much as anyone else.

Nevertheless, he paused, one foot on the first railway sleeper whilst the rest of his body was caught in an awkward twist when he swivelled around to get a better look at the car. After a moment or two of contemplation he finally realised that it was the darkened windows that were worrying him.

Coppers didn't like cars that had gone out of their way to prevent you seeing inside them. To him they represented either celebrities or royalty who didn't want the paparazzi to spot them, or villains. He knew this bias was probably unfair, but he didn't care.

Slowly, he removed his foot from the sleeper. The fact that such a car was parked here just when he himself had arrived to take a look around was making him a little uneasy. *Paranoid much?* he asked himself dryly. But now that he thought about it, wasn't it *this* car that had overtaken them right after Hillary had pulled in off the road? How long might it have been behind them?

He approached the car cautiously. For all he knew, the driver might still be sitting inside, watching him getting closer and closer. That was another thing that gave him the creeps. Of course, he might well be letting himself get spooked for no good reason at all — in which case he'd feel like a right prat.

He stopped about a foot away, considered his options, then took out his mobile. He got through to his office and read out the numberplate and asked for an immediate DVLA check.

When, nearly a minute later, he heard the name of the owner of the car, he felt the back of his neck go cold.

* * *

Hillary quickly discovered from the many informative notice boards lining the pathways that Beggar's Leap referred to the main and highest waterfall at the site, but that there were many other falls, ranging in size from not much smaller than the Leap itself, to mere rivulets trickling their way through the cracks in the rocks.

She'd managed to get a few photos of the view from over the Leap itself, but she wanted to see the fall of water from the other side as well. To do that, she'd read, she needed to take the steps leading laboriously down and around to one of the other viewing spots. Since it was cool under the trees and the exercise would do her good, she set off down the daunting range of steps, pausing for a breather here or there and to take more photos. Here, she had no objection to using her camera phone, since (unlike on the train) she had all the time she wanted to appreciate her surroundings as well.

She was about halfway down the final set of stairs when she noticed a very minor trail leading off to her right. Her mental map or compass had always been excellent, and she reckoned that the little track through the trees would lead her to a view of one of the smaller falls to the east. She could tell by the undisturbed grass at either side of it that the track was seldom used, and the thought of finding a spot to herself was attractive.

Although there were relatively few people around, she'd already almost fallen over an excited four-year-old boy, and had her crotch investigated by the nose of a very inquisitive Dalmatian, and a little guaranteed alone time with all this beautiful scenery was appealing. So she set off through the trees with a growing sense of well-being. The fact that she had to duck under some beech branches reinforced her feeling that this little offshoot wasn't much travelled.

A tiny flash of movement in the predominantly evergreen pines caught her attention and she immediately stood still, trying to track it. Eventually she was rewarded by the sight of a goldcrest which she half-suspected was the smallest bird in the country.

She'd grown up in the countryside, and her father had been very much a countryman who'd taught her the names and habits of much of the wildlife in their small patch of north Oxfordshire. But she'd not seen many of these tiny, beautiful little birds before.

It was as she stood utterly still so as not to frighten it away that Hillary heard stealthy footsteps about fifteen yards or so off to her right and behind her. Instantly, she stiffened.

Normal footfalls had a pattern to them that, to her, were unmistakable. Your average person's tread, over unfamiliar ground, was slower than usual, but the walker wasn't making any effort to be silent. Why would they be? But the sounds she could hear getting slowly nearer to her were barely audible and had a caution about them that was chilling because it meant that someone didn't *want* to be heard. And since she could think of no good reason why anyone out and about on an innocent excursion would need to be so careful about it, common sense told her that she needed to take notice.

Normally, most people in her situation refused to believe that they were seriously in danger. She'd read as much, time after time, in the witness statements by survivors. Their mind, trying to protect them from growing panic, would speculate that they were hearing things. Or that the maker of the sounds would turn out to be some frail old lady walking a frail old dog.

For some reason, the idea that you were seriously in danger was something people found very hard to believe. Almost absurd, in fact. Bad things happened to other people, but never to you.

But Hillary Greene had no such doubts, even on such small evidence, that she was in serious trouble, and she was going to act accordingly. And if it turned out that she was overreacting, so what? What was the worst that could happen? She'd rather be embarrassed over making a fool of herself than dead because she'd allowed an enemy to get too close to her.

Quickly her mind flashed to one particular resident of the Riverside Inn. Had she been followed here? Did the killer of Imogen Muir somehow suspect that she had guessed their identity? And were they, even now, trying to edge closer to her to prevent her from doing anything about it?

Hillary glanced quickly around, assessing her position and refusing to panic. Panic, she knew, was more of an enemy than whoever it was who was out there, hunting her. She needed to keep calm, keep a clear head, and she needed to think rationally. Which was often easier said than done when your throat had gone dry and you were feeling nauseous with growing terror.

Instinctively, she reached for her mobile phone, praying that the notice she'd seen about lack of connectivity was an old sign, and that good old BT might have fixed the problem by now. She glanced at the tiny screen.

No signal.

So much for the wonders of modern technology then, she thought grimly.

Alright. Focus. She was alone, surrounded by dense trees. But she knew that people were nevertheless all around her, scattered about. If she started shouting for help someone might hear her. Usually, she was a great advocate of hollering your head off if you were in trouble, but that strategy worked best if you were in a town or open countryside. But how far would the sound of a human voice travel amongst all this dense vegetation? Especially when there was also the general roar of falling water as background noise to contend with.

Also, by shouting now, she was alerting whoever was out there that she was on to them. Whereas, at this moment, they were probably feeling confident that they had gone undetected. Losing an advantage without a significant gain to offset it was foolhardy. So — yelling for help was out.

She was aware that her heart rate was accelerating significantly as adrenaline continued to flood into her system, designed to give her added strength or speed, depending on whether she chose flight or fight. So, with the disconcerting sound of her heart beating loudly in her ears, she took long, slow, deep breaths and considered both options rapidly.

Proper flight — that is, full-out running — was problematic; she had, realistically, only the narrow path available to her to get her out of harm's way in the quickest time possible. And if she did that, who knew where the path let out? For all she knew she could end up running right out and over a ledge that would send her toppling down the mountainside. But if she started to run back the way she had come, who was to say that she wouldn't be running right into a killer's arms?

Alternatively, she could abandon the path altogether and try to dodge and weave through some of the bigger pine trunks in the hope of remaining hidden from any pursuer; but from all her many past sojourns through the woods back home she knew that there would be many hazards out there in the rough. Dense patches of wild garlic that could slow her down, protruding roots to catch her running feet and trip her headlong, not to mention the sudden dips and holes in the ground that were the result of long-uprooted trees that, being overgrown, would look deceivingly as if they were level ground but weren't. Fall down one of *those* and she could break an ankle or a leg, leaving her easy prey to whoever was out here with her.

No, a cold, calm voice told her firmly. Flight was out.

Which left fight.

Or did it? Flight didn't automatically imply speed, the same cold voice in the back of her head reminded her. She could always do what the person stalking her was doing. She could use stealth.

Although it felt as if she must have been stood frozen and thinking for minutes, she knew from past experience that this wasn't the case. The human mind could think far faster than you realised, especially in times of stress and peril. In truth, she'd probably worked all this out in less than a second or two.

But in those two seconds, her stalker had also gone quiet — the stealthy footsteps had stopped. Which was not surprising. If it was the killer of Imogen Muir out there — and Hillary thought it was highly likely — then they would have been listening keenly to her movements and would know that, for some reason, she was no longer moving.

And they'd want to know why.

Slowly Hillary looked around, doing a complete 360-degree turn. All she could see were trees, foliage and dappled sunlight on leaf litter.

She was pretty sure that, when she'd first heard the footsteps, they were coming at her from about the four o'clock position. Which meant that she needed to turn to the seven o'clock position and move.

Hillary moved.

* * *

Also moving was DI Ian Jones — but unlike Hillary he had nothing to impede him as he ran hell-for-leather down the road towards the booth leading into the falls. He was already reaching for his wallet and ID as he had to force his way, apologising profusely but firmly, past the small queue of people waiting to filter in.

The startled teller went pale as she was suddenly confronted by a white-faced man barking questions at her. He gave a rapid description of Marvin Bodicote, which the woman remembered, for he'd been dressed in a very smart suit and tie and was rather handsome — although he hadn't given her a second look. When Ian asked if she'd seen which way he went, though, she could only vaguely point the way that all the tourists went at first: the small square wooden platform below, which showed a map of the site.

He got out his phone, knowing he'd put Hillary's number into the memory, only to find any call he made to it stubbornly refusing to connect.

Cursing, Ian raced down the gravelled path, wishing that he hadn't been transferred to this part of Wales only recently. It meant he didn't know this place and had no bloody idea of the lay of the land here.

* * *

Unaware that her colleague was searching for her, Hillary Greene made her way slowly towards a hazel bush. Pine trees had the habit of saving most of their greenery for the very top, where the sun was, leaving the rest of their length uncovered, which meant that the hazel bush, with its concealing splodge of greenery, was the only real cover for some distance.

She crouched down beside it, looking around, and slowed down her breathing so that she could hear better. By her calculations, she'd been very slowly and cautiously making her way back the way she'd come whilst maintaining a distance of at least twenty feet away from the actual path for about ten minutes. In that time, she had stopped and listened six times, as she was doing now. And during each of those six times, she'd heard movement behind her.

As she did now.

Any hope that she might have had that the person hunting her through the woods was unaware of what she was doing was now gone. She peered over her shoulder into the brown-and-gold light filtering down from the densely packed trees but could not make out an actual figure. Then she heard a small 'thwack' sound and recognised it at once. Her pursuer had brushed past a bendy twig, and it had just realigned itself into its usual position.

And the only bush that could have produced that sound belonged to a hawthorn thicket about fifty yards away. Whoever it was out there was inexorably closing the gap between them.

Grimly, Hillary rose from her hiding place and moved forward. She didn't think she could have walked all that far along the little-used track before she'd become aware of the danger, which meant that she shouldn't be that far away from the main tourist routes. If she could only . . .

It was just as she was thinking this that she heard a sudden thrashing sound behind her and gave an involuntary yelp of fear; her pursuer must have spotted her and decided to abandon their cat-and-mouse game in the woods for a more full-on assault.

Hillary began to plunge forward, instinctively heading towards the lightest part of the horizon. More light meant a clearing, and a clearing meant — hopefully — people. People taking pictures of the waterfalls, people eating ice creams and chatting or just sitting on a bench and taking it all in. People who would be witnesses to anything that might happen to her, and thus provide her with a way out of this nightmare.

* * *

Jones hadn't found Hillary at the big waterfall itself. A quick glance at one of the maps on the viewing platform told him there were at least four more large falls he could visit, as well as over a mile of trails that led to lesser falls.

For a second or two he had wasted time on despair, before forcing himself to think. From all that he'd learned about Hillary during their more idle, personal chats over the last few days, it seemed to him that she was the type who would prefer not to be a part of the crowd. She lived alone on a narrowboat, for Pete's sake, moored up away from it all in a hamlet of just a few houses or so.

So she would probably head for one of the more remote spots, right?

He picked an out-of-the-way area by random and made his way there, checking around him every time he could see people moving about. So far, though, he'd seen neither Marvin Bodicote nor Hillary Greene.

Everything he'd heard about Bodicote was now swirling around in his head, pushing his blood pressure and anxiety levels ever further through the roof; Marvin was a nutter, a fantasist, but he was also a man of extreme cunning and ambition. Worse — he was as vicious as a trapped sewer rat.

As he found himself running down more and more steps with no idea whether he was getting anywhere nearer to either one of them, Ian Jones wondered if he wasn't a little off his head himself.

* * *

Hillary spotted the open area of light, just above a patch of flowering Jack-by-the-hedge, and pushed on through towards it. Behind her she could hear a definite and regular pounding of running feet and knew that it meant her enemy had to be very close now, and that she could be tackled to the ground at any moment.

With a near shout of profound relief she broke free of the treeline and found herself, indeed, in a clearing. In front of her was the now familiar view over the valley down below, guarded by the equally familiar railing that kept people back from the edge of the cliffs. These particular barriers consisted of stout diamond-shaped wiring from the ground up to just over waist height, and were topped by stout wooden rails. This allowed the view to be uninterrupted, whilst providing a secure buffer between viewers and the abyss below.

There was only one problem.

Although the view was spectacular, and the area was clear and open, there was not another person there to enjoy it. Worse — the trail it was on bent quickly away to both the left and the right, which meant the only witnesses who might be able to see her would be those far on the other side of the viewpoint. And to any of those who might just happen to be looking this way, she would be little more than a cream and blue dot.

Fight it is then, the cold clear voice spoke calmly from somewhere deep inside her, and Hillary turned quickly to face the onrush of movement that was erupting from the treeline behind her. Instinctively, she put one foot back to anchor her body weight more firmly and spread it out, giving her more balance, and raised both arms a little in preparation.

She knew that her age and recent surgery were distinct disadvantages, as was her stiffness and soreness after her bout with the skinhead who had attacked Jasper; but on the plus side, she'd taken several self-defence courses over the years, starting with her police training in college. Even better, if she was right about who had killed Imogen Muir, her opponent would have disadvantages themselves.

But almost before this last thought had gone through her brain, her eyes were processing what was in front of her, and she knew that she was not dealing with anyone from the Riverside Inn.

The man who had now come to a panting stop a few feet away from her, and was grinning delightedly as he saw that they were alone, was someone she'd never met before.

But she knew who he was, of course. She'd seen his picture when DI Ian Jones had sent it to her phone. Besides, who else would wear an impeccable dark blue suit and look at her from eyes as mad as this?

'Mr Bodicote, I presume,' Hillary heard herself say.

CHAPTER FOURTEEN

Marvin was feeling good. Very good. Not only had he spotted Hillary Greene soon after entering the grounds, she had only gone and obliged him by setting off into the greenery on her own. He was a little less pleased that she had somehow twigged that he was following her, but that game of hide-and-seek in the undergrowth had been a real thrill, and a truly delicious appetiser for the main event he knew had to come.

And now, after the chase, came his reward. He couldn't have asked for better than this — alone, unobserved and unlikely to be interrupted, he could savour every single moment.

He made a show of putting his hands nonchalantly into the pockets of his trousers and sauntered casually a few steps closer.

Hillary watched him silently, constantly assessing. He was lean, which was good (really heavy men could simply use their bulk as an effective weapon), but he looked fit, which was bad. He was clearly riding high and super-confident, which was good (it often led to unnecessary mistakes) and instead of attacking at once he obviously wanted to play first (which was even better, since it meant she could play too — for time).

'I daresay you want to know why I'm here,' Marvin began smoothly.

Hillary gave a mental shrug. Well, if he wanted to talk, why not? Every moment that passed was another moment gained when someone might come around the corner and interrupt their little tête-à-tête. 'I *am* rather puzzled,' Hillary agreed, making damned sure she sounded good and calm. Giving the bastard any kind of psychological advantage was absolutely not on her agenda. 'You can't have had anything to do with the murder of Imogen Muir, which is all I'm interested in.'

She held his gaze steadily, not wanting to break eye contact. The more information she could get from his facial expressions and body language the better.

'I don't give a shit about some murdered old bint on a train,' Marvin informed her with a sneer. 'But you're messing about in my business. And I can't let that pass. Jasmine Van Paulen is my property. I can't have you arresting her, can I?'

Hillary cocked her head a little to one side. 'What makes you think we'll arrest her? Has she said anything about killing Imogen?'

Marvin shook his head playfully. 'You've no idea, you cops, have you? I've never even met the girl personally. I prefer to do my business from a safe distance.'

Hillary didn't think much of his idea of a safe distance right now but let it pass. 'Well, I can tell you that as far as I know, the local police have no immediate plans to arrest Jasmine or anyone else for that matter.' Although she hoped that would soon change. 'So enlighten me as to the reason for all this, exactly.' She made a vague gesture at the woods behind them but was careful not to make too sudden a movement.

Marvin smiled. '"Enlighten me." I like that. Posh words — you don't often hear them in my line of work. But then, I can tell you're a real lady.' He wasn't being facetious about that either. She was wearing a pair of cream trousers and a sky-blue top that suited her colouring and made her look effortlessly elegant. And although she must be a good twenty odd years older than himself, he rather fancied her, which only made things even more exciting. 'But I'm forgetting — you're an author as well, aren't you? I'm reading your book now, as a matter of fact.'

'Thanks,' Hillary said dryly. 'I'll remember your contribution when I get my first royalty payment.'

Marvin's smile began to falter. This was not going how he'd anticipated it would. At first, he'd quite liked it that she was pretending to have it all together and wasn't secretly bricking it. He liked her spirit — it was making things more interesting. But now she was beginning to needle him.

'Oh, you won't be around to get any royalty statements, Inspector Hillary Greene,' he said softly. And slowly, he withdrew his hands from his pockets, pointed to the railing behind her, then pantomimed his intentions of tossing her over it.

Hillary went cold, then hot, then cold again in what felt like less than a second and was suddenly aware that her reality had just totally altered. Gone was everything mundane and normal and familiar. Now she was facing death, and she really didn't like it.

Oddly, she didn't feel afraid as much as furious.

She wasn't aware of it, but her upper lip turned up in a sneer and her sherry-coloured eyes went flat and cold. And when she spoke, she was almost as shocked by her words as the man confronting her. 'If you think you're going to throw me off this mountain without coming with me, then you really haven't been paying attention.'

And then she moved. Fast. *Towards him.*

Which wasn't quite as foolhardy as it might have seemed, since it took her further away from the danger zone of the rail and the edge of the cliff beyond. Not only that, it gave her more fighting room, and would also force Bodicote to work all that much harder at getting her back to the edge.

Also, by going on the offensive, she had gained not only the element of surprise but now psychologically had the upper hand. She doubted that anyone had ever presumed to challenge the dominance of Mr Marvin Bodicote in a situation like this, and for a split moment, he would be bemused and hesitant.

Only now that she had committed herself, she needed to make the most of that split moment and decide what to do with it. If they were in a kung-fu movie, at this point she'd probably leap into the air, turn sideways and deliver him a kick to his chest, head or jaw.

But Jet Li she was not.

Instead, she went low, and once she was within grabbing distance of his hands, dropped to one knee, swung her right hand back and up underneath her breasts and put all her impetus into an uppercut towards his groin.

And if the blow had landed fair and square it would have been all over then and there.

But Marvin was younger, faster and fitter, and just managed to twist his thigh fast enough so that her fist bounced off the big muscle there and only managed to connect to about a tenth of her intended target. This, nevertheless, was enough to cause him immense pain, and Hillary heard his squeal of shock and outrage with immense satisfaction.

But she was now in real trouble. She was down on one knee and getting back to her feet without him laying hands on her would be almost impossible. Already, through his vicious and visceral swearing, she saw him fighting to get himself together and his right hand was descending, no doubt intending to grab a painful bunch of her hair and bring her head snapping back up.

So instead of trying to rise, she did the opposite and dropped her second knee to the ground and hunched down, hugging her arms underneath her so that he couldn't easily get his hands under her armpits in order to heave her up, and only when she felt his angry breath on the back of her neck did she put all her weight on her knees (making it her turn to yelp in pain) and heave upright, making sure to keep her head thrust forward.

This time, the top of her rising skull made solid contact with his groin and again he squealed. Hillary immediately threw herself onto her side and rolled frantically away to her right, feeling the movement of air as his arm swept barely a centimetre over her body as he tried to grab her.

Had she made the mistake of trying to get her feet under her, he'd have had her.

As she continued to roll frantically over and over to get some much-needed space between them, stones and twigs digging painfully into her, she had a kaleidoscopic view of him. He was half-bent over and hugging his privates, his face suffused an ugly red colour with pain and rage. And he was lumbering towards her.

It was now or never. She only hoped her knees wouldn't fail her now. She put both hands firmly on the ground and levered herself up. She got one knee under her and yelped as it protested violently, and then the second.

She was up.

But the victory, she knew, would only be short. Already Bodicote was pushing past his pain and coming for her, murder in his wild, hating eyes. Worse, her rolling had taken her back almost to the railings again.

She had taken him by surprise once with her willingness to fight as dirty as any Neapolitan dockworker with a flick knife, but she knew that trick wouldn't work twice. And she had no time to try and flee — always supposing her badly used knees would let her gain any kind of speed. Besides, in order to run she'd have to turn her back on him. Which would give him the ideal opportunity to race her down and get his hands around her neck from the back. And then it would be game over. She knew it, and she could see he did too, for a smile of anticipated victory was already crossing his face.

But Hillary had meant every word she'd said to him — if she was going over this bloody railing, then so was he.

So once again, she did something that Marvin Bodicote was not expecting.

Hillary Greene sat down.

It brought him up short enough to halt his onrush and for one, almost comical moment, they simply stared at one another — Hillary sitting fully on her bottom, both legs out in front of her, her arms crossed tightly against her chest; Marvin bent double in front of her, dragging in great noisy gulps of air, putting their faces barely inches away.

Bizarrely, Marvin began to laugh. He couldn't help it. Then the moment passed, and he slowly straightened up and looked down at her. 'Now I'm going to chuck you off this mountain,' he said. 'Do me a favour and scream all the way down, will you?'

'You first,' Hillary said, and reaching out a hand, wrapped it around his calf and yanked.

He almost toppled over, but not quite. With a snarl he reached down and grabbed her, hauling her upright, then looked comically surprised as he felt her push upwards with her own legs. He'd assumed the reason she'd sat down was to try and use her body weight to keep her anchored to the ground and make him work to lift her, so he was totally unprepared for her seeming cooperation now.

But in the next second, Hillary leaned her back against the railing and spread both arms along it, then using it to support her upper body, she bent and swung both legs up and locked them around Marvin's slim waist. She felt her ankles cross and lock satisfactorily in the small of his back, and before he could stop her, she threw herself forward and put one arm either side of his neck and locked her hands together behind him in a grotesque parody of a playful lover's embrace.

Once again their eyes were only inches apart. '*I* go over, *you* go over,' Hillary said flatly.

And then bit him on the nose.

Hard.

Instantly his blood spurted into her mouth, making her want to gag, but she screwed her eyes up in disgust and only ground her teeth harder together. Her heart was now beating so hard and fast that she barely heard his roar of aggression, but she felt him spin around and try and shake her off. She had no idea, realistically, of how long she could keep her pose, for already her leg muscles were trembling with the effort to defy gravity and shock was beginning to set in.

But at least Marvin was moving backwards, away from the railing. Then he seemed to pull himself together and she felt his hands move up to her waist, then rise further. With an inner jolt of despair, she knew what he was going to do. He was going to yank her head back by the hair, and then—

She heard a scream of outrage that seemed to come from neither herself nor Marvin, and a moment later a body slammed into them, forcing them both sideways onto the ground and back, once more, against the railing.

Hillary was now sandwiched between the wire and Marvin's body. She grunted as the air left her lungs in a rush and she inelegantly but very gratefully turned her head and spat out the blood that was in her mouth. Suddenly Marvin was jerked away from her and swung up and around to face Ian Jones.

The next instant the two men were grappling together, fists swinging.

It took her a few seconds to realise what was happening and to fully comprehend that she was now safe. But, just as before, when the knowledge that she was about to die had seemed surreal, now the idea of safety didn't seem real either.

It took her a moment, when all she could do was lie there and breathe and let the glorious, wonderful knowledge that she wasn't about to meet her maker after all filter through. And she felt utterly grateful.

Then, slowly and painfully, she got her hands under her and levered herself half-up. Everything seemed to hurt.

And then she heard Ian give a yelp of pain as Bodicote slammed a fist into his solar plexus. Now it was her colleague and friend who was in trouble. Instantly she hobbled forward and just as Bodicote measured him up for a sock under the jaw, Hillary drew her own hand back, forced her fingers to curl together, and aimed the punch at his face.

Her goal was simple: he was already bleeding from his nose, and now she wanted to break it, if possible. Because it was hard to kill someone when your throat was clogged with blood and you suddenly found yourself fighting for breath yourself.

But Bodicote saw her just in time, lurched around and changed the direction of his own fist. Hillary ducked it, and as she did so, Jones launched himself at his opponent a second time, and both men hit the railing hard and fast. It resulted in Bodicote's back bending at a painful angle against the rail and turning him into a near-perfect fulcrum, as, in an instinctive attempt to try and relieve the pressure of it, his left knee came up, leaving him see-sawing precariously half-over the rail.

Not surprisingly, he grabbed out for something to stop his backwards momentum, which, unfortunately, happened to be one Detective Inspector Ian Jones.

In dismay, Hillary saw Bodicote's scrambling hands fix on Ian's belt, jerking her friend violently forward, which meant that Ian's feet also left the ground as the counter-weight of Marvin's own bodyweight had him swinging, stomach-first, over the railing on top of his opponent.

And now both men were just a split second away from see-sawing over the railing and plunging to their deaths.

Hillary, for what felt like the hundredth time in just a few seconds, fell to her already bruised and swelling knees and desperately wrapped her arms around Ian's legs and threw herself backwards, letting out a moan of relief when Ian's feet finally touched the ground again.

But Marvin's feet were still flailing around in mid-air and in blind panic, and as Jones hauled on his suspect to try and bring him fully back over the rail, Marvin's flailing shoe caught Hillary smack under her jaw.

She felt her teeth snap together in one white-light-of-pain instant, and she could only hope her tongue hadn't been between them. Her head rang and she could have sworn she heard literal bells. Then, yet again, she felt blood fill her mouth — only this time it was hers, not Bodicote's.

She crawled away, humiliatingly aware that she was whimpering a little in shock and wanting to hold her jaw with her hand but not daring to. She quite literally didn't know what to do with herself. Tears scalded down her cheeks, but after a few seconds the white-hot sensation of mind-blowing pain receded, and she finally became aware of her surroundings again.

Someone was saying something, and the words had a curious sing-song quality to them that were oddly familiar. Then the words coalesced and made sense, and she looked carefully and slowly to her left where Jones was kneeling on a squirming Marvin Bodicote's back as he slipped on the handcuffs and recited his rights.

Something about the feel of the handcuffs and the meaning of the words seemed to pierce Marvin like a knife, for he suddenly lay very still and closed his eyes. And Hillary saw, with a sense of unease and a weird kind of embarrassment, that the man was silently crying.

Ian leaned back against the railing behind him, his chest heaving as he dragged in air, and cupped one hand protectively over his no doubt aching ribs. He was looking a little green and was probably about to be very sick.

Hillary, her hands taking most of her weight as she knelt on her poor knees yet again, watched him with some concern. She wanted to ask if he was all right, but when she went to do so, felt an ominous little movement within her mouth, and with shaky fingers, she reached inside to pull out the object that had just fallen onto her tongue.

But she'd already guessed what it must be.

She saw Ian's gaze focus on her as he too concentrated on the small object now resting in the palm of her hand.

It was a blood-covered tooth.

Hillary regarded it glumly. She could only hope that it wasn't one of her front teeth, because if she ended up talking with a lisp because of the likes of Marvin Bodicote she was going to be seriously pissed off.

Or pithed off, as the case might be.

CHAPTER FIFTEEN

Five hours later, Hillary was sitting in the emergency room of the nearest hospital and kicking herself for letting Ian talk her into seeing a doctor. Naturally, some cuts, bruises and a missing tooth had hardly impressed the nurses, and she was probably — quite rightly — at the bottom of the triage queue.

Jones had deserted her almost immediately, but she didn't blame him for that. She knew that the paperwork alone created by the arrest of Marvin would keep him busy until the early hours. Thankfully, he had promised to delay getting her own statement taken until tomorrow, for although she'd quickly discovered her missing tooth was a back molar — so no lisp — her jaw was swollen and aching, and talking was not the most pleasant of experiences for her right now.

For about the fourth time, she gingerly levered herself out of her chair and took a careful, hobbling turn around the waiting room, just to stop herself from stiffening up even more. Just as she was finishing her circuit, she saw a uniformed constable arrive, look around, and then approach her tentatively.

'DI Greene, ma'am?'

Hillary couldn't be bothered to correct him about her civilian status and somewhat wearily nodded. 'Inspector

Jones's compliments, ma'am. I've brought your car back down from Beggar's Leap — a green Volkswagen Golf, yes?' At Hillary's second nod, he smiled and handed over her car keys, along with her bag. 'The inspector thought you might like this too.'

Hillary accepted the bag happily and with yet another wordless nod. The constable didn't hang about either and quickly left, whilst Hillary took her bag back to the chair and checked its contents.

Her phone gave her the most pause for thought, and after a few moments, she brought it out and checked the battery time remaining. Another couple of hours at least. Perfect. Whilst she was waiting, she might as well do something useful.

She sat down, created a file, and paused for a moment to collect her thoughts. If she'd gone over that mountain today, her theory as to who had killed Imogen and why would have gone with her, and her conscience was seriously bothering her about that. So now was as good a time as any to give Ian the benefit of her wisdom and advice — such as it was.

She sighed and began to type:

'Imogen Muir — case number . . .' And here she had to stop. She had no idea what the case number was. It still felt odd to be investigating a crime without being a part of a proper team and with none of the usual access to evidence or resources that that entailed. Well, Ian would just have to fill that bit in himself.

She sighed, rubbed a hand against the back of her neck and stared at a poster opposite warning her about liver disease. It didn't make for enthralling reading.

She forced her attention back to the white screen with its demanding, waiting cursor, then checked the time and noted it down, along with the date and her own name. Then, trying to fight off the growing desire to just have a hot bath, take some aspirin and curl up in a nice soft bed and go to sleep, she began to marshal her thoughts into some semblance of order.

Since this wasn't to be an official document, but merely her take on the case for Ian's benefit, at least there was no need for her to use formal jargon. After a moment, she nodded, and began to type.

'The case against Patrick Unwin.'

I suspected Patrick almost from the beginning, simply because he was the one to suggest the outing to Beggar's Leap in the first place. Of course, it was always possible that one of the others simply took advantage of this, but bearing in mind Occam's razor, it was inevitable that he went straight to the top of my list. Since he alone knew in advance what he was proposing, who else would have had more time to prepare things than Patrick? (This presupposes that he anticipated everyone agreeing to go, but I think, had anyone decided not to, he'd have been confident of his persuasive powers. As you'd have observed yourself, he has a lot of confidence in his charm and 'gift of the gab'.)

I also remembered that Patrick was the first of the guests to arrive at Riverside, with Imogen arriving later the same day. Which, if you check the weather survey, was a cold and wet day, with the hot spell only kicking in the following morning. The others then arrived over the following two or three days — which meant that, of them all, Patrick had spent the longest time with her and would have had more chance to get to know her routine and habits. Now, one of the first things that struck me when I examined Imogen's body initially was how the bloodstain was barely noticeable because Imogen's top was such a dark colour. If you remember, I later asked to see the list of Imogen's possessions because I had a hunch about her outfits, and saw that she had brought with her very few dark-coloured clothes — and that those tended to be warmer items. Which was as I had suspected. The long-term weather forecasts predicted very hot weather for at least two weeks, so most of her wardrobe consisted of light summer wear in a variety of pastel colours. But Imogen mentioned on the journey that she'd been advised that the higher altitude of the station might be chilly, especially if the clouds came down. If you can find an independent witness that it was Patrick who told her this, that would be helpful. Remember, he'd have been the only one of the residents to have seen her in her dark warm outfit (on the day of her arrival) since she'd worn only light summer outfits ever since. (You can check this by asking Judith Pringwell, or any of the others.) So he, of all of them, could have predicted what she'd wear. (NB: If Imogen had ignored his advice and worn something summery and pale in colour, it's possible that she would not have been killed on the train, since the bloodstain would have shown up at once and her death might have been immediately discovered — and someone might recall that Patrick had been the last one near her.)

I was also struck by the method of the murder. Your team quickly found out that none of the suspects had any formal medical training, including Unwin, but of them all, I realised that Patrick might have had a certain expertise in the strategic use of thin-bladed weapons. By his own admission he had been kicked out of horseracing for taking bribes and backhanders and 'handicapping' horses. I think if you send people into that fraternity and do a thorough investigation of him, you'll find proof that Patrick, despite his protests at being an animal lover, wasn't above nobbling horses far more brutally than just giving them too much water to drink before a race. I think thin blades can and have been used to nick tendons and needles used to puncture all sorts of organs in order to cause pain and slow down racehorses. And if I'm right, it means that Patrick must have studied the anatomy of horses at some point in order to become adept at using sharp blades; and not only that, he must have done so whilst concealing what he was doing from fellow jockeys, alert trainers and suspicious stable lads. And if he could study animal anatomy, he could study human anatomy. And if he could be quick enough to 'stick' a horse and not be detected, why not a human being?

If my theory is right, this tallies with the timing and location of the crime. All along, it has bothered me that the killer of Imogen should opt to kill her in the train. It narrowed the suspects down to such a small number, whereas killing her at Beggar's Leap itself would have been so much easier (as you and I both know from personal experience). But since Patrick was confident that he could kill Imogen quickly, instantly, and not be spotted, then there must have been an advantage to him to do it that way. And I think that advantage was in setting up an obvious scapegoat.

I'm talking, of course, about Jasmine Van Paulen. As we now know, the writing experts don't believe that Imogen wrote the anonymous letter accusing Jasmine of a drugs buy. I strongly recommend that you get Patrick to write something in block capitals (or even better, find a previously existing example of his block-letter writing) and get it compared to the anonymous note. I think you'll find they match. He had a bit of luck spotting Jasmine cosying up to her supplier, and it wouldn't have taken him long to see the possibilities it presented. By accusing Jasmine in the letter and then planting the idea in everyone's mind that it was Imogen who had written it, he had to think his chances were pretty good that the police would concentrate on Jasmine as the prime suspect. And by re-questioning the others, it's possible that you could track the original source of the rumour that it was Imogen who was the stool pigeon back to him. He must also have gone out of his way to stoke the vendetta between Jasmine and Imogen, and again, you might get some testimony to that fact.

And this brings me to the psychology of it all. Of all my fellow guests at Riverside, by far the one most at home taking risks is Patrick. Not only did he start out in the high-octane arena of horseracing, even when he got a 'regular' job, we strongly suspect that he was doing a fair bit in the way of dodgy dealing on the side. Again, taking a risk.

I considered all the others in turn: Barry Kirk is almost the antithesis of a risk taker — he's measured, careful, considering, and more of a thinker than a doer. He would be well out of his comfort zone plotting something as outlandish as what happened on the train. Belinda is living the good life, but as we know, has a secret past that she wants to keep secret. Her default setting all these years must have been to live in the limelight, enjoy herself, and to protect herself at all times. I think she'd have paid blackmail before risking life imprisonment for murder. Jasmine is wild, spoiled and reckless — she alone of the rest of them might just have been tempted to kill — but her motive is far too weak. Even if she found herself on a drugs charge, she'd have known her father would get her out of it. And Jasper is a rich man, used to dealing with lawyers and payoffs rather than physical violence. Rich businessmen very seldom get their own hands dirty, as you know.

Now, I know what you're thinking — all of this is so much pie in the sky. It might be interesting and even suggestive but taking this to your super (even if you can pin Unwin down on the horse-rigging scenario) won't earn you a pat on the back. Which is why I suggest you concentrate your investigation from this point on proving his motive.

And it's a simple one. We already know that Imogen's husband dealt in scrap metal. And we know that Patrick Unwin is responsible for the purchasing (and presumably the disposal) of a fair deal of oil-rig equipment. I think it's highly likely that Unwin and the late Mr Derek Muir did a fair bit of illegal business in the past. It's an odd thing, Ian, but whenever genteel, well-heeled 'little old ladies' are murdered, we almost automatically and instinctively think of them as innocent. We don't do that for almost any other victim, have you noticed? If it's an attractive woman, we instantly consider whether or not she might have been cheating on her husband. If it's a middle-aged businessman, we instantly start to wonder if it's money-related, and if he'd been fiddling the books. Teenagers — are they in a gang? But little old ladies . . . It's so easy to assume that they could have done nothing to bring an attack on themselves. But what do we really know about Imogen? Her husband (we strongly suspect) was no angel in business, and how likely is it that she was really in ignorance of how he came by his lucrative deals? We know that lately she was beginning to feel the pinch, financially. We know that Unwin has risen higher and higher in his company and is now very nicely placed when it comes to income. You can see where I'm going with this? What if Imogen's 'holiday' to Hay-on-Wye, and her booking into the Riverside only to find one of her husband's former cronies also in residence, wasn't a coincidence?

I advise you to go over the last month or so of Imogen's life with a fine-tooth comb. You might find evidence that she'd hired a private detective to locate Unwin's location. Or she might have had his contact details from her husband's files. If she was in any way even a little tech-savvy, you might discover on her home computer (if she had one) browser history that she'd been trying to find him or learn more about him. And — best of all — there would be, somewhere, financial trails linking her, or her husband — to Patrick. I wouldn't be surprised to find that Imogen had already approached Patrick to suggest that he start paying her to keep silent. If you recall, when we talked to Patrick, Barry Kirk mentioned that he was about to get a big promotion so we know that he had even more 'scrap' to illegally sell on to whoever took over from Derek Muir as his middleman. Which means he'd have been even more desperate not to rock the boat and lose this very lucrative sideline, should Imogen blab. (NB: Imogen would have been very wary about being alone with Patrick at Beggar's Leap. She was no fool and would know better than to be alone with her blackmail victim at such a dangerous spot. But if you will recall, she'd asked Belinda to stick close to her when they got to the waterfalls — and no wonder! This could be an added reason why Patrick needed to kill her on the train — he knew she'd be too wary of him to be caught alone with him otherwise. But she'd feel safe in a confined space with other people all around her. Incidentally, the fact that she chose Belinda to be her unknowing protector made me put Belinda right at the bottom of my suspect list.)

I think the chances are pretty good — if you get the accountants and financial wizards on the case — that you'll find the solid proof and link-up that you need.

And, by the way, I suggest you get Barry Kirk alone and give him a good grilling. He's the sort who sees everything and says nothing.

And don't forget the newspaper angle — if Patrick did use a newspaper to protect himself against possible bloodstains (and I still think it very likely — if he'd had blood anywhere on him he knew he'd probably be arrested on the spot!) you have to find it. It'll provide a much-needed forensic link.

She signed off with a sigh of relief and saved the document.

She then reread her somewhat rambling memo and mentally shook her head. It wasn't exactly up to her usual standard of coherently presented paperwork but she was still groggy from the after effects of shock, ached all over, and was almost too tired to think straight.

What's more, damn it, she was supposed to be on her holiday! Let the official team do all the donkey work, she told herself grimly.

Just as she was feeling at her most bolshie, her phone pinged. She checked and saw Ian's number. Holding the phone up to her ear she said briefly, 'Yes?' And even that made her jaw ache.

'Hey, I just thought I'd give you an update. I know you can't talk much right now, so just listen. Marvin's only trying to go down the old "insanity" route! He's pretending to have had a complete mental breakdown. Naturally, his fancy solicitor is all over it, demanding he get medical attention and be sanctioned for a couple of days, pending a full assessment. But I'm not buying it,' Jones added scornfully.

Hillary merely grunted. She was by no means so sure as her colleague that the drug dealer was shamming; after all, what had happened at the waterfalls must have been devastating to his ego. Not to mention that, in her opinion, the man was as crazy as a rabid bat to begin with.

'You still at the hospital?'

'Yes. I'm sending you a document to chew over,' she mumbled.

'You're doing what?' Ian asked uncertainly. 'Lending me a what? And what do you want to "do over"?'

Hillary sighed. 'Check your phone,' she tried again, enunciating as clearly as she could in the circumstances, and hung up. Her hands were a little sore and scraped, but she could still use her fingers all right, and a moment later her thoughts on the Imogen Muir case were winging their way to the SIO.

It was then that she heard her name finally being called, and wearily got out of her chair and shuffled off to a waiting cubicle. There the nurse settled her down on a narrow hospital bed and left. When the doctor arrived about ten minutes later, she was already fast asleep and he had to wake her up.

After a quick examination he cheerfully assured her that her jaw wasn't dislocated, and advised her to go to bed with an aspirin. She refrained — just — from glowering at him.

* * *

The following morning she awoke in her bed at the Riverside Inn, not at all surprised to find that it was gone noon.

She lay for some time in bed, reluctant to move (knowing that it would hurt) and stared out of the window at the treeline beyond. Eventually she roused herself enough to check her phone and saw, not surprisingly, that she had a text from Ian. She opened it and had to smile as she read it. It was short but to the point.

'Bloody hell! How did I miss so much? I'm putting a rocket under the team. Wish us luck.'

Hillary certainly did that. She knew that they had a big task ahead of them, but she was confident they'd get enough on Patrick to charge him.

With the odd swear word or two and a couple of winces, she got out of bed and stood for a moment looking out of the window over the River Wye and the meadows and mountains beyond. It was a lovely view, but she knew in her heart that she just wanted to go home. Back to the peace and quiet of the canal, and the cocooning comfort of her narrowboat.

She'd stay for the rest of the day, give her statement about the incident at Beggar's Leap, and then, after a good night's sleep (hopefully) she'd set off after breakfast tomorrow.

In the bathroom she regarded her reflection in the mirror with a wry smile. Her jawline was red and puffy, she had a scratch on her cheek from when she'd hit the ground yesterday, and there was a yellowing area around one of her eyes that she strongly suspected would eventually turn a not-particularly-charming shade of purple.

In short, she looked like something that no self-respecting cat would even dream of dragging in.

So much for taking a relaxing holiday and recharging her batteries. She gave her reflection a ferocious stare. Right now, she was feeling as if she needed another holiday to get over this one!

* * *

The next morning, feeling marginally less stiff and sore, Hillary made her way downstairs. Yesterday, after making her statement, she'd deliberately stuck to her room to give herself a chance to recover. She hadn't really had the energy to pretend that nothing was amiss in front of Patrick and the others, but luckily, the news had got around about the latest attack on her, so she had the perfect excuse for not putting in a public appearance.

Now, bags packed and ready to go back in her room, she entered the dining room quietly, but was, of course, quickly spotted. Jasper got up and somewhat tentatively approached her, whilst a bored-looking Jasmine looked on.

'Hillary, goodness gracious, you have been in the wars! I hope all your summer vacations aren't usually this rough,' the American said, with a rather nervous smile. 'I trust you're feeling a little better now?'

'I am, thanks,' Hillary said, not altogether truthfully. 'But I've decided enough is enough, and I'm going back home today.'

Jasper nodded. 'We'll miss you here, won't we, honey?' he said, turning to look at his daughter, who looked blankly at him for a second, before nodding desultorily.

'Yeah, sure,' she said.

At that moment, Belinda came through the door and immediately checked her stride as she spotted Hillary. Jasper made a strategic withdrawal as the chic Canadian woman hovered at Hillary's table.

'We heard someone attacked you again,' Belinda said, almost accusingly. 'But the police won't say anything about it. Was it the same man who attacked Jasper?'

'No,' Hillary said, then mitigated the rather abrupt answer with a brief smile. 'I'm sorry, but I can't say anything much about it. It's an ongoing investigation you see.'

Belinda sighed, unimpressed by this, then glanced around uneasily. In their usual corner, Hillary could see that Patrick and his regular tablemate Barry Kirk kept shooting them curious glances. She could imagine that Patrick, in particular, was straining his ears to try and pick up any titbits Hillary might be passing on to his fellow hotel guest.

'Did what happened to you have anything to do with what happened to Imogen?' Belinda begged, lowering her voice to a near-whisper. 'Can you at least tell me that?'

Under the perfect make-up, Hillary could see that Belinda was pale, and her body language screamed tension. She wanted to reassure her that things would break soon, but she knew she couldn't.

'My own opinion is that it was unrelated,' she compromised reluctantly. Which was true enough — Marvin and his gang of not-so-merry men had had nothing to do with Imogen's death.

Belinda nodded pensively, not sure whether to be relieved or discouraged by the information. Then her head swivelled sharply to her right and at the same time, Hillary heard a familiar voice.

Out in the Hall, Ian Jones was giving orders to two uniformed PCs, and when this trio stepped into the dining room, an instant silence fell. Although this group of people had had plenty of dealings with the police in recent days, and their presence at the hotel was hardly unheard of, an almost atavistic sense of impending danger now seemed to grip them. It was as if something was warning them that the moment they'd all been waiting for was now upon them, and the very air felt explosive.

Belinda abruptly sat down at the empty table opposite Hillary, as if all the strength in her knees had left her.

The American father and daughter abruptly stopped their conversation mid-word and out of the corner of her eye, Hillary saw Jasper quickly reach out and grip Jasmine's hand. He also instinctively moved closer to her, as if trying to shield her from the sight of the newcomers, leaving Hillary in no doubt that if Jones were to approach their table, he'd be on his feet in an instant, threatening him with a barrage of lawyers and promising to bring down the wrath of the American consulate on his head.

But Ian was not looking their way. As he passed Hillary's table he glanced at her, smiled briefly in acknowledgement, but didn't stop walking — all the way to the far corner, where Barry Kirk watched his approach with slowly widening eyes.

Everyone watched, fascinated.

Hillary thought it was rather like observing a herd of prey animals, spotting a predator and waiting to see which of them was being targeted for the slaughter.

Jones fixed his gaze on the Irishman. From where she was sitting, Hillary saw the surprise in Patrick's eyes, before he paled a little, and then the shutters came down. His shoulders went back and his chin jutted out pugnaciously, and Hillary knew he was going to brazen it out. After all, what choice did he have?

'Mr Patrick Unwin, I'm arresting you for the murder of Mrs Imogen Muir . . .' As Jones recited the words made familiar to everyone in the room by numerous television programmes, films and crime novels, everyone seemed to exhale at once.

Belinda leaned back in her chair, and Jasper let go of his daughter's hand. Barry Kirk pushed his chair back a little from the table, as if trying to distance himself from what was happening so close to him.

Patrick listened to the end of the recital, letting a small, whimsical smile light his face. When DI Jones was finished, he let the constables take him, each by one arm, and then actually laughed.

'You're making a mistake, Inspector, you know,' he said, almost sounding sympathetic. 'I never touched the lady. And nobody can say any different,' he added, looking around at his fellow passengers in the train that day.

None of them would meet his gaze.

Ian shrugged, unimpressed. 'Please take Mr Unwin to the station,' he told the constables, who cuffed Patrick efficiently, and escorted him from the room.

Patrick shook his head gently from side to side, all the way out.

Jones glanced across at Hillary, and as he approached, Belinda bleated out some quick excuse and made for the door into the hall. After a quick mutual glance at each, the Van Paulens also rose and left their half-eaten breakfasts behind them.

Only Barry Kirk remained seated in the far corner table, and after a moment's hesitation, continued to eat his breakfast. But Jones, sitting opposite Hillary, kept his voice low.

'You were right. We've been following the money. We're going to get him, for all his cocky confidence that we won't be able to touch him.'

Hillary nodded thoughtfully. 'It'll be a tricky trial though. Murder in plain sight, but no witnesses? The prosecution will have to handle the jury carefully.'

'I know. But with none of the others having a motive, and Patrick having plenty, they'll see sense. Juries like a solid motive. And greed is as solid as it gets,' Jones pointed out, leaning back wearily in his chair.

'Been up for a second night in a row, huh?' Hillary said.

'Yeah.'

'You know what they say about all work and no play . . . You should take a walk in the hills to clear your head, or have a meal with your partner, unwind a bit.'

Ian shrugged. 'I don't have a partner.'

'Divorce?'

Jones sighed. 'It just doesn't seem real still. I keep thinking she'll come back . . .'

Hillary gave a shrug, then winced when it hurt. 'You can waste a lot of time on regrets,' she said softly.

Ian blinked, then slowly nodded. Funny, it was sort of obvious and yet he'd never really thought about that. 'Yes, I suppose you can.' She was right, of course, this woman from Thames Valley. As usual. He'd been letting himself drift. Well, to hell with self-pity. He was getting heartily sick of it. And it wasn't as if he hadn't had any interest in him! There was that rather attractive brunette at . . .

'Well, I'm off back home after I've had breakfast,' Hillary interrupted his more pleasant musings.

'Not going to be sending off any postcards saying "Wish you were here" then?' Ian asked with a grin.

Hillary grinned back. 'Only to my worst enemies.'

And she couldn't help but feel rather gratified to have been proven right in what she'd always maintained. Holidays were highly overrated. Next year, she'd stay on the boat, as usual.

THE END

THE JOFFE BOOKS STORY

We began in 2014 when Jasper agreed to publish his mum's much-rejected romance novel and it became a bestseller.

Since then we've grown into the largest independent publisher in the UK. We're extremely proud to publish some of the very best writers in the world, including Joy Ellis, Faith Martin, Caro Ramsay, Helen Forrester, Simon Brett and Robert Goddard. Everyone at Joffe Books loves reading and we never forget that it all begins with the magic of an author telling a story.

We are proud to publish talented first-time authors, as well as established writers whose books we love introducing to a new generation of readers.

We won Trade Publisher of the Year at the Independent Publishing Awards in 2023. We have been shortlisted for Independent Publisher of the Year at the British Book Awards for the last five years, and were shortlisted for the Diversity and Inclusivity Award at the 2022 Independent Publishing Awards. In 2023 we were shortlisted for Publisher of the Year at the RNA Industry Awards.

We built this company with your help, and we love to hear from you, so please email us about absolutely anything bookish at feedback@joffebooks.com

If you want to receive free books every Friday and hear about all our new releases, join our mailing list: www.joffebooks.com/contact

And when you tell your friends about us, just remember: it's pronounced Joffe as in coffee or toffee!

ALSO BY FAITH MARTIN

DI HILLARY GREENE SERIES

Book 1: MURDER ON THE OXFORD CANAL
Book 2: MURDER AT THE UNIVERSITY
Book 3: MURDER OF THE BRIDE
Book 4: MURDER IN THE VILLAGE
Book 5: MURDER IN THE FAMILY
Book 6: MURDER AT HOME
Book 7: MURDER IN THE MEADOW
Book 8: MURDER IN THE MANSION
Book 9: MURDER IN THE GARDEN
Book 10: MURDER BY FIRE
Book 11: MURDER AT WORK
Book 12: MURDER NEVER RETIRES
Book 13: MURDER OF A LOVER
Book 14: MURDER NEVER MISSES
Book 15: MURDER AT MIDNIGHT
Book 16: MURDER IN MIND
Book 17: HILLARY'S FINAL CASE
Book 18: HILLARY'S BACK
Book 19: MURDER NOW AND THEN
Book 20: MURDER IN THE PARISH
Book 21: MURDER ON THE TRAIN

MONICA NOBLE MYSTERIES

Book 1: THE VICARAGE MURDER
Book 2: THE FLOWER SHOW MURDER
Book 3: THE MANOR HOUSE MURDER

JENNY STARLING MYSTERIES

Book 1: THE BIRTHDAY MYSTERY
Book 2: THE WINTER MYSTERY
Book 3: THE RIVERBOAT MYSTERY
Book 4: THE CASTLE MYSTERY
Book 5: THE OXFORD MYSTERY
Book 6: THE TEATIME MYSTERY
Book 7: THE COUNTRY INN MYSTERY